Mundane's World

MUNDANE'S WORLD

A NOVEL BY

Judy Grahn

✳

The Crossing Press, Freedom, California 95019

Cover illustration by Karen Sjoholm
Cover design by William Houston

Printed in the U.S.A.

LIBRARY OF CONGRESS
Library of Congress Cataloging-in-Publication Data

Grahn, Judy. 1940-
    Mundane's world : a novel / by Judy Grahn.
       p.   cm.
    ISBN 0-89594-317-4 : $20.95.   ISBN 0-89594-316-6 (pbk.) : $8.95
    I. Title.
PS3557.R226M86 1988
813'.54--dc19   88-15024
                                                      CIP

Reversing A Perilous Situation
Doesn't Necessarily Mean Skinning The Cat

Five mostly brown young girls moved down by the riverside, stirring the bushes with the motions of their bodies. They ranged in age from the eldest to the youngest and they spoke quietly, disturbing little around them, for it was late in the day and they were tired. They were not all together very often, but on this particular evening they were all together and they acted completely as a unit. They ranged in color from the extremely dark one through medium brown to the one who was oddly mottled white.

They were late for home without having done what they had been sent out for, and they knew it. Their chore was to each pull up a bundle of reeds or wickers growing in the shallow water close to the bank. The reeds were to be dried and dyed and used to make baskets, mats and trays for the midsummer festival only two weeks away. The eldest moved the fastest, frantic to collect the hard stubborn plants along the river. The reeds that had been admirable and friendly in the morning now had turned into deep-rooted enemies who surrendered to the tugging with ill-will. She knew they were being rude and hasty, so that the plants bit them.

"Come-up, come-up," the eldest whispered desperately as she yanked on them, and her hands began blistering, however she couldn't stop before they had gathered each a good load, because she knew that the youngest child, who was very literal about directions, would not give up until they had gotten the proper quota of reeds.

In a few minutes the earth had turned away from the sun, and they were doing their work in near darkness. When she thought they would all agree with her, the eldest said, "That's enough," and they started for home.

Nobody had complained, though she thought she heard

1

somebody's nose running, probably from the pain of the blisters; her own hands stung from the fury of biting plants, but she forgot them as they quickly pulled themselves up the slippery bank and found the narrow trail after a few false fumblings in the underbrushes.

They walked swiftly in long-legged strides, single-file, only a few yards down a trail which was exactly as wide as they were, and then the eldest stopped dead short and all the others ran into the one ahead.

Facing them on the trail, and on her way down to the river for a drink of water, was a mother lion. She stopped too, and there they stood for the longest time, all examining each other with big eyes. The lion smelled them and knew they were from the town two miles west of where they were now, that they were frightened above everything else, and that they had been in the water; she also knew they would taste very good if she put her mind in *that* direction, and she did, because she nearly always did, that being her occupation.

They smelled her and knew that she had kittens somewhere, since she had a milky odor under the dusty lion smell. More than that they couldn't tell.

The eldest and first in line kept her eyes on the lion's eyes and mentally rehearsed everything she had ever heard about the pride of lions, because in split seconds she would have to make the decision of what-to-do-next.

It occurred to one of them that this might be the lion who had eaten her uncle's favorite goat last year, but she couldn't afford to be mad about it at the moment. The oldest and first in line tried to spread her vision to see if she could make out the outlines of kittens behind their mother, and could not. They must be very little, and home in bed. She tried to smell if the lion had eaten recently, but could detect no bloodsmell.

The eldest knew that their only weapon was a knife, and she was not carrying it, and couldn't remember who was; a mistake she would never make again. Then she remembered what was important about today, that it was the hottest day anyone could remember since last summer, a day so blistery that they could not resist swimming it away, and that meant the countryside was dry, and that meant the mother lion was probably more thirsty right now than she was hungry.

Having decided on a solution, she took a breath and dropped one hand slowly from her bundle of reeds, and reaching behind herself, she pushed the leg of the next girl backwards, as a signal. Then the next dropped her hand from her bundle of reeds and pushed back on the next and the next on the next until the youngest child got the signal and took one giant step backwards; then they all took one giant step backwards while at the same moment the lion took one giant step forwards. In this manner, and with none of them making a sound except when their feet touched the ground, they all backward walked to the river until the youngest child stood on the bank and took one more happy step and fell into the river.

The eldest, still with her eyes staring at the yellow eyes, knew when she heard the splash that she only had four more steps to go, and sure enough, soon they were all in the water, reeds clutched every which way, frantically swimming downstream. The one who could not swim pulled herself along with vines and roots hanging from the marshy bank. The mother lion watched them go with no comment, sniffed the air, walked to a low place in the bank, and drank enough water to drown anyone.

A Woman With A Wandering Eye Can Cause It To Rain

A city seen from a great distance looks inedible and like square sandstone blocks, white sandstone tumbled into the crook of a river; a crooked river seen from a great distance by a buzzard circling above it looks like a crooked blue line drawn through green and tan fuzz spilling down to the sea with a few sandstone blocks tumbled into one bend of the mouth of it, but a wise buzzard always looks closer.

A wise buzzard passing high over a lively plain cut by a river that rages in one season and nearly disappears in the others, passes first over some thin shepherds sitting in their dry hills with their thin herds; a wise buzzard watches for something that ought to be moving and isn't.

Thin shepherds all day watch the hot sky with their dry faces; sometimes they spit in the weeds and say, "A woman with a wandering eye can cause it to rain." They do not notice their own motion or anything from too great a distance.

Way past the shepherds, across the river and closer to the city, a buzzard will certainly notice something which ought not to move, but does; in this case a wooden cart made of tree trunks with a tall woman sitting on it pulled by a donkey. Her head is gradually bending lower as though she is burdened. A wise buzzard doesn't waste time puzzling the motion of tree trunks, but passes over until he is circling the city from not such a great distance. Eyesight behooves a buzzard.

The oldest of cities is named "Mundane" and is one of many on the river though it is the only one located where the river spills into the sea. It is not made of sandstone and it is not made of milk and honey either, it is made of hundreds of white plastered one, two and three story brick buildings, richly painted with colored pictures, and a few elaborate five and six story buildings, with gardens. All among these are thick walled workyards with green shrubs and water wells. Everything is connected together while outside these closer connections are drooping green orchards and rugged slumped fields, outlined with canals which today are not full of water.

At one end of the town there are many shops, stables and work-places. There is a large market with chickens wandering, and just beyond the market stands a brick factory yard made lumpy with large ovens and stacks of fuel, where no fires are lit just now but people are working. They see a flat shadow passing over the ground; the slight trace of a buzzard.

Near the center of the city enclosing many well-shaded workyards and fainting gardens full of sleepy children and slowly working older women who are often making baskets is one of the largest sunken workyards where lives an oak tree of outlandish age.

Many of the dark green leaves of the oak tree face the sun, on a few of them are little white bubbles of eggs who have been laid there by some large brown beetles. Up and down the gulleys in the bark of the oak tree run the members of a colony of ants, also of outlandish age, though not as individuals. Two of them have found a new clump of beetle's eggs, some twenty in a lump stuck underneath a green leaf; they have lifted one of the jar-shaped eggs away from the others and are trying to carry it down the tree but somehow their coordination has gotten boggled. When one pulls the other pulls also, at opposite ends, yet they have not dropped it. They are joined by a third ant which doesn't appear to help. In the clutches of three brown ants and inside the white sack a larva is writhing in danger of never becoming a beetle.

All of this can be seen from a great distance. Eyesight behooves a buzzard but motion is not interesting; what he finds irresistible is something that ought to be moving but isn't. The buzzard floats seeking something of interest, past the fields with drooping greens and the yard with women working, past the roofs and the busy oak tree and past the young girl playing with her wandering eye.

Outside the last blocky wall and seen from a closer and closer distance, something lies up on a platform of interest. For three days something which used to be moving has been watched by a wise buzzard. Three days of hot sun tends to make matters more and more interesting and less moving.

From his close distance the buzzard has decided it isn't. He has dropped down straight out of the sky, and has been followed at once by eight more buzzards who have been watching his motions, who are followed by sixteen more buzzards who have been watching their motions. Now there are twenty five buzzards who are all interested and no one is watching.

Remembering Is One Way of Writhing In The Clutches Of Three Large Aunts

In a city of dreamers the women say they dream babies into their bellies from spirits and the men dream of hunting animals who no longer live around the vicinity.

Off the street within the walls of a small workyard of the Snake clan, the clan of healing and balancing, a female child is neatly unobtrusively playing. Her elder cousins are all grown up and gone to work as shepherds. She herself has dark brown skin and kinky black hair near her head, a sturdy body with a slightly round stomach and large hands, large eyes and heavy eyelids. She has one eye set straight in her head, the other eye wandering off to the left. She is squatting and arranging ceaselessly a wide variation of small bottles and jars on the ground in front of her, and is mumbling to herself; and is very serious and is called: *Ernesta.*

She had turned her head to the right to listen to a donkey arguing with someone in the distance but when she is called: *Ernesta,* she turns her head to the left, so that her eye wanders up even more, seeming to be staring straight at the sky; and anyone looking is tempted somewhat to laugh but controlling it, then seeing the rest of her face, the solid-featured heaviness of it, anyone puts away their laugh and takes the face more seriously than they would if it did not have a wandering eye, which is a form of justice.

"Mama?" Ernesta asks, although the caller steps out of the

shaded doorway and is not exactly her mama being rather her aunt, Aunt One, whereupon the eye wanders more and is huge.

Aunt One knows that Ernesta was first in a line of girls from various clans who recently escaped a perilous situation with a mama lion who had nearly undone them, being perhaps even the notorious Lion of Mundane.

Knowing this lengthens her square face of concern. She says, "What are you doing out here? You aren't using any more water are you?"

"Oh, I'm just waiting for something to happen," Ernesta says. Actually she has been remembering five girls walking in a line three days before; she has been lining up the pots and jars on the ground before her naming them, "First there was me, then Jessi-ma from the Bee clan, then Fran-keen from the Lion clan. Next was Dee. No, next was Margedda who is such a weird person and then Dee was last, and both from the Tortoise farming people." This arranging of jars was helping her remember who was who and how it had all gone that day when everything changed.

Aunt One moves with a soft-footed marching motion, she wears a long dull red dress of filmy material of her own making with pins holding it together at the shoulder. Her niece wears a faded red skirt with no top and very little bottom. Aunt One's hands are full of dried plant fibers, yellow and tan which she calls her wickers.

"Waiting will not cause something to happen," she says sharply. "Nor prevent it either."

She crosses the courtyard to a place with a bowl of water where she sloshes her wickers. Aunt One is making a basket, she sings while she does this.

Aunt One often sings. Everyone sings for many reasons, Aunt One often sings for her own amusement. She sings to remind herself what she is doing. She sings to placate the spirits of noncreation. Today Aunt One's song is about a crane who stood for so long in one place on one leg that she hardened into that position, and was unable to lay eggs or get about at all until a supple green snake came along who she persuaded to stiffen itself and be her second leg, whereafter she could walk with not so much trouble although everyone made fun of her and called her a green legged crane.

The entirety of Ernesta's clan, the Snake clan, is happy these days, everything is in harmony with their ways, nothing is in dissension with them. By midsummer's eve their own major clan workyard will have a complicated tile mural picturing some

6

of their more important stories. These included a story of Aunt One and her three sisters and their mother Mundane importing fig trees in a procession carrying the tree bundles from the sea side dock and transplanting them into one of their medicine gardens. Soon the story of the procession would be part of a brilliantly colored mural, glazed and shiny with a permanent record of Snake clan power, the power of certain people to effect transformations on living matter.

Aunt One and two of her sisters had brought the mural matter up with the council of elders recently wrangling it through with no problems except a slight argumentation from the Bee clan. The wonderful story tiles would be baked by the Bee clan as was proper and then set into place in the wall of the major workyard by the time for the midsummer festival.

The tail end of Aunt One's basketmaking song includes this current information which she sings loudly as she weaves her wickers. The more recent version of her song has forty-two verses taking the better portion of one hour to sing and she enjoys every one of them.

Ernesta does not hear the end of the long song. Her attention has returned to her rows of little baskets and jars, miniatures of the ones used by adults, made long ago when she was a small child, each one a child's size with a child's contents of dust or selected pebbles or barley meal leftover from the cooking larder.

Ernesta has made variations of the mixtures, and the discovery that sprinkles of water mixed with dirt and grain and left in the sun for a week or so renders a baked mass that will neither go in nor out of any jar, and is ugly looking besides. Information so useful it never needs to be remembered again yet having something to do with learning the nature of cooking. Memory is important to Ernesta and so is cooking. In Ernesta's clan, cooking and the making of chemical mixtures are one and the same thing.

How Cooking Took A Long Time To Learn

Ernesta knows that cooking took a long time to learn because she herself is a primary example. Ordinarily many people do the cooking together but one time left to her own devices in the kitchen, she had put honey in the vegetables and salt in the fruit. She had boiled the milk and left the bread dough nearly raw, just lukewarm. Her relatives had threatened to make her eat the whole composition by herself, all of it, to better appreciate her own creativity.

"I didn't burn anything," she protested. They were not impressed by this.

Ernesta's family have a thorough understanding of how cooking took a long time to learn, because they invented it, or so they say; the entire hundred-thousand-year-long process is analoged in their songs with many variations including the difficulty of combining fire with water.

When Ernesta had put so much salt in the fruit her mother had said, "Ernesta has imagination."

"Not so," Aunt Two said, "that's not imagination. She just doesn't pay attention when she is taught. Ernesta has only a scattered memory, therefore she makes things up as she goes along."

Ernesta worried about this a great deal, for in her family a good memory was an imperative. She worked on her memory, reciting avidly when no one was looking: salt for vegetables and curing; salt for cheese but not for teas; honey for bread and open wounds, honey for milk only in the morning or when someone has a stomach ache; onions and garlic for nearly anything though not for melons or rashes. She worked on her memory when she was very young and anxious until it became a habit with her mumbling to herself the litany of whatever she might be in danger of forgetting. This habit gave her an excellent memory which her doubting aunts tested her on considerably.

"Smell this," Aunt Three would say, holding a little jar of crushed petals under Ernesta's nose. "What is it called? What foods is it used in and what medicines? How much do you use, where does it come from? If you boiled it with cloth, what color would come out?"

"Feel this powder, Ernesta," Aunt Two would say. "What liquids does it mix with? What did I tell you about it yesterday, where does it come from?"

A puzzle remained to her for some time about cooking, why some things are never eaten raw, like barley, and some are never cooked, like lettuce. Beer appears only at festivals, berries only in the early summer. Why don't you put butter on *everything*, for instance oranges. Why can't you ever put onions in the apple cider. Why are there a hundred ways to eat squash but only a few ways to eat melons when in the fields the squashes and melons look almost the same. These things are peculiar about cooking; these and thousands of other details Ernesta had to learn concerning mixtures which took a long time in the beginning as well as presently.

In the meantime she lined up her jars, a thin one for Jessima, a heavy one for Margedda, a short one for Dee. She was not so much playing since she had actually outgrown this sort of toy as she was trying to puzzle out a thought. She put in place in the little line an unpainted jar to stand for Fran-keen and then a most interesting and decorated elder one first in the line, for herself. Then she reconstructed her memory.

Here they were walking up the trail from the river where they had pulled each other out soaking wet. She scratched a long slender mark beside the line of jars for the trail; she scratched other marks off to the left where the foundation for the new temple was being built by the Bee clan; and then down the center she made a wide scratch for the river road, past where everyone now knew a dead woman had been found that same afternoon, three days before. She laid a short woman-representing stick on the spot with reverence.

An enclosed space in a city with light and air is for young children; in this city the walls of every four ground-floor rooms form courtyards of many sizes. These are often with trees or shrubs for shade and company, more often they are with gardens and henyards.

There are four clans in the city altogether, the yards of this particular one are lined with pots and plots of herbs and nursling plants. Ernesta's clan being the healing people always smell of sharp powders and spices they use in their processes. All her babyhood she has played with old or imitation powders and has been warned sharply away from the places in the area where the Aunts and her mother Donna keep their more volatile drugs and venoms. Fear that their babies could eat the leaves of overly powerful plants have caused the women of Ernesta's clan to build a sturdy formal moon temple with a plant nursery on the second floor, guarded by heavy doors that can not be pushed open by little fingers easily.

The four clans altogether in the city of Mundane are: The Snake clan, of transformation, balance, healing and mixtures. The Bee clan, of constructions, water bearing women, and the keeping of measurements. The Lion clan, of animals, movement, transportation and trading. The Tortoise clan of farming, provision, distribution of necessities and the keeping of records.

In addition are the pan-clan societies of which the largest are the Spider Society of predictive women and the Arrow Society for crafty men. In a city of dreamers the clans are held

9

together by a mutual knowing of numerous natural powers and especially one whose name they usually call: *Ana* and who is a lady of many faces, some other names and a great deal of body.

Handiwork Is Just Another Name For Manual Labor

Anyone who makes baskets all day long for several days will get blisters, but not Aunt One. Aunt One has hardly callused hands and is an expert. The thin green branch of a willow tree wound around in a circle and woven together with itself by skinny water-soaked strips of long sharp wicker leaves will eventually form a sturdy basket but almost anyone who makes baskets all day long will get blistered. Except Aunt One, who has made so many and who is however annoyed at the amount of work it takes to make a good midsummer festival. She has sworn not to make any more containers though everyone knows she will anyway because her two younger sisters can always think of more things to put in them. Aunt One wonders if it is wise to have sisters with so much imagination.

Aunt One has been working on the same basket for six months. It is now so tall that only the black top of her hair shows as she stands inside of it, working. She hums a song to help herself along and also to breathe a good spirit into the container. She wants nothing to ever rot secretly at the bottom of it, she wants nothing to ever leak out of its sides. She has incorporated a pattern of red and black into the walls, intermittently a long wavy snake figure and a crane with red body and black legs and head; there are nine of these figures all the way around. The head of each crane is as large as the palm of Aunt One's hand. They stand for transformations of the spirit, something which their designer is hoping for herself, who has been depressed lately on account of arthritis in her hands, and is dreading the chill of winter.

Even a Snake clan woman of transformations can be in need of transformations. Ernesta does not know that her first aunt is depressed by what is happening to her hands; she believes that Aunt One's new gnarly knuckles and oddly bending fingers are an invention of her person, Aunt One's creation of a variation in her own form. She is amazed by this, for she herself even practicing cannot get her hands into such positions; it seems to her a further proof of Aunt One's complete control over her own physical matters.

Ernesta fixed her wandering eye on Aunt One's head, barely showing. Aunt One had told her that meeting a lion on the trail was the reversing of a perilous situation, and from then on that was how she remembered it. It was important to Ernesta that she had been the first in a line of girls who reversed a perilous situation because she had been the one called on to think up the solution. She wondered if this being first in line would happen to her again, was that the kind of person she was.

All the people of the Snake clan of transformation have great control in physical matters, in this family they have learned much of it from Ernesta's grandmother, the great Mundane, who is currently on a lasting journey. She has left behind her five children in the city, four women and a man, Blueberry Jon. Of the four sisters the youngest is Ernesta's tender-hearted mother Donna and the elder three are her formidable aunts.

Ernesta examined the pattern of jars and scratches she had made to help herself recall what had happened on the particular day. There was one element missing, something so mysterious she had discussed it with nobody, not even her mother who sometimes listened or appeared to be doing so, under her lowered eyelids and nodding skull.

Of all the dreamers in the city Ernesta's mother Donna was the most unusual. While other women dreamed their children from stars, domesticated plants or people, she had dreamed hers from a strange wild bush growing deep in some rocky hills east of the city. Someday Ernesta would meet this plant, who was called by her mother a spirit mate and called by her aunts a greedy little weed.

A Charming Woman May Not Want A Social Life

Anyone has a genius, a spirit double who represents the best of oneself. Donna's genius is a weed living tenuously high in the hills above the city on an outcropping of alkaline rocks. Having dreamed her first and only child while looking at it one midnight, naming it her spirit mate she brought parts of its leaves home to show her family. Thereafter her sisters harped so long on its dusty stench and uselessness she stopped her visits to the rocks shortly after Ernesta was born but lately had taken to making them once again. Dreaming of wild vegetables she keeps her charms in leather sacks under her pillow, practicing a nighttime skill of transformation that has to do with herself. She is not a member of any councils or groups and is not particularly close to any people, avoiding the gossipy everyday political life of the city which so engages her older sisters.

"Ernesta," she whispers, "sometime we will go meet the spirit mate who caused me to dream of you. Then you will never again be satisfied."

Ernesta can see the top of the Moon Temple where her mother, the youngest of four Snake clan sisters nods over her poppies; she is a charming woman devoting most of her attention to herbs and certain animals. She is also an expert at disappearing, vanishing into sleep during the day or into the Moon Temple tending sprouts and captured snakes while entrancing herself with dreams.

Having many charms some of which are dangerous, she teaches them to her daughter surreptitiously, sometimes taking Ernesta with her on early morning visits to the river bank which thrives and thrashes with living matter. Here they practised some of the secrets of disappearing, which are used by many kinds of animals for different purposes. The art of disappearing was the first step in any transformation her mother said, to disappear in one form and only then to reappear in another.

"Watch me," she would say at the start of the lesson, how could anyone watch someone who didn't intend to be there any more, but "watch me," her mother would say and then she would disappear as easily as a guinea hen.

"Everything takes up its own space," the charming woman said, "but then there are spaces in between things which are not often used. If you slip into one of those, nothing can notice you." It was a way of becoming neutral. It is very important to know ways of becoming neutral if you often handle poisonous snakes and in this she was an expert. They were a part of her charms.

The aunts do not approve of any of these habits; they say Ernesta will simply become a charming woman and have no social life if she follows the ways of her mother.

A full Snake clan person, they say, has bearing and balance. A full Snake clan person of transformation and balance sings well with understanding of harmony, and knows the physics of all the people and creatures together as well as separately, to say nothing of minerals, water and crystals.

Ernesta is talking to herself softly so as not to disturb Aunt One's basket song, or else Aunt One might begin using her name in the song. Not drawing the attention of three acute aunts is a hazardous skill though necessary. Someday she would become an expert at disappearing. Her second aunt has lately been negative in her remarks, she has noticed Ernesta's whimsical tendencies and is bound to correct them. She often uses the word, 'responsibility' to balance with 'whimsy'.

"I would rather be like my mother," Ernesta thinks. "She always dances and bushes understand her. My mother laughs as often as a duck."

"Your mother is whimsical," says Aunt Two, and her wide mouth droops when she says this. "A full Snake clan person does not use her life for whimsy."

The three aunts are gossips by profession, transferring news, opinions and advice along with poultices, diets, splints, teeth, teas and other condiments for comfortable harmonic living. Their brother Blueberry Jon is the pharmaceutical grinder and mixer of their household.

He is a man of transformation among the shepherds and other men of the out lands who sometimes come to ask favors of him. He gives his favors to them and they in turn give him presents. When he stays in the city he does not spend his nights with his sisters and their children very often, going instead to the house of a woman named Gedda of the Tortoise clan of barley and millet, or over to the men's lodge to spend time talking to the fellows of the Arrow Society.

Ernesta has scraped a deep swathing band in her drawing pattern on the ground, a sweeping cut of river flowing past the jars with their names. She fills this trough of river with imaginery water. Tracing the side of her hand down the line of it, she stops at the bending part, thinking about the elements which are missing from her picture. How can she tell about it? Cautiously she draws a circle with two dots, then stops. Who is there to tell about what she and Margedda saw that day when it bothers her so much and she has no words for it?

Her mother would listen, and say nothing; her mother so rarely speaks, and when she does she so often bends close to Ernesta's ear whispering.

"Something about the child is different from what you might think," Donna drops this idea into the household quietly, wrapped by its insidious softness around the clattering opinions of the aunts, sly as silk the idea winds across the floor to wrap around and around the conversation until the aunts will think they have thought it.

"Ernesta has an odd way of solving problems," Donna says

one day, and the aunts stare briefly at the ordinary rectangular shaped child with her wandering eye before continuing with their constant comments on other clan affairs. But by evening they have tested her with a dozen problems, searching for what is so uniquely different in her solutions.

"Phoo," Aunt Two always says, "I don't see anything different."

"Don't be so sure," Aunt Three answers, "you know what they say. A woman with a wandering eye can cause a dry spell, or a wet one."

Ernesta's mother is not sleeping today, she is working up in the cool greenhouse on the second story of the Moon Temple. She is so connected to the plants, she says they are more individual to her than animals or humans; she says sometimes they speak to her of their confinement. The three aunts believe it is contrary to the reality of the world to carry a sensitive nature to such extremes. They also believe that it is the nature of plants to love confinement; rootless mobility, they say, is what a plant hates most. Why else do trees shriek in the wind if not in terror of losing their roots?

Ernesta is licking the little bubbles of salty water that form on her upper lip and underneath her big lower lip. She does not know how to disappear without her mother. She does not know how to describe bothersome things to anyone, even in pictures. She does not know how to draw the spirit of an idea to herself. The air hums with sunshine, a buzzing noise that seems to come from the ground. Like the air the inside of Ernesta is acutely buzzing, aware of sights and sounds, motions and meanings, even if she cannot draw the pictures of them yet too well.

From her mother she is understanding empathy and variation in all things, and from her aunts determination, ruthless self-examination, sociable exactness in all things. From her uncle she is learning deliberation, for Blueberry Jon could take four hours to mix three powders together, much to the scorn of the aunts, who considered such deliberation irrelevant in a transformational person.

"Why does he have to think about it so much?" they asked each other. "Two pinches of the first, three of the second, four of the third; does it take so much thinking to count from two to four?" But Ernesta watched the ponderosity with fascination. She loved slowness in events, and minute quantities given their due in the course of human afternoons and illnesses.

"Too much whimsy," the aunts say of their youngest sister Donna, and their mouths droop in Ernesta's direction. "Too much deliberation," they say of their brother Jon, and their mouths droop in the direction of their mother Mundane's closed-off room as though she alone is responsible. "Too much whimsy and too much deliberation do not make a full transformational woman."

All three of her aunts have philosophical opinions which are for everyday use, and which are certain in their minds from a long time ago. Ernesta is certain they would not even bother to answer a question about whether it is possible to be whimsical and useful too.

Ernesta knows that her aunts want her to become a full transformational woman. Her own mouth droops toward herself when she thinks this. She is afraid that means she would become more like them: square shaped and stern, and terrifying to children. The aunts laugh in prescribed patterns and are seldom wrong. Seen from underneath, their great protruding jaws are cluttered with teeth and guttered below with wrinkles of brown skin running down to their necks, and little black or white hairs grow on the edges of their chins in solitary strands that wiggle up and down as they talk.

Why is it not possible, Ernesta wonders, to be whimsical and useful too. She lowers her head over the row of jars while her wandering eye darkens, shooting off to the left in a frenzy of hard wondering. Even in Aunt One's half-muffled basket song Ernesta seems to hear her name: "Ernesta, do something useful. Are you doing something useful? Are you learning to count, are you thinking about the names of herbs, are you remembering songs?"

Hearing some loud humming, she looks around. Her second aunt, Aunt Two stands in the doorway with her hands held out stiffly in front of her. Aunt Two's hands are always dripping something, wet clay or wet corn meal or wet paint. All three aunts have strong square shaped hands with thick fingers and a muscle that bumped up at the side of their thumbs, from all the handy work they did all the time. Besides the usual pounding and grinding and lifting that anybody did, Aunt One had a muscle from making baskets with tightly coiled and tied material, Aunt Two's muscle made big thick pots and Aunt Three's muscle made expert false teeth held together with flattened strips of metal and tiny nails.

Aunt One has climbed out of her basket to fetch more wickers from the soaking bowl.

The basket has gotten higher, it now consists of three tall sapling willows wound around and bound together with themselves by thousands of strands of wet and dyed wickers. Aunt One's finest weave contains thirty four stitches to the inch but this basket is woven more coarsely. The saplings are strong and springy, thick as Ernesta's wrist at the butt, then tapering to the thickness of two of her fingers. They always want to straighten out again, they cannot bear their confinement. They are as hard to hold in position as it is to hold a struggling calf. Aunt One must use the whole length of her arm as well as her tight muscled hands to hold them, Aunt Two says Aunt One will get calluses up to her elbows.

Aunt Two's jaw is working.

"What are you doing outside why aren't you napping?"

"Oh," Ernesta said, "I am just waiting for something to happen."

"Nothing will happen," Aunt Two said.

"Oh you never can tell," called Aunt One. "Everything always changes."

"Nothing ever changes," Aunt Two said, shaking her messy hands. "And I'm glad for that. I love the peace of it all." To Aunt Two change meant disorder and disorder meant evil and that took up a lot of time. Aunt Two does not like to give up her time.

"Oh yes it does," Aunt One said, vigorously nodding. She swatted the thick wet wickers against the ground.

"No," Aunt Two said. "Nothing ever does change, everyone knows that."

Aunt One held the wet wicker strands in her mouth as she climbed on her short stool over the wall of her basket. "Yef ik dudds," she said speaking through the wickers.

"No," Aunt Two said, shaking her hands and going back into the house.

"Yef," sang Aunt One from inside her handy work.

Three Can Have A Large Fight With No Victor

Leading into a courtyard of major size there is an entrance to the city where an oak tree of outlandish age is living. The green leaves of the oak tree turn gradually to follow the sun; this motion is perceived by the ants who work up and down the oak tree as a tilting of their landscape so they adjust their balance accordingly. Three of the ants have stumbled half way down the broad trunk of the tree with the larva of a large beetle which is slightly writhing in danger of no longer becoming a beetle. They are cooperating in this effort though no one would know it. Several yards away from them and under the ground some roots of the oak tree are tangled in water.

A tall woman driving a cart pulled by a donkey has entered the city; she has stopped by the well in the courtyard and thrown down the bucket for water. The big wooden bucket is bumping and thumping the roots of the oak tree which are tangled in the well, and the woman is annoyed because of the obstruction and alarmed that the water level has fallen so low. The tall thin woman has a particular responsibility for the wells in this neighborhood.

At the moment she also has a responsibility to the donkey, who is thirsty and annoyed that water is always kept out of her reach down a long hole by the humans.

The tall woman has turned shouting to the oak tree that it is indecent and morally wrong to fill up a well with roots during a time of drought is it not possible to move them?

"You're drinking too much," the woman is shouting; the oak tree replies with a mammoth number of drooping greens.

Outraged that the human is spending so much attention on an immobile tree when anyone can smell perfectly good water right down there in the hole, the donkey repeats this statement out loud many times. The oak tree has been alarmed to have her roots knocked about with a bucket; she is offended and determines to grow a thicker wood callous around her more vulnerable places. Amongst the three of them they are making a great deal of racket.

Now looking again down into the well the tall woman's head is bent as though by a burden. As the oak tree's dark leaves turn imperceptibly with the sun they are disturbed by nothing, certainly not by a shadow which passes over them at such a distance it is hardly larger than each of them is.

The woman straightens to watch the shadow, she has one hand up over her eyes. She hopes the shadow is a buzzard. She knows that on a platform far outside the eastern border of city buildings lies a dead woman who is hardly resting; and her spirit is in turmoil. The tall woman's name is Sonia and her own sister is a dead woman. Among the living a dead person's presence attracts much attention and is not neutral. She herself has been in a donkey cart to visit their brother, a Bee clan quarryman on the plains to the west of the river staying among goatherds and shepherds with their flocks to tell him of their sister who has died of a peculiar head injury.

She has other problems in addition, among them a drying up well and a drying up donkey for whom she is responsible.

Sonia raises one hand to shade her eyes watching the shadow; she understands the tension of the flesh which must passively wait on a drab platform for deliverance when deliverance has the unbearable patience of wise buzzards.

A donkey tethered to a well cannot drink the water in it but an oak tree several yards away can. There is a relativity in motion.

"How soon will her spirit leave us?" Sonia is talking out loud about her sister Lillian. Sadness drags at her throat. Three days her sister has laid dead on a tall platform and everyone hates an encased spirit without its freedom. A dead person has a freedom of spirit but even in death a person is weighted with property which must first be divested.

"I hope it's today." Her arm has dropped to her side, her neck bent. She is tired, sad and irritated. The first three days of losing someone you love can be the most violent, for the holes they leave in you. Suddenly she is pulling at her hair and clothing in a fit of weeping that surprises her, upsets the donkey and leaves the oak tree indifferent. Presently she sighs and wipes her face with the palms of her hands and again lowers the bucket.

Sonia has managed to salvage half a bucket of ugly looking water by knocking further about in the roots of the oak tree who sends out unpleasant vibrations.

"Here," she says to the madly talking donkey but distracted beyond hearing the donkey has knocked the bucket out of her hand and the water is spilling.

The water from the bucket has seeped down and lies beneath them in tiny juicy drops trembling between the grains of sand in the soil; nearby root hairs from the roots of the oak tree push into these large drops and leave themselves open to absorb them.

Up on ground level she slaps her between the ears whereupon she butts her head into her chest and she is spilled backwards onto the sand like the water. Sonia is a woman who does not like to be knocked on the butt by a donkey or anybody, and she leaves to go to her house; she is so angry she is running. She does not care what ever happens to the donkey.

In small juicy drops the water lies between the grains of sand in the soil; root hairs from the roots of the oak tree have pushed into these drops and left themselves vulnerable. In tiny amounts the water along with other edible minerals is sucked between the cells of the hairs as they had been sucked between the grains of sand and not sucked between the cells in a donkey's stomach of which she is keenly aware.

18

Being Dead Is A Matter Of Internal Turmoil

High on a platform and coming to no easy rest on the eastern edge of the city lies a dead woman having internal turmoil while on the western edge of the city her live sister is losing a fight with a donkey. In this turmoil between two moving bodies the donkey has apparently won by knocking the woman over because she slapped her because she pushed the bucket out of her hands and has left the scene altogether. Whereby it now seems more likely the donkey has lost the battle because a bucket of water was the prize actually, and it is streaming down through the dry earth to the roots of an oak tree who knows very well what to do with it. Whereby the donkey is bawling, a combination rasping and squeaking carried easily to the ears of the tall woman as she enters her own courtyard and has caused her to lose the satisfaction of mind that comes to a person who successfully gives water and other things to the animals in its care and feels responsible.

A tall thin woman named Sonia is beset with many problems, one of them is her donkey but the others are more pressing though not so noisy.

Outside the city and high on a platform of heavy meaning lies a dead person, a dead person is not neutral. As a body becomes less and less moving on the outside it becomes more and more moving on the inside. Three days of hot sun tends to make matters more and more interesting and less neutral.

Having a living sister who has just had a fight with a donkey on a day when you are dead and in turmoil is only one reason for no easy resting. Twenty five buzzards waiting have such perseverance but patience can also build turmoil. Waiting in them builds up a kind of tension, waiting in what they are watching builds up another. Two kinds of tension make a special patience that can have so much perseverance as to be explosive.

The problem of a dead woman is too much property encasing the spirit because a wise buzzard does not care for hard surfaces or difficult entanglements. A buzzard who is built for neatness and is fastidious in all matters depends on proper timing and good judgement. The sun is a good stove for certain kinds of cooking since cooking changes the properties of matter, a matter of internal mixtures and tensions. The softening of matter is one property of cooking, a property which has been advantageous to both babies and buzzards.

A dead woman and her useless flesh that laid so heavy now that it could not move of its own volition has no other volition but the release of her spirit. Trapped in her only property, a spirit cased in hard muscle and firm fat will not find an easy way out. On a platform heavy with meaning and internal turmoil there can be no easy resting but a wise buzzard is full of hesitations and patience.

As a body strives to release its spirit from the stuff of its former existence, it becomes more placid and unfeeling on the outside, but more moving on the inside. Deep down inside the body a new motion works vigorously preparing the body for the release of its spirit, churning and working at the hard places, softening and blending, merging and smoothing away the hard defined lines of its former life and means of motion. This straining for a release from hard definition begins to show in a certain strained puffiness which is closely watched by a wise buzzard. A different will is working, differently moving, different from the one which had walked about and worked and shared itself with others like it. Now it is a sharing of itself with others unlike it. The body which had all of its time in life used its willfulness with others like it must now use its willfulness with others unlike it because the flesh does not always give up its spirit easily.

High on a platform of uneasy resting a dead woman has been busy working at blending. Although there is more internal turmoil there is now less and less waiting and more tension.

A Tall Woman's Idea Of Justice
May Be Different From A Short One's

Inside the city and into the workyard of the Bee clan, a tall thin woman is slowing her angry pace. She has returned to her courtyard having lost a fight with her donkey, and has found her workyard in a worse condition than she left it. A tall woman who has just returned from a sad overnight journey and ought to be cooling off with her daughter, a fan and cold lemonade is instead agitated. True her sister has recently died of a head injury and that is sad but that is the least of it. Although a death is sorrowful it doesn't make her helpless and angry.

All her burdens are on her at one time, as a tall woman she

has begun bending. First her head began on the long journey, then her neck and shoulders. Now even her back is bending. She straightens when she sees her tall daughter and it is a false motion.

This is the situation of the Bee clan, to which the tall woman Sonia belongs: they are in charge of foundations. They are in charge of brickmaking and public ovens, waterworks, wells, canals and plumbing. They are in charge of all new constructions, including a new temple planned by the river. They are famous for not getting along well with animals but that is the least of it.

As water bearing women Sonia and her dead sister Lillian had once been in charge of draining a large marsh at the end of the river road to make way for more gardens. However they had argued for a new measuring temple instead that would link the city of Mundane to the great metropolis to the far south and were now busy planning the blessing of the ground for the new construction.

The workyards of the Bee clan people smell often of wood, metal and plaster, their spaces are crowded with bricks, tubing, planks and instruments of various kinds. In the city at large people say that the Bee clan has a marvelous sense of disorder. Of this they are proud and comfortable.

However the situation of the Bee clan is this: the Snake clan must have a colorful mural to display at the midsummer festival, they say their sense of memory and history depends on it. They were impatient to have it finished, they argued eloquently for it at the last council of elders. They persuaded vehemently for the glory of their mural in spite of the Bee clan protesting they could not easily do the work on it. The Bee clan must bake all the hundreds of tiles for the mural and all their large public ovens were being cleaned and repaired during the summer. The large public ovens for baking tiles are cleverly located outside the limits of the city so the noise and heat of them will bother no one, unfortunately during this period they cannot be used.

"Nevertheless," said the transforming women of the Snake clan, "we want our mural, it must be ready."

In particular had three younger sisters of the Snake clan argued this sentence, not the fourth who is known for whimsy, the three who are so well known for their solidarity. Sonia remembered now the stern solidarity of their faces in their argument. Remembering makes her grit her teeth together as she looks around at the confusion now in her workyard. Her imported lemon tree has fainted. Stacks of tiles which must be baked

21

at home in the cooking ovens outside their own Bee clan houses with burning fires, day and night are destroying all coolness and bringing confusion.

There is a difference between having confusion and having a marvelous sense of disorder which other people in the city do not understand about the Bee clan.

The usual cool smells of wood and plaster have been replaced by the acrid stink of too much smoky fuel burning too quickly, the workyard is a squalor of unhappy babies and bickering adults. Sweat pours down every body and dogs yap in irritation. Heat rashes have erupted on all the children and food spoils, no one can sleep and everyone hates the waking hours.

Across the city the Snake clan is not swearing and bothered by their own cranky children, Snake clan children are not sweating and bothered by their own cranky adults. Snake clan children still had plenty of space to play in, and warm meals in the cool indoors of the evening. Bee clan children were eating dull millet cakes with lukewarm goat's milk because no one could bear to light another fire, no one could bear that many sweaty bodies milling about indoors, and outdoors was blistering with the heat from the ovens.

Seeing this scene as similar to how she had left it yesterday Sonia draws back her upper lip in a gesture of anger. This exposes one of her front teeth, a startling expression. She will use this startling expression more and more throughout the day until the exposed tooth becomes very dry. She is watched from a roof above by her tall thin daughter, who often imitates her.

Alternately bending her head or raising it and snarling, Sonia stalks through the workyard and curses. She lays out the whole list of her and all their troubles; lethargic ears turn away from her. Heavily working the bellows, her cousin turns his head to mumble, "It is never any use to argue with a donkey." Sonia spits in the tile dust, but no one is responding. Clearly she has a strong sense of injustice, not completely developed.

Sonia has noticed her daughter on the roof and momentarily adjusts her terrible posture. She climbs the ladder to stand beside her. Jessi-ma is a skinny spider of a daughter to have with knobby knees, elbows and knuckles. She is a parody of her thin graceful mother; with their eyes they always seem to be laughing at each other. Sonia hugs Jessi-ma's bony self but does not dance around, she follows her into their second floor room with her head bent down.

They hold each other and cry briefly as they do often now remembering the absence of the dead woman from their house

22

when they see her bed and belongings or her friends or her son or each other.

A house is constructed for coolness in the summer. A series of rooms can be so well built that milk will turn cold in the lower chambers, cheese will remain hard, drops of cold water will run down the walls. The Bee clan spent centuries developing such architecture, meticulously engineering cities perfect in their regulations of temperatures, balancing the changes of heat and cold almost as scientifically as the bees themselves do in their hives. Now it is wrecked by one foolish decision in the council.

Inside the close stifling room a little boy sleeps with rosy cheeks splashed over his brown skin. He is Sonia's nephew, the child of a dead woman, her sister.

"Jon Lilly believes that you can fly," Jessi-ma says.

"I probably can." The mother sits wearily in the doorway leading to the air shaft, fanning herself with a wide brush fan. With the light falling behind her she is a dark shadow, the fan is her wing.

Startled, Jon Lilly snaps awake from his nap in the corner of his mother's bed. He stares at his aunt, who has the appearance of a terrible bird landing in the airshaft. He begins to cry.

"Take care of your cousin," the mother says.

Jessi-ma plays with Jon Lilly's hair, and tickles him.

"Why are you crying," she whispers.

"I don't know," he whispers. "I saw a shadow." He has stopped. They wrestle. The mother is her own shape again, bending over a group of wilted vegetables her daughter has traded from the gardeners at the market: parsnips, onions, peppers so limp from the heat they have lost much interest in living.

Sonia grunts at their limpness, her anger returns to her. She stares at nothing. Sweat runs into her eyes unnoticed, and this is disturbing to the daughter. Jessi-ma lets Jon Lilly tickle her and pull her hair until it hurts. Then she throws him off her stomach in nasty irritation. He screams. The mother is thinking so hard she hears nothing.

The vultures that circle in Jon Lilly's dreams, circle in reality over the wooden platforms set up on the east end of the city, outside the last habitation. There lie waiting for their time to be ripe, the city's yearly crop of dead, given over to the carnivorous birds of horror and usefulness, awkwardness and grace. For flesh is of the earth, and should be given back to the birds who are such fine flesh-keepers, while bones are of the bones of earth and should be buried in it and kept. The spirit then is free to return to the wind.

At the end of each ceremony of returning, the bones were collected by their respective families, cleaned and painted, honored and put in jars. The jars were buried under the bed in remembrance though never before the dead person was celebrated in dances and paintings.

Under Jessi-ma's bed lay a cousin who had died in infancy three years before, after taking the trouble to be born to her Aunt Lillian. The bones of Jon Lilly's mother would go under Sonia's bed, since they were sisters and their mother was not living in Mundane but rather in the great metropolis of Celeste that was their Bee clan place of origin.

Now Jon Lilly saw birds everywhere, especially in his dreams. In a few days the nightmares would disappear and Jon Lilly would become surely happy like everyone else in the Bee clan, whose people are irrepressible in their love of their own motion and fascination with everything that lies still and can be handled. They had also a great impatience toward material matters so that they could not let a mountain be a mountain or a tree a tree but must take them apart and put them together in some other form of their own measuring.

Some people thought their tendencies to do this were entirely too frequent and unwarranted while others said that it was good, that Ana herself built and restructured things and that the Bee clan came from Ana. Certainly she blessed them, since nothing bad could happen but what they would turn it to some advantage, and celebrate its happening. Even when the ancient volcano far northeast of the city had newly erupted, the Bee clan was directly there, riding on donkeys borrowed from the Lion clan, gathering the ash to mix another kind of cement and bathing in steamy pools of near-boiling rainwater, or so the clan story tellers say.

As water bearing people, the Bee clan concerned themselves with rain in all its aspects, with plumbing and the course of the river, especially how to get some of it into the fields for irrigation. This was peculiar given that they had a reputation for being terrible swimmers. Jessi-ma upheld their reputation, sinking in bodies of water with honor and dignity at every opportunity.

Presently Jessi-ma brushes at her mother's hair carelessly. Jon Lilly has fallen back asleep, his face twitching now and slippery with sweat.

"How is Uncle Jad?" Jessi-ma asked formally. Her mother's tiredness and unusual scowling frightened her.

"He is fine, he is dry like all the shepherds and like all of them he spits in the dust and prays for a woman with a wandering eye to help him." Sonia's brother was usually tending the family herds in the countryside but lately he had a special temple project as a stonecutter cutting foundation blocks in a quarry which needed summer rain to keep the dust out of everyone's eyes and noses.

Sonia began pacing up and down sometimes bending and sometimes straightening as though she could not decide which attitude to have. She explained her many problems to her listening daughter: concerning the donkey, the heavy dead tension, the clogged wells, the new temple to have been blessed and formally measured by Lillian and herself at the festival, and mostly about the terrible ovens burning day and night in the clan yards.

"Now what is it about justice," Sonia asked. "Everything being equal, there would be justice. But where is it in all of this? If justice begins with equality." She straightened when she said this.

"But there is no equality involved in this situation with those damned tiles. No none at all." She bent when she said this. "The tiles are for the Snake clan, so they are so happy. Their milk is not clabbering, their children are not covered with heat rash; their babies do not have diarrhea from lousy cooking. No, they are happy. I'll bet those three cronies are so happy they're sitting over there in the shade making baskets and singing while I curse in my own daughter's presence."

She paused with her head cocked to the left listening to the workyard sounds below them, of bad tempered people slamming things around.

"We could take the babies for them to cure," Jessi-ma suggested, thinking hard of what would help. "They're the ones with medicines, cures and changes. They know about alterations of the body and the mind. They could take care of the rashes and bad temper."

Sonia straightened. "We might have to take the whole damned clan over there before these next two weeks are over." She creased her forehead. "You've given me an idea."

She bent. "But it would never work."

She straightened. "But maybe it would."

She bent. "I'd have to persuade all my relatives—they're so sluggish."

She straightened. "On the other hand, I'm so mad, I could persuade anybody."

"Mama, what *is* it?" Jessi-ma was bursting.

"Equality," Sonia said suddenly smiling. "Justice begins

with equality. We'll take all you children over there and let you stay with the Snake clan."

"For keeps?" Jessi-ma was horrified.

"No, just until they reconsider the implications of their decision, after they have a chance to share their happiness with us who have so little." Sonia grabbed Jessi-ma's arms. She kissed her hands, she swung her off her feet. Giggling, they danced wildly around the room until they fell down sweating and puffing on Jessi-ma's bed.

"Why don't we take you over there first to get started and you can make your presence very apparent. You know how to do that don't you?"

"Make my presents apparent? What presents shall I bring?" Jessi-ma asked. She looked all around the room.

"No, no," Sonia said, raking a tall ivory comb through her own hair carelessly. "Your *presence*. That means just be yourself—only more so. Be the way you would be at home if no one ever stopped you." She laughed.

"Oh," Jessi-ma said with interested eyes. "I know how to do *that*." She bit her lip as Sonia tossed her the delicate pick comb.

"You think I don't know? Here, fix your hair while I find someone to watch Jon Lilly. He's sleeping again. Sleeping and crying, that's all he ever does. Love him all you can, Jessi-ma, until he feels better."

She dashed out of the room in long slender strides. Jessi-ma's eyes shone. She loved her mother's many ways. Holding a hand mirror, she forgot about her tangled hair, instead practicing curling her lip until one tooth showed.

Water Bearing Women
Walk With Watery Movements

A wooden latticework trellis which Aunt Two had stuck in the ground last year in the certainty that it would attract her to plant some pod vines, although she has not gotten around to doing so stands between Ernesta and Aunt One's basket across the yard. The trellis throws square shadows onto the scene Ernesta is re-enacting on the ground with bottles and jars. She places them sometimes with great concentration, sometimes with one ear cocked to the side listening to passing street noises for some girls to be going by who would be of greater interest than this solitary form of thinking.

In the Snake clan yard watched by three formidable aunts Ernesta is a rectangular shaped person when she stands up but now she crouches. Mumbling to herself she has manipulated her five jars with names through the day at the river to the point where they fell in, and after pouring a little imaginary water on the girl jars for authenticity, she is bringing them back to town on the river road, which is a long scratch on the ground leading nearly to the trellis.

Past the mounds and ditches of the new temple foundation, past the marshes where Aunt One sometimes collects special wickers with her toes, past the boggy mud where all the basket-makers bury their wickers for days in order to dye them black. The five jars with the most elaborate lidded one named for Ernesta herself in the lead, then the graceful skinny one for Jessi-ma, the colorful stubby one for Margedda, the plain one with broken handle for Fran-keen, the littlest potbellied stripey one for Dee, all dripping water and walking tip toe into the city as they had in the evening three days ago, numb with shock.

Ernesta drew the city as an irregular circle with X marks for her three aunts and other concerned adults who had met them in the marketplace. Everyone was in an uproar, and it seemed half the city was there and all erupting at the five girls. In their jar shapes Ernesta stood them in a circle of explanation surrounded by X marks.

Then she placed a square of cloth on the ground and laid a twig on it, representing a dead woman. This was Jessi-ma's Aunt Lillian, someone rocking and pulling her hair explained to them, who was found dead by two young men of the Arrow Society on the river road only an hour before.

"We thought you were *all* dead," someone else moaned. This was Sonia, Jessi-ma's mother, a tall woman holding a screaming young boy and clutching each of the returned children in turn.

Ernesta slid the Ernesta jar away from the circle of X marks, gliding it to the square of cloth. The jar leaned over the twig. She had never seen a dead person up close before.

Aunt Three's high voice of concern interrupted her thinking. "Oh, that's terrible. How can you bear it?"

Startled, Ernesta looked up, seeing through the squares of the trellis and across the yard that someone has come to the gate knocking and has been answered by Aunt Three. Both Aunt One and Ernesta have been too engrossed in their work to hear her come from the house and cross the yard. This took a lot of concentration on their parts, Aunt Three being a heavy-walking enthusiastic person who displaced a great deal of space and wore bells on her clothing by inclination.

The rectangular shaped girl stood up to peer through the trellis, putting all her fingers into the squares. A tall thin woman from the Bee clan has apparently brought her daughter to play and gossip with Ernesta. Their faces are sweating and their hair is carelessly tied in tangles. The tall woman Sonia is talking very loudly and joking with bitterness in her voice.

Looking at her, Ernesta remembers that she is a water bearing woman, full of balance and bearing who is responsible for wells and waterworks and also she had been working with her now dead sister Lillian to build a new temple building. Was there, Ernesta wondered, such a thing as having too much bearing because of having too much to bear? She does not think it strange that she had just been thinking about Sonia and her daughter Jessi-ma and now here they are.

"It's bad, you can bet," the Bee clan woman leaning on the gate nodded vigorously into Aunt Three's face, with her upper lip pulled back to expose one tooth. "We're melting completely into the walls." She looked around as though hoping for other sets of ears to hear her, but Aunt One was not stirring inside her big basket.

"Clay tiles!" The Bee woman laughed suddenly. She had a loud voice. "You haven't seen anything yet. We're going to bring you some that are made with human fat!" She slapped her long thigh, then clutched it, jiggling the spare flesh. "See this? How many tiles do you think this will make?" She laughed raucously.

"Not many," Aunt Three said. She slapped Sonia's thigh too and laughed too, actually she liked the humor of the Bee people, although her two older sisters thought them too pointed and spare and irreverent of broader feelings.

Although nothing ever changes, it often happens that if you see a person once, you will see them again soon. It is the way of looking that matters. Or perhaps, Ernesta thought, it is a matter of willfulness. As Jessi-ma crossed the yard toward the trellis, Ernesta remembered her as someone who had been second in the line of them who played down at the river and met up with a mama lion.

They had not seen each other since that spectacular day, when they were all five picked out as though at random by Aunt Three when she found them milling around the public bakery collecting leftover fruitbread for the Bee clan dovecote Jessi-ma had promised to show them, and had sent them on the errand to gather reeds for the midsummer festival.

Now, seeing Jessi-ma again through the trellis, Ernesta could not resist whooping with excitement. Her wandering eye turned as straight as the other one, and both eyes glowed.

The whooping sound brought Aunt One's head jerking up out of the top of the basket; she went ssssst and glared at them briefly before disappearing inside again. Aunt One has certainly gotten carried away with her basket. Soon she will need a ladder to get into it and a stool to stand on while working inside. The basket is presently eight feet across but she as she is working it is increasingly clear that it will narrow at the top to six feet across.

Her design is nearly complete, a combination of the universal and the personal. She will not sign it, though she will leave a rectangular gate of space undone in the top rim so that any bad thoughts she had while making it can get out. Otherwise, the grains might rot near the bottom, closed in with evil thoughts. Sixty bushels of millet or wheat will fit into it, the basket can easily be in use fifty years after Aunt One is dead and if it is buried with her bones, scraps of it could possibly be found thirty centuries hence to prove her and all their existences as long as Mundane stays in a dry climate, and this coming winter will surely be easy on her arthritis since she exercised her fingers so thoroughly on its weaving.

"Jessi-ma," the tall woman calls across the yard with no trace of severity, "don't break everything at once." She smiles a big toothy smile at Aunt Three and leaves walking away with watery motions.

"Oh my," Aunt Three murmurs softly with increasing interest. "I wonder if something is going to happen."

Jessi-ma smiles a big toothy smile at Ernesta through the trellis. They were both very excited though no one could get more excited than Jessi-ma. She was so clumsy when excited that she had been forbidden to express extreme emotions when she was within five feet of breakable objects by everyone in the Bee clan. Jessi-ma was so clumsy that she had once knocked her uncle's goat completely unconscious by accidently clipping it under the chin with her elbow while drawing back her arm to throw a rock. The young goat, who had been reaching up to the branch of a hackberry tree, never ate hackberry leaves again and displayed suspicion of trees in general.

Ernesta remembered a lot about Jessi-ma including that she could not swim, that she was born and would die skinny. When she got into the water she appeared to sink because no part of her was either round or flat enough to form a surface that would buoy her up. Jessi-ma said she had learned this the first, second and third times that she tried to swim and knew she would learn it better and better throughout her life.

At the moment they both remembered the lion, they looked at each other now through the trellis with big eyes, wondering if each other knew how much the lion had grown in size the more it was discussed by the adults, who called it "The Lion of Mundane." They laughed spontaneously and covered their mouths. "It was a terribly large lion?" Jessi-ma asked.

Ernesta burst out laughing and hopped around, "Yes I believe it was enormous, and with blazing yellow eyes." She held her arms out pretending that such a distance was the width of the lion's head. She was agitated and could feel the excitement spreading from her through the square spaces in the trellis all the way to Jessi-ma, who at once leaped into the air, screaming and throwing her arms and legs in a whirlwind of directions.

"No, red eyes and as big as a house!" she shrieked and came down full force on the trellis of round branches tied at square angles, tangling all her hands and feet in the spaces.

The trellis broke at the bottom falling forward with her body mixed up in it, squishing Ernesta flat on the ground underneath in one surprise motion. They lay face to face with the trellis between them, screaming into each other's mouths. Jessi-ma could not untangle herself at all even though she was on top, it was Ernesta who finally found a way to wriggle out from under and then had to help unravel Jessi-ma's twisting feet from the latticework. She had never seen a body so loose or bony.

Having rolled every which way collecting dust, the jars with names had wiped out the X mark scratches and other designations. Ernesta noticed also that the twig named "Lillian" had snapped in two.

Disturbed out of her work, Aunt One's dry form loomed curiously over them for a moment with her chin bobbing and then she marched back to her basket.

Ernesta was enraged at the dust on herself. She sat in a glaring huddle next to Jessi-ma, brushing at her arms and with her eye wandering off to the left in a huff.

Ernesta likes having shiny dark brown skin for which she has been praised. A thin layer of dust tends to turn shiny brown surfaces grey as ash, which Ernesta does not like and she does not like the feel of chalk either. Oil behooves Ernesta; she has a bottle of her own which is not for drinking or cooking. Ernesta's skin when it is oiled shines like a beetle's back and makes her feel prosperous.

In the dry summer days when dust fell down upon the earth like dew and settled over everything, Ernesta could escape the feeling of chalk only by staying in an upright position. Now she felt as though she had been rolled in chalk as sliced vegetables are rolled in flour for deep frying. She pushed with angry hands in her hair to get the cloud of dust out of it and brushed snappily her chalky feeling arms.

Jessi-ma's hair is frizzy too but it sticks up any which way in several directions at one time. Her hair is not self contained or especially shiny black like Ernesta's rather it is a dull dark brown and unruly similar to her face, so it is not a contrast to her face, it does not keep her face from looking skinny with a pointed chin.

"I'm sorry if I hurt you," she said, rubbing her ankles all around the scraped places.

"You didn't hurt me," Ernesta said sourly and as if that would have been better. "You messed me up altogether."

They sat side by side for a while in an atmosphere of mistrust.

Ernesta's name doesn't have a special meaning but Jessima's does; and Jessi-ma confides this finally as a peace offering: that her own name means 'beloved of Ma,' Ma being an ancient vampire who lives in the mountains that no one treasures so much as Ana more. Her name is considered a slight joke in her family, a family that likes to make fun of itself. Ernesta absorbs this gifted information without forming an opinion or an expression.

In a usually slow pre-festival summer season, too many things are happening meanwhile Ernesta is concerned with the matter of leaderships and balance. Having been first in a line of young girls who efficiently overcame a perilous situation, she must test for herself whether this is going to be a habit with her. Already Jessi-ma has set a certain pace for the afternoon by squashing her with a trellis; she is determined to reverse the direction.

"Let's play house," Ernesta suggested.

"Okay," Jessi-ma agreed, and immediately began searching the yard for material to work with and make a house. This was new to Ernesta, who always used her imagination for the 'house' and then stocked it with whatever small neat objects she had found or made for toys.

Not so the Bee clan, who took the word 'house' very literally.

Jessi-ma was plainly soon disgusted with the neatly kept,

overly swept yard of the Snakes. Her own Bee yard was rich with tools, wood planks, new cut stones and broken bricks.

A City Is Alive To Its Constructors

In the eyes of the Bee clan, and in its moving hands the city was a large live body, a personal great sow of a being for whom they were responsible. None of them could shudder in the wind without feeling it as the breath of the city, the very rich smells of it from all the openings of a body. All the city's physical substance of clay, plaster, stone and wood they perceived as living muscle, in their eyes the flesh of the walls breathing, fattening, changing, sloughing of plaster and paint like a snakeskin in the hardly raining rainy season, cracking with old age in the sun needing massage, comfort and repair as any body does.

In the minds of the Bee clan the tunnels and piping for water and sewage, the rise and fall of the water levels in the wells, the moaning of the wind down the streets and around corners were manifestations of the physical substance of the city with its upkeep, usefulness and beauty falling into their keep. Grooming, repairing and reshaping as was necessary, the Bee women slapped plaster over the bricks they had laid with the quick smooth motions of a mother spirit who was deliberately shaping skin over bones and muscle. They laid out the ventilation systems with the certain knowledge that they were insuring the very breath and temperature of the rooms within.

In the quarries the men cut their stones as carefully as anyone cuts a cake for children, with that amount of equality and much more delicate exactness to say nothing of sweating and swearing. Donkeys hauled their quarrystone cakes for them though not too willingly. Helping the other clans to lay out gardens, pipes, hutches and granaries as they would imagine in the belly of a sow the innards lay harmoniously functioning, and designing the multiple complex temples to be the keenest eyes, ears, spine and thinking glands of a city which for them never rested or stopped living and to whom they were never indifferent, however impatient, the Bee clan people sang and chanted of love for physical substances, stone and metal, and the geometrical progressions of hot and cold molded clay.

"There is nothing to play with," Jessi-ma announced disgustedly. After scouring among the neat beds of flowering herbs and medicinal bushes planted symmetrically under Aunt Two's supervision in Ernesta's yard she could not find so much as a stray ribbon or a string blowing in the corner.

"Can't we just make up the house?" Ernesta asked.

"No."

"Why not?"

"Because," Jessi-ma said sounding like her dead aunt Lillian had once sounded, "we," she said, speaking with her hands for her entire clan and its thousands of years of continual persistence, "we are the constructors, and the constructors always have to build the house before anyone can play in it or do anything in it."

Ernesta groaned. "Well, what about this piece of charcoal. We could just draw the bottom of the house and then make up the rest of it. What I mean is, we could draw the floor plan and pretend it isn't built yet."

"It *isn't* built yet," Jessi-ma said.

"We could just admit that," Ernesta said, "we could play future-house." That solution was suitable to the constructor. Ernesta turned a piece of household charcoal over to her and watched as she drew precisely straight lines around the yard for a four room house. She drew in extra lines for doorways, windows, bed platforms, pillows, cooking pits, fireplaces and plenty of roof and yard space for outdoor working and lounging. Ernesta watched in amazement. "Don't you think it's a little large for the two of us?"

Jessi-ma suddenly looked secretive. "Other people might show up," she said. "You never know."

When she had finished, Ernesta took over the game. She took a step forward and said, "Now I'll be Ernesta and you be Jessima. And I am a Snake medicine woman, good thing for you, because you have a disease, a fatal wasting disease, and I'm going to treat you."

"I don't want to have a fatal wasting disease," Jessi-ma protested. "I don't want a fatal anything." Ernesta could see that she was thinking of her Aunt Lillian dying recently of a fatal head injury on a day when they had gone to the river and been very close without seeing her. However in a fit of realism Ernesta pushed down on her friend's shoulders until she collapsed inside the charcoal lines of a bed platform.

"Pretend this is all in your life chart," Ernesta began again slyly, "and that every once in a while you simply go out of balance. And pretend it's also in your chart that someone comes along to heal you, so you feel like living again, someone, say, who looks a lot like myself." Ernesta dusted off her hands briskly and

33

gathered her jars together in a new row without names.

"Now suppose," she continued, "that she is such a full medicine woman of the Snake clan, who is so well balanced herself, and has so much much bearing, and so little little whimsy, that she does persuade you to heal your wasting disease. And then you will owe her a favor. Maybe," she added enticingly, "she could fix it so you never do get another fatal wasting disease or go out of balance or be clumsy or anything. And then you will bring everything you need to finish building her house for her." Jessi-ma lay propped in suspicion on one elbow, watching Ernesta run in and out of the doorway to the house bringing ingredients to mix various conglomerations into her row of containers.

"How do you know what the sickness is?" she challenged.

"Open your mouth," Ernesta said. "See that tongue?"

"No," said Jessi-ma.

"Well I do, and it definitely has fatal disease spots on it. A rotten-footed spirit has been walking on your tongue."

"What color are they?"

"Blue." Ernesta brought three transforming medicine mixtures to the bedside.

Jessi-ma fingered her tongue dis-easily while Ernesta drew pictures of the rotten-footed spirit on the floor by the bed with the charcoal. She had Jessi-ma draw and then lay on the pictures and she said certain sentences, mumbling to keep her secrets. Jessi-ma began to look impressed, especially with the pictures.

Ernesta began to sing; Jessi-ma did not look so impressed. "You sing awful," she said. Ernesta glared at her, then sprinkled a mixture of stale oil, powdered pollen dust and crumpled garlic roots onto Jessi-ma's tongue. Jessi-ma choked.

"See there, you're nearly dead already," Ernesta persisted with her game, but the choking unexpectedly continued. When slapping her on the back didn't help Ernesta told her to go over to the wall standing upside down for a while which Jessi-ma did balancing herself on her hands and with her feet walking up the wall. Shortly she coughed spitting out remnants of roots and recovered.

When they had gone back into their unfinished house Ernesta looked at her now puffy-faced companion and relented. She, who was kind so often to everyone had been mean to Jessi-ma in a fit of realism.

"I'm sorry," she said.

"It's okay. I feel much better. I just drown easily." However, then she began to cry for her aunt who had not recovered from *her* fatal unbalancing and so Ernesta wrapped her arms around her and sat on the chalky ground with her while she cried.

After a while Jessi-ma finished crying and produced another idea, an idea about making walls. It is definitely not easy to play house with anyone from the Bee clan when they take it all so manifestly.

Ernesta wanting to cheer her friend up raised no protest when Jessi-ma began putting all the five pots who had once had names in a row, the beautiful round jugs made so apparently easily by the adults. She put them all in a row standing up and then Jessi-ma mixed spit and dirt dug from the yard with her long thumbnails. With this mixture they plastered the jars together at the bottoms. As the clay dried it cemented the bottoms solidly, single jugs no more but an intricate short wall inlaid with the round stomachs of five jars.

They are pleased. They are pleased to run their hands, giggling, over the round clay stomachs of the jars which now remind them of a row of human stomachs, brightly colored and without belly buttons. They do this many times, shrieking and looking at each other with bright eyes of girls who know that growing up is not too far away.

Now Jessi-ma has another refinement of her idea; digging out the contents of the jars she fills them with tiny flowers and stands them like a row of breasts or a short water pipe harmonica. The two friends lean far down to the ground on their bellies, they cover the tops of the jars with their mouths to see if they can suck the flowers out; they play fierce melodies; they blow air harshly into the jars to make the petals bubble and dance. They suck sticky flower parts out and blow them into each other's shrieking faces.

The two are doing all of this when Aunt Two and Aunt Three come together to stand behind them. Aunt Two's potter hands are dripping with clay from the careful ware she is making. Clearly Aunt Two once made all the little jugs in the yard, herself made them with their pretty painted designs with no intention that they should be stuck to each other with mud and used for flower shrieking games.

The wrath of the almighty aunts is a terrible thing to Ernesta. They wave their arms and shout, their garments whip through the air, their big chopping chins are terrifying to see from below. Their hands are pushy and strong against the young flesh of the two children, their very flesh crackles.

Jessi-ma now must go inside and lie down as though for a

nap. Ernesta must lie down as though she is a still younger child for a nap. She is forbidden to play with jars, jugs, baskets or water. They are sent to separate rooms to lie down on pallets as though for tiny babies. Not even the warm ancient faint pee smell of the pallet comforts Ernesta who cries pitifully for herself and for her in-between age. Her jars, baskets and imaginations have been taken away from her, and her afternoon has been taken away from her. She hates Jessi-ma.

Certainly she should never have trusted anyone who is so skinny and has a funny name anyhow, anyway anyone who is called the beloved of a dirty old bloodsucker who lives in the mountains is bound to be a disrupter. Ernesta fell asleep lightly dreaming first of living uneasily in Aunt One's basket, trying to keep out of the way of constantly moving crane feet. In the middle of her sleep sweat came on her face as she saw in her head a face she had been unable to draw on the ground earlier. It had a twig in its mouth with a pink stain and caused her to grind her own teeth in dismay.

A Mad Donkey Makes Unhappy Noises

In a busy major courtyard where someone has left a mad donkey, other things are happening. In moving a jar-shaped sack down the complicated trunk of an oak tree, three ants who appear uncoordinated have actually come a great distance. They have not been so much hunting as they have been gathering, they have gathered in this case one of the fruits of a large beetle.

Just outside the entrance to their deep underground city the three hardly working ants have become exhausted, they are one by one wandering in strange circles wobbling and waving delicate knobby antennas and falling. Soon they are lying down around the large larva as though dead. Shortly they are found by other ants from the underground who notice the writhing larva but paying no attention they instead run to the three exhausted ants and grip them, wrestling and appearing to murder them.

However they are not murdering them, they are feeding them a soft sweet liquid food with their mouths in order to provide energy and information which are often the same thing. In a short while the three exhausted ants are standing strong and recovered, they again take hold of the larva moving it down into the entrance and along the winding streets to a chamber in the underground city. No workers have been left staggering on top ill or deserted.

All of this business and more is known to the oak tree and to her is not a matter of indifference, as too many beetles in one season have been known to eat everything in sight. Nobody loves the absolute greediness of too many beetles.

All day long the millions of feet which tromp about on the body of the oak tree are not ticklish to her or irritating; they keep her trimmed, groomed and orderly. For her part she provides them with most of the essentials of life never eating them until they are already dead and disintegrated. By and large all living things return in some form to the slowly growing oak tree who is of an outlandish age, and this is one reason she has such a massive store of energy and information. Those who have known her bring stuff back to her according to their alterations. Currently the dark green leaves turn imperceptibly sapping in the sunlight, while deep below her rooty toes wriggle among carbohydrates and iron.

In a little while outside her window Ernesta woke from her miserable nap hearing more adult voices. Raising up she peeked out in time to see the tall thin woman Sonia again standing at the Snake clan gate with Aunt One who has left her basket. Sonia was holding a little boy in her arms and looking distracted. The other two aunts came out so they stood all three in a row together, broad backed and stern in their similarity. As usual they are all three dressed in dark red and white dresses, a formidable color of their own making. Again Ernesta heard the loud voice with its complaints about the overheating, complaints said as though to be heard all over town, understood and acted upon. Again Aunt Three's expression was being slightly sympathetic while her two older sisters stood solid faced and unwavering.

Looking into the heavy faces of their solidarity, Sonia had a sinking feeling which she let go all the way to the bottom of her stomach and then let rise again in a bubble of determination, remembering that justice begins with resistance on both sides. In the in between wavering of her willfulness she decided to act quickly.

Quickly she thrust Jon Lilly into Aunt Two's folded arms. "Can you watch him a minute? I've got to run home and tend my ovens."

At Aunt Two's shocked look she has added, "For the tiles, you know—we're trying to hurry with them, and we're afraid meanwhile the children will get sick.".

Sonia was hustling back down the street as Aunt Two grumbled, "If you don't want to get baked, don't get in the oven," by which she meant that some things could never be changed, and that if you were born into a family of bakers, baking was the least you could do about it.

Aunt Two put Jon Lilly down because he was screaming. He stopped as soon as she was no longer holding him.

"Bee clan children," Aunt Two remarked, "are plainly disruptive." The adults left him alone in the courtyard except for Aunt One who gave him a hug and a kiss and went back into her handy work. Jon Lilly sat dreaming in the shadow of the basket tracing the outlines of the design with his sticky fingers. He began telling stories to himself.

In a few minutes Jessi-ma the disrupter stuck her long head through the window above Ernesta's round head.

"Pssssst," she said.

"You stink and all of your teeth are going to fall out," Ernesta said fiercely.

"What?" Jessi-ma asked.

"You stink and worms are going to come out of your neck," Ernesta continued.

The hair rose on the back of Jessi-ma's neck; even though Ernesta wasn't a full grown Snake woman still the cursing of Snake clan people was considered powerful stuff if not transformative.

"Stop that," she said.

"Your belly is going to swell up and a big ostrich is going to kick out of the middle and take all your guts with him, and you'll be moaning and rolling on the ground and no one will help you and _____"

"Stop cursing me, Ernesta. Spirits might hear you and make it come true."

"I hope they do."

"Oh come on, don't be mad at me. I have another idea that won't get us into any trouble. Take back what you said and come with me."

"I hate your ideas," Ernesta said, which is not true. And because it is not true Ernesta crawled through the window and crouched outside whispering with her friend.

"I have some business at the well in the main plaza," Jessi-ma said. "I'm going to take Jon Lilly. Do you want to come?"

"What kind of business?"

"It's my mother's business, it's about justice and it's very interesting."

Ernesta could not resist, so they took turns holding Jon

Lilly's hand climbing three ladders and two walls, meandering two streets and four roofs until they reached a wide major courtyard with a well and a donkey and an oak tree.

The still-tethered donkey was making a terrible nerve-wracking sound by bellowing down the well where there is a strong echo. She was extremely sad with little crusts in the corners of her eyes.

"Poor donkey!" Ernesta said.

"That's the tacky donkey who knocked my mother down," Jessi-ma said ferociously. She drew her lip back.

Ernesta saw the donkey jerk her head in reaction to the sight of Jessi-ma's tooth which caused her to display all of her own teeth being much greater in number though not in ferocity.

"Let me handle this donkey business," Ernesta said firmly.

In the neutral manner of another donkey approaching with nothing on its mind except the mutual affinity of donkeys, Ernesta walked lifting her feet high to untie the tether in one smooth motion. The donkey backed off several feet, not exactly startled though wary and still in a bad temper. Then Ernesta pretended her face had a long nose with muzzle and sniffed the donkey who sniffed back through dry nostrils.

Now under Ernesta's direction Jessi-ma and Jon Lilly lowered the bucket into the well and with difficulty confiscated a quarter of a bucket of mucky bad water. This bucket Ernesta had them put on the ground in what she considered a neutral area.

"Now turn your backs," she directed. All three of the children solemnly turned their backs on the donkey and soon heard her slurping. Jon Lilly giggled. The slurping stopped.

"Sssshhh," Ernesta whispered.

The slurping went on.

When the donkey had finished, Ernesta again walked up to her head in a donkey manner, and held the rope tether loosely in the casual manner of holding a friendly snake. Then she pretended to be walking somewhere very interesting, and while she did this she thought about stacks and heaps and piles and fields of grasses and hays. The donkey went with her past the tree across the courtyard up the stone steps and down a crooked street to the stable. Jon Lilly and Jessi-ma discretely followed, awed that Ernesta was thinking so hard that her eyes were bugging out of her head while meanwhile walking as casually as a friendly snake handler. At the stable Ernesta turned the animal over to a donkey keeper, a member of the Lion clan. The girl Fran-keen was there also in the stable helping him, and they were both very pleasant to Ernesta, and she was pleased with herself as they walked back to the major courtyard.

Jessi-ma kept looking at her. "Where is your wandering eye?" she asked.

Ernesta looked confused. "Isn't it here?" She pointed to her left eye.

"No, now it's straight."

"Oh. Maybe it straightens out when I feel good. I think it does."

"What does it mean, to have a wandering eye?"

"Aunt Three says a wandering eye can dry up a flood," Ernesta said.

"That's strange. My mother says just the opposite."

"I guess our people don't get along very well."

"That's only because your aunts are so selfish. They want to burn us up with their damned tiles."

"No my aunts are not, selfish," Ernesta protested. She knew that her aunts were stickery, sharp, stubborn and traditional; that they were dogmatic, rigid and formidable in their solidarity; and she knew that they scared her out of her wits with their terrible chins and fierce eyes but she was not prepared to hear that they were selfish.

"Yes they are."

"No they are not," Ernesta said.

"Yes they are, they are shellfish," Jessi-ma said, tangling her words.

"You are calling my aunts shellfish?" Ernesta said. This idea struck them both the same way; they put their arms around each other cackling and roaring.

Jon Lilly laughed too, having a high pitched giggle that sometimes caused crickets to answer him. His own laugh startled him so he waited until the others had quieted down with his hand over his mouth.

"I want to go down there," he said. He pointed emphatically several times.

"He wants to go down into the well," Jessi-ma explained.

"He can't do that." Ernesta knew that the walls around the tops of wells had been designed in the very beginnings of well-digging to keep small children out of the hole.

"Well, this isn't exactly a well." Jessi-ma became a constructor again. "A well has water in it and this one doesn't, this is more like a mine."

"Are children allowed in mines?" Ernesta asked. Jessi-ma's family worked several quarries and mines up in the hills as well as some clay mines farther down along the river.

"Sure," Jessi-ma bragged as though she had access to each and every clan project. "I go into them all the time."

So they sat Jon Lilly's round bottom in the bucket and lowered him until the bucket rested on the tangled roots of the oak tree.

He was very happy to be down there, he chortled to himself and rubbed green mossy slime into his hair from the cool rock sides of the well.

Not Every Form Of Justice Works

"There is something we have to do now," Jessi-ma said, "to help out my mother. As a water bearing woman, my mother is responsible for this well which is all tangled up with roots so nobody can get to the water. It's a matter of equality, see, because the rooty old oak tree is getting everything while the people who use this well are getting nothing."

"So?" Ernesta said, who hadn't thought about the situation that way.

"So we have to show this oak tree an idea about justice. You wait here a minute." She stuck her head down the well. "Don't pee in the bucket, Jon Lilly." Then she raced across the courtyard to the main entrance of the Snake clan temple. Being a Moon Temple, it was laid out in a circle with pillars arranged for sighting the moon in its cycles. Sometimes people called it the "House of Blue Lights" because certain stones glowed blue when the moon's light touched them, signaling that next month there would be an eclipse. The pillars supported a second story. Jessi-ma paused at the stairs leading to this part, unable to resist the temptation to investigate.

She dashed up. On the second floor to the right stood a heavy wooden door where the drug plants and seedlings were kept. She couldn't open it. To the left a short hall led to a trance room where people dreamed gathering energy for special purposes. She peeked through the woven screen. Across the room and under a tall statue of Ana, Ernesta's mother Donna sat rocking gently from side to side, eyes closed, face lifted, lips moving, and lap full of poisonous snakes who were gently sleeping or sliding here and there with their dry heads knocking under her chin.

Jessi-ma clenched her own arm to keep herself still. Even so and from this distance across the room she knew the woman's trance was sensitive and would know it had been observed. Reluctantly she pulled her arm away from the screen not speaking to herself as she went down the stairs or tripping. In the main chamber below which served also as a public meeting room, a fire burned forever, tended by two young women from the Snake clan who were learning to be full Snake women of transformation. They were dressed in brilliant beads and were very helpful handing Jessi-ma the brazier of fire she asked for with a cover and long cool handle. Peering under the lid she saw four small coals huddled together and turning red when she blew on them as she smiled in satisfaction and serious intent.

"I saw your mother upstairs," she said when she returned to the well. "She was entranced."

"My mother is a whimsical dreamer," Ernesta said not using Aunt Two's worried tone of voice or Aunt One's gesture of dismissal.

"What does she want to sit with all those snakes for?"

"She brings them in from the countryside once a month and talks to them. This keeps them from biting people who accidently step on them the rest of the time, and they give my mother something to think about. They give her ideas."

"Oh."

"My uncle does that too, he helps her gather them up in a basket and take them back to their homes again."

"Let's bring Jon Lilly up now," Jessi-ma said, bored with Ernesta's family. "He's ready anyhow." They pulled the little boy up on the rope and lifted him out of the bucket.

"Now I want to go down," Jessi-ma said.

"What for?"

"This is what is going on," she explained with exaggerated patience. "This is about justice. Now the oak tree is not hot and sweaty, she has all the cool water she needs so she doesn't know what it feels like not to have any and to be burning up in the heat. So I'm going to take these coals down there and show her." She drew her lip back to show her tooth.

Ernesta said that was a very interesting idea though extreme.

"Just a little bit, I'm just going to warm up the roots a little bit; you'll see how it works, she'll get the idea right away."

She climbed into the bucket swaying and which began to slide rapidly down into the well. Ernesta caught the handle of the pulley just in time, and with Jon Lilly hanging on to it too, they managed to give Jessi-ma a not-too-terrifying drop down to the bottom.

She set the coal brazier on one of the bigger roots. "See?"

Her voice hollowed up to them as they squinted down at her. "See? It's nothing. Soon there will be a big change, when this tree lets go of the water with all of her feet."

A tangible horror emanated from the oak tree that Ernesta immediately felt turning to stare at the trunk for a moment before being pulled away by her overpowering desire to know what Jessi-ma was doing.

"Anything happening yet?" she called down.

"No, not yet." Jessi-ma turned the brazier upside down so the coals could lie directly on the roots. A few of them hissed into the water below, but most of them stayed glowing enthusiastically on the wooden parts. Her intention was to warm the oak tree into a sweat, and then do some explaining, following which she was certain the understanding tree would remove its roots from the well. She examined the naked root parts around her anxiously.

"Do oak trees have trouble sweating?" she called out. Smoke began curling and then billowing around her.

"Jessi-ma, what's going on?"

"It's working," she shouted up the well.

"No it's not, it's on fire," Ernesta screamed. "Jessi-ma get back in the bucket!"

Beginning to choke, Jessi-ma climbed into the bucket. But even using all the strength of both Ernesta and Jon Lilly, they could only raise it a distance of three feet with Jessi-ma in it.

"Help!" Ernesta shrieked, swinging with all her strength on the handle; by this time Jessi-ma gave up on any help and skinned up the rope with her hands and thighs and feet, appearing with huge eyes in front of Ernesta's face surrounded by a swirl of smoke.

"Demons!" she yelled, "Run!" They all three ran.

Fearing nothing more than fire, the cells and nerves of the oak tree shuddered and emanated and were helpless against it. The sap within and the water level without finally put the fiery coals back to sleep though not without consequence.

Justice Often Appears In The Form Of Many Bodies At Once

A dead person is not neutral and also has a hatred of confinement. High on a platform of uneasy resting a dead body swells to the extreme limits of its new existence. A dead body may be internally moving but for external motion it must depend on other creatures. Other creatures have been closely watching the internal motions of a dead person, they take the form of a wise buzzard and some others who have been building a kind of tension. This tension is broken when the wise buzzard moves closer to the body and begins a kind of bobbing which means no more waiting. A bobbing motion in a buzzard may seem funny looking to some others but to a dead person it is the only release from the tension of no easy resting or volition.

All matter tends to dislike confinement, a buzzard is no exception. Once there has been a bobbing motion from one buzzard there is likely to be much bobbing motion from some others; it is not long before the hardly resting body is again moving as it gives over the stuff of its former existence to some others who are now no longer made greedy with waiting but efficient, fastidious and somewhat in a hurry. About the dead body there is now a stiff waving motion like a child having heavy garments taken off by another; it is an eager and stiff motion like a waving and a giving over of expectation to the buzzards who are all bobbing and altogether the platform of no easy resting and heavy meaning begins to resemble a garden of red flowers, all bobbing and then all resting and having very little tension. This is a characteristic of the exchange of energy which is the essence of matter. At this moment the spirit of a dead woman is released from its now former existence of confinement in the form of no motion or volition, and rejoices.

In the feelings of her live sister Sonia there is a change of fortune. In the course of the afternoon, increasing numbers of her relatives had taken their children to Snake clan houses with instructions. She felt that her hard work of persuasion was beginning to accelerate. A procession of water bearing women and men appeared at the gates of the Snake clan, smiling and bearing gifts aged one to thirteen. By this time their courtyards would be wall to wall with milling Bee clan children and something was certain to happen. Sonia squeezed lemons into a quarter pitcher of water and took it to a nearby roof sitting pleasantly in the shade. She felt much better, she felt almost relieved about everything. She began singing: "Three wishes have I, only three wishes have I, and one of them is a blueberry pie. Take your own finger and stick it in your eye; so much to think about I don't know why; some like watercress and some like to be sly; all I like is a blueberry pie."

Sonia's Bee clan relatives who ordinarily consider that she makes up the worst songs in the neighborhood, thoroughly enjoyed her singing this afternoon, climbing to the roof with her and being encouraging. She kept it up for hours while her favorite looking cousin fanned her and her other cousins sang the chorus lines, clapping time and telling derogatory jokes and stories, especially about the Snake clan, though also about Sonia and Lillian of the Bee clan as they all waited for the flesh and spirit returning ceremony for the dead Lillian that was bound to begin soon.

Three children stood in the doorway of the Snake clan court-yard staring at the turmoil. Aunt Two stood in the middle say-ing, "Too many babies." She could not be heard. It was suppertime and everybody was hungry. In addition, all the chil-dren had been coached to say that they were not ever going to go home.

A children's chorus formed a ring singing:
"Who designed, my mother designed, to send me,
Where the palm seed clings you will climb the palm tree,
Near the sweet comb honey you'll find the sting bee—
Shoo with a sling pea."
Then they sang, "Hop on the left foot, hop on the right foot."
The littlest ones played this by hopping on Aunt Two's left and right foot. When Aunt One found four small Bee clan chil-dren climbing into her basket with her she gave up working on it. She joined Aunt Three in her kitchen, rushing around filling great boiling pots with water and grain and vegetables. The chil-dren had already eaten all the fruit, they had even eaten the in-edible orange berries off the southeast corner berry bush and one very small toothy one was chewing wetly on a bulged-out crane figure woven into Aunt One's basket design.

Aunt Two pulled rapidly at one of her long earlobes and be-gan losing her head. "Why don't you go home," she screamed, and everytime she did the children sang, "We're never going home again. No one loves us at home, or feeds us. We want to live with YOU." And then they would burst out laughing and hug the legs of the aunts, who trembled with anxiousness.

"Someone is putting words in their mouths," Aunt Two declared. "Words in the mouths of little babies."

Little babies crawled everywhere with more interesting things in their mouths than words, while older children crowd-ed into the cooking room hunting for bowls and spoons, they sat in huge piles watching every move the cooks made, waiting with terrifying patience for their supper. Crawling children tugged on every passing skirt or leg, and someone had found Aunt Three's false tooth collection. Making and fitting splendid sets of false teeth is Aunt Three's specialty for which she is renowned. She stood in the middle of the room vainly trying to persuade Snake clan children to confiscate the teeth from Bee clan children. Then she gave up and sat down but even big Aunt Three could not hold five children in her lap while watching out for seven more plus a tooth collection. She soon surrendered under their wriggling weight and laughed with frustration and heavy implications.

"We're never going home again, no one loves us, no one feeds us, we want to live with YOU," they sang.

"I know, I know," Aunt Three said.

In the meantime more people of the Bee clan took fans and musical instruments up to neighboring roofs where they lounged around indolently and insolently, singing and telling stories; occasionally they watched the uproar below them in certain courtyards. Some of them began a slow procession toward the east of the city. Their own houses were completely deserted, no one could locate any of them.

Jessi-ma, Ernesta and Jon Lilly stopped at the gate when they saw the turmoil in Ernesta's yard. "Let's don't go in there," Jessi-ma said. "We're probably in trouble anyhow."

"Demons are after us?" Jon Lilly asked hoarsely.

"Shhh, there are no demons after us." Ernesta gave Jessi-ma a meaningful look. "You shouldn't accuse demons when you know you did it yourself. That's lying."

Jessi-ma stuck out her chin and showed her tooth, and although she is very good at it her tooth does not dry out in an interesting manner like her mother's.

"Can't you stop doing that?" Ernesta asked peevishly. "Let's do something whimsical and far away from here." She had decided that Jessi-ma was unbalanced and needed some harmony. "I wonder why my aunts are giving a party without telling me."

"Do they do that very often?" Jessi-ma asked.

"They've never done it before. It makes me furious."

"Well, where should we go now?"

"Let's take Jon Lilly out to see his mother. He would like that."

"Yes," Jessi-ma said, "he might. I don't think he understands what happened to her. Do you know about dead people?"

"Oh yes, of course," Ernesta said. "I could explain to him. At least, my aunts have told me some things, and my mother has told me a lot more. You have to know a lot about dead people in the clan of transformations."

As they left they could hear Aunt Two's most piercing voice saying, "Something must be decided about those tiles."

"See," Ernesta said. "My aunts are really very fair." Jessi-ma grinned at her.

What If The Wind Forgets To Pick Her Up

As they went through the streets Jessi-ma noticed how many times people called Ernesta over to them in order to ask or tell her little things, even though she was still a girl and had only one bell sewed to her dress. Aunt Three had a dozen bells tied to her clothing because she was a major gossip of the Snake clan. When she walked down the street people came out onto their roofs to call down to her, and to exchange the news. This was a part of the major calling of the Snake medicine clan, to be a street gossip, for to them the city is a constantly fluid but mar-velously stable network of human activities, each one interlinked which was its strength and also its vulnerability.

Her mother Mundane was such a great gossip she had got-ten tired of the number of bells she had collected. "I can't hear what anyone is saying anymore," she said. She cut them all off her dress and one day stood in the bakery courtyard saying to every passerby, "No more bells, no more bells."

In the correction of any disorders and imbalances Snake clan took into account all the different factors of human variation and politics. Persons could as easily fall sick because their relatives had secretly cursed them, or because they had so many enemies. Having many enemies can cause any one to fall sick because of so many bad feelings being generated inside one's person at one time. Or it might be that a person had an unbalance of respect owed to Ana's natural interlinking worlds, or simply that a stray demon wandered through town with not much to do, or a bad water supply went worse, or bad cooking from ill tempered sisters, or other signs that people were neglecting the mundane parts of their worlds.

For these reasons some members of the Snake clan kept track of the intricacies of everyone's lives as well as the news from other areas, considering the imbalance of one to be the im-balance of many. In their festival theater they expressed this with juggling balls. In their daily lives they took care of it with gos-sip and then more gossip.

It was nearly sundown when the three children reached the outskirts of the city. They sat near a high platform, each girl holding Jon Lilly's hand. Many members of the Bee clan sat

47

there also no longer singing. Everyone was waiting for the certain actions of the death birds circling upon them from the dome of sky.

High above them they could see the outside timbers of the platform rim, and above the wood rim they could see the tips of blue-grey wings bobbing up and down; the sun's rays tinted the wing tops a golden brown color. Other light rays dropped in shafts among the support timbers of the platform with many deep rich brown shadows and light tan places, while the earth all around glowed pink. Everyone and everything was very quiet except for a light breeze whooshing and the thudding sound of heavy bird feet occasionally on the planking.

Later in the night and later still in the weeks ahead when Lillian's bones were gathered for polishing and burial there would be mourning, there would be screaming and rolling and tearing at one's own flesh. There would be drumming and howling of the Howling Society as it lead the mourning. But for now, in this still place of descending and disembarking, the ceremony of returning flesh to living flesh was officiated only by the birds. And for their purposes, this was never heavy mourning, this was quiet rejoicing and releasing.

Jon Lilly nestled between the two girls as they sat side by side against an ancient wall, while Ernesta explained that there are three different kinds of vultures, or death birds, and they are each built uniquely for the effort of making certain that the spirit is freed of heavy flesh and returns to the air where it can be a free life spirit. The listeners shivered with the terror and harmony of it, and the justice.

"Your mama's spirit will soon be able to spread out anywhere in the peaks of the mountains," Ernesta said, feeling the grandness of this releasing, "where the wind will be certain to find it. The wind will pick her spirit up off a rock somewhere, and blow it down to some other city or maybe even back to this one, although we can't be sure of THAT, Jon Lilly," she added, lest he wait forever for his mama's return.

"What if it doesn't," he whispered. "What if the wind forgets to pick her up."

"The wind never forgets. Sometime we will go up on the top of a mountain and you'll see how the wind remembers to blow everywhere. The wind will bring the spirit down off the mountain and blow it across the face of some woman, and she will have a little baby who will be your own mama all over again."

"Why doesn't the wind blow now?" Jon Lilly wanted to know.

Ernesta said, "Because Ana doesn't blow air in and out all the time like we do, just sometimes."

"Like belching?" Jon Lilly asked.

"Yes, like belching. Ana has a lot of things going on all at once and they all happen some time. If something tries to happen out of time, it doesn't turn out well."

"Like eating a green plum?" Jon Lilly asked. He had gotten sick on green plums the week before.

A huge buzzard dropped awkwardly off the platform and sat a distance from them, his stomach swollen with his new burden. His wings were half raised and his mouth was open, panting, waiting for enough meat to digest to make his midsection a smaller lump and give him the strength to fly home with the rest of it. A buzzard's lifework is not easy. Two more waited for him at home, and he would give them most of what he had gotten, his own never filled hunger driving him out tomorrow for more.

He was a glowing blue grey color with a white breast and thick white neck ruff, a naked raspberry neck and bald head. He was the most beautiful and most frightening bird they had ever seen, stately and solid looking.

"See how honored that big buzzard is by your mother's presence," Jessi-ma said. "See how he spreads his wings and pants with the power of it."

"I thought he was just too hot," Jon Lilly said.

"No, he is overcome with meaning, it is a buzzard's way of showing veneration." Jon Lilly squatted, spreading his arms and opening his mouth to show veneration. Tears ran down his round face but they weren't screaming frightened tears, they were simply the tears of missing someone most dear.

"What did my mama look like?" Jon Lilly asked, crying harder because he couldn't remember.

"Your mama looked just like me," Jessi-ma comforted him and bragging a little.

Ernesta looked at her friend's face with long features, at the intense eyes set close together and big elastic mouth, skinny bone shoulders and double jointed wrists, big knuckles, crooked fingers and long thighs, swollen scabby knees and scarred toes. She began to laugh and presently they all began to laugh and to cry at the same time, for who could believe that two people in the world would look like Jessi-ma, and if true, how dreadful that one of them is dead.

"Sonia will be our only mama now," Jessi-ma said to the boy. Softly they began to sing a song about Lillian. Jessi-ma sang the first verse and then Ernesta but Jon Lilly sang three because he had the most feeling about it.

Those Of Us Who Forget The Greatest Influence Are Liable To Be Shaken

At dusk the three wandering children returned to Ernesta's yard where the Bee clan children had organized intricate games. All the adults were attending a big emergency meeting in the public hall of the Snake clan temple where a fire burned day and night. After barely tasting the thin soup which was all the food left for their supper, the three went over to eavesdrop the meeting, which mainly consisted of dozens of testimonial stories of how Bee clan children had suddenly appeared in the most unlikely courtyards with their usual raucous behavior and threatening to stay on for the duration of their childhoods.

Above the clatter of too many adult voices going on at once they heard Sonia yelling into Aunt Three's face: "That's not solidarity. That's solidification!" Jessi-ma went over to sit by her mother looking pleased.

Then Aunt Two glaring at both of them delivered a speech on the special unbalancing done to her usually orderly and sedate niece Ernesta, who had been induced to throw things around, rumored to have nearly drowned a little boy in the drying well, and CEMENT PERFECTLY GOOD JARS together in her own yard. Wasn't it obvious that the heat was adversely affecting the proper development of the children of the Bee clan and causing them to spread much madness about in the general population, plainly the situation must be reversed immediately, it was not so much a matter of the tiles, she herself had never been THAT much in favor of hurrying up the tile mural, after all a story takes its own decent time to tell and next summer would do just as well since nothing ever changes, the story would stay the same whenever it went up on the wall.

Furthermore, a midsummer festival surely depended most and foremost on the prosperity and general good health of its participants, and as a Snake clan woman she spoke for health and welfare when she said what were a few decorations, when compared to the deteriorated states of mind of the poor Bee clan, Ana and all her friends knew what evil effects were released by all this fuss to be saying nothing of rumors that some children had set fire to the oak tree, surely that was an omen enough for the day, and heads nodded all around as the people reversed their previous decision with regard to the baking of the tiles without a single dissenter.

After further dialogues the Bee clan offered to replace the food which their startling children had eaten. This offer was accepted by the Snake clan who then said they would give half of it back at harvest time as compensation for the discomfort they had caused the Bee clan. Following this everyone passed around shallow baskets of nuts and figs, having used much energy in the argumentation and events of the day.

Aunt Three took advantage of this socializing opportunity to surreptitiously snatch both Jessi-ma and Ernesta by their arms, propelling them forcefuliy out of the meeting and across the courtyard outside, which also contained the oak tree having been built around it's venerable woody body. Guiding them ferociously past the now ashy-smelling water well, past the drowsy ant city deep underground, she marched them to the foot of the oak tree. Aunt Two may not have gotten all the facts ordered in her mind, but Aunt Three had much imagination and no whimsy.

"Oak tree," she said loudly and reverently, "you know that we are only human beings, we know very little. You know that we are graced with animal bodies, we are dependent. We do not have your immobility, your storage of memory, your longevity, your connections to other forces, your excellent judgement. In addition, some of us when we are younger animals, we are silly."

Tugging and shaking their arms, she thrust Jessi-ma and Ernesta forward. "Some of us when we are young and silly, and trying things out, we do not remember what you have done for us; we forget that human beings produce nothing but other human beings; while you and your kind produce everything good and nourishing that there is on earth, with the exception of clams," (Aunt Three loved fresh clams,) "in abundance enough for everyone else to use. Some of us forget that but for you there would be no food, no shelter, no clothing and no fuel for fire. No cooking.

"Some of us," Aunt Three continued loudly, shaking her hands in front of each girl with vigor, "forget in our lust for influence on the face of the earth, and in too great a hurry to grow up, some of us do not remember that yours is the greatest influence on the face of the earth, that you are the first provider and that without you the face of the earth itself would be a wonder ful though barren rock, lovely to see but with no one

51

close by to see it.

"Oak tree, we promise that those of us who have forgotten will do better at remembering you, by practicing, for THIRTY days, to bring you gifts every morning including various healing waters to help your burn which hurts you, and various manures from the stables and gardens to increase your days and the number of your leaves, and to chant lovingly and sincerely to you for twenty minutes at least. I trust this will be a good restitution to you," Aunt Three paused to listen to the leaves talking in the wind, nodding her head, "and that the matter will not come up again. Thank you, most blessed vegetable of our hearts, without which we would not exist." Still nodding, Aunt Three backed away, releasing each of their pinned arms. True to her word, she would never mention the subject again, and seemed to be the only person who knew why there were ashes in the well for a week.

"I never knew that the oak tree meant so much as all that to my aunt," Ernesta whispered to Jessi-ma.

Overhearing, Aunt Three stopped solidly staring down into Ernesta's face. "She is more than that to me," she said, "she is my ancestor."

How did the oak tree and Aunt Three get to be related, Ernesta wondered. But she didn't ask.

Reaching A Large Storage Chamber
Of Their Own Making

As the people at the meeting in the temple began going home, Ernesta found her mother among them having come down from upstairs and seeming very alert after her entrancing day with a lap of snakes. Ernesta snuggled up beside her mother, who has thick eyebrows like the aunts and is younger than them and with a smaller face. She walks with a little forward lurch and also has fine black hairs growing all around her forehead near the main body of hair.

"Today I spent almost the whole day with somebody special, somebody who is both whimsical and useful."

"Mmmm," her mother murmured as though still somewhat entranced.

"But she would make a lousy Snake medicine woman on account of her extreme clumsiness."

"Where did you get this word lousy?"

"From Jessi-ma."

"And that's the person you are talking about."

"Yes. Mama, how come people say opposite things about wandering eyes? How come they say well, a woman with a wandering eye can do this, and then she can do that?"

The older woman thought about this for a while, one hand touching the leather sack of charms she wore around her waist, the other twined in Ernesta's hair.

"I think what they mean is, that everything changes or nothing ever changes, but some people can cause things to happen or not to happen. And a woman with a wandering eye can do that, or so they say, and so can sorcery. Besides, when anything, is different about you, people either think great good or great evil or both at once but not neither one. I don't know why that is but it is. Besides, the eyes focus tremendous personal energy, so if one of your eyes wanders you are able to focus a different kind of energy than other people can."

Out in the old sunken courtyard the oak tree has settled down, rustling to herself. Although the fire in her roots had gone out soon after the children went away, she hurt still, and withdrew all her generous feelings toward the city and its people for a month, which would make them uneasy and cold of heart everytime they passed through the main courtyard where she lived, and caused a mild outbreak of unaccountable dissension which contributed to a few squabbles among the Bee people in particular.

Deep under the ground around her, meticulously twisting and turning down along the tunnels of their underground city, three hardly working ants have succeeded in bringing a writhing beetle larva a great distance from its birthplace on the underbelly of a leaf.

Reaching a large storage chamber of their own making, they have dropped the white sac as they rummage around in their stored food, some of it the already made and packaged eggs of wrapped creatures who will serve as their supper throughout the summer. Apparently randomly rearranging the neat stacks in the chamber, they create a space for the larva near the second entrance where it will not become a beetle but will wait to become a writhing dinner. Falling about in their weariness, the ants move down another tunnel to a sleeping room which is still warm from the daytime, and curling around each other, they rest. And all in the nest rest, and the larva, no longer writhing in the grip of three ants, turns once with its sac, and wonders.

Shortly after sunset a great howling noise began at one end of the city, a high mourning sound with wavering up and down harmonies. It would continue deep into the night, as it had for two nights already. It was the mourning noise of the Howling Society, robed and weeping for Lillian a woman of the Bee clan who had died so unexpectedly of a head injury. It no longer startled the buzzards to hear this howling noise. They had heard it often; it celebrated their good fortune.

Before the moon rose and in the last light of the day a wise buzzard at last went home with his heavy body, to provide for his nesting mate and their huge constantly starved fledgling. Already as he passes over the city he is remembering ahead to tomorrow, to another set of sandstone blocks that bear close watching, where he yesterday thought he saw something that ought to be moving but wasn't, though you never can tell when you are looking from such a great distance.

The Night Has A Thousand Eyes
And Millions Of Feet

In a summer night the number of bugs who would give anything to get into Ernesta's room and roam all around, walking on her or dying in the candle were something like four thousand not counting unborn young growing in the various egg sacs carried by some. Ernesta's narrow slot of window overlooked Aunt Two's spice garden and rows of acacia and fig trees where most of the insects had been born consigned to a luxurious garden life.

Not lighting the candle or otherwise enticing any crawly creatures Ernesta lay pleasantly in her pallet bed low to the floor, watching shadows and lights giving a purplish blue luminosity to the white plaster that the moon was casting on the wall.

Ernesta loves her mother's room, the map of plaster in the wall reminding her of rivers, roads and lines on the earth as on a face she has yet to see. The round brown timbers of the ceiling have been made from the bodies of northern forest trees who are continuing their lengthy living or beginning their lengthy dying in her mother's room, supporting the ceiling as graciously as they once supported the tons of their own long branches and weighty turning leaves. Their big bodies are helping to regulate the thought patterns and events in the room as they had once done in the forest where they grew up during their primary life on earth. Ernesta knows this because her mother has explained it, how now in their secondary life on earth the trees continue to form, influence and regulate the lives around them.

Ernesta loves seeing the marbled brown polished surfaces change in every kind of light, imagining that she sees creatures peering from the knotholes or snakes slowly sliding in the long grains of the wood; and that they are really all living in a forest together, an inside-the-mind forest.

From the narrow slit of window in the east wall where the mats of increased warmth have been taken down for the summer, she can hear the beginning evening noises of the city. Crickets are shrieking love songs of location to each other while nightbirds are whooshing low over the yards and the roads where there is also a rustle and clank of human activity.

Her uncle, Blueberry Jon is passing her window having left the front part of the house where he was talking to Aunt Three and going now up the road to Gedda's house spending the night as usual. Ernesta can hear the soft slap of his pouch hitting against his round, interesting thigh.

For a while she had sat outside the living room doorway with the bead curtains tickling her neck as she listened to her uncle Blueberry Jon talk to two of his sisters. Aunt Two had come in from her garden to brag about the deep color of her kohl plants to Aunt One as she sat humming. Blueberry Jon had come in just then from a long day at the river. He had been searching with men from the Bee clan, he said. He was carrying a little sack. For what was he searching, Ernesta wondered, shivering under her beads as he opened the muslin sack of his efforts. His hand came out full of speckled brown feathers as his hiding niece jerked with strong feeling and his sisters looked in idlest curiosity. Then before they could harp further on his findings a second wad of speckles hopped from the sack, this time of its own effort.

"What!" sang Aunt One while Aunt Two clutched her green kohlrabi to her chest. The newest effort rolled to the floor and became a little feathered person as Ernesta could see very well, a little comical feathery thing.

"I found this child owl," Jon began to tell, however his sisters did not then let him finish his story. Ernesta remembered that Snake clan people do not have interchange with owls as a way of respecting snakes.

"I won't allow one of them in my house," Aunt Two declared making herself larger and more and more of a proud gardener. "I don't want one of them under my roof. No indeed, never."

"Take it out of here," Aunt One instructed, waving her long fingers like a fan blowing Jon out the door. He scowled and stuffed all his feathered efforts down into the sack backing out the door. Aunt Two put down her kohl plant and began sweeping where he had been standing.

"Bringing an *owl* in here," she called after him. "What would Mama Mundane think if she were here."

"Yes, you're right, you're right. Though she might love it," Ernesta heard her uncle's voice receding, sounding annoyed. Scurrying back to her mother's room she arrived in time to see him pass the window on his way to Gedda's house where he usually stayed with her and her daughter Margedda. Ernesta would have liked to see the banished owl up a little closer to her face before becoming a full grown balanced Snake clan woman with bearing and a natural prohibition toward the owl family.

Soon a whole group of nightfishers is passing on their way to the river loaded with mysterious gear; outside the window they meet up with a couple of dayfishers on their way home who are chuckling something while a sharp fish smell cuts the air around Ernesta's nose. This exchange is followed shortly by the muffled footsteps of the Howling Women who have finished with the citywide lamentation over the dead woman Lillian. They are on their way to the Howling Society house for hot tea to soothe their wailing throats telling stories far into the night concerning spirits and other immaterial nonmatters.

In a while Ernesta heard the unmistakable accents of some Spider Society women, probably passing down the street swinging their night buckets, specially made with wire mesh across the tops, traps for the nocturnal creatures they used in their divination and potions. Snake transformation women of her own clan often carried such buckets too, going out to gather the stuff of which their medicines and ointments have been made.

Spider Society women attracted Ernesta more than anyone, not only for their yellow turbans, more particularly for their peculiar eyes, sharp and sideways looking. Because of her own wandering eye Ernesta noticed how people carry their eyes and use them. For days before a baby was born, her mother Donna said, Spider Society women come to the swollen mother and spin out a likely story in signs woven into a baby wrapping shawl, because they know much that is about a person's position in the universe and how a life is likely to go. That, Donna said, is why they are so often stooping and snooping.

Ernesta knew the passing group were Spider Society because they used phrases and intonations peculiar to themselves, a kind of dialect they alone spoke. Donna told her that all the women of the oldest clans once spoke that same way but lately the women spoke more and more a general language that included the way the men spoke too. Once upon a time, Ernesta knew, her uncle Blueberry Jon would have spoken one way and her mother another.

As the moonlight increased in intensity Ernesta became restless in her bed filled with a longing for motion. She could hear the muscles in the inside of her thighs twitch. She could hear Aunt Two bumping around outside in the small back garden picking snails and slugs for one of her favorite ointment formulas. Lucky thing for the garden she had this recipe, she said, "Otherwise we would never have any green vegetables. I would be the primary gardener for snails," she said. Aunt Two likes to do several efficient things at one time especially if this includes putting her hands into something. Tonight she was putting her fingers down into the leafy lettuce plants plucking out the sticky snails for her bucket. The delicate whorled lines on the backs of their shells reminded her of decorations she had seen on the face of Margedda and her mother Gedda.

Ernesta thought for a while about Gedda and her daughter however she preferred thinking about the evening and the night air and whether her mother would ever take her anywhere. Aunt Two thought about Gedda also since she had been talking about the woman to her brother. However neither of them thought about Gedda one one hundreth as much as Blueberry Jon did, especially as he was walking up the road to spend the night with her as he so often had. Since they had been arguing too much lately he thought each night might be the last one that he was walking up the road to Gedda's house, and so he thought about their differences.

Gedda was a farming woman growing vegetables and grains as a member of the Tortoise clan but she wasn't always. She didn't always look so happy about her farming either even now after several years of doing it and living in the city. Gedda had been an outlandish woman from a northern country having arrived one day at the busy river dock where Aunt Two had taken her vegetables in baskets to trade for preserving spices and oil coming off the ships. Aunt Two had been the first person speaking to her in the city that Gedda had heard when first she arrived by one of the ships.

Dancing Now On One Foot Now On The Other

Putting her cracked and dirty fingers on her hips there are days when Gedda stares at the marshy waterbirds standing now on one leg now on the next, missing everything for long moments. Tears run along her cheeks of longing, as she remembers other moments and other marshbirds in another land of her derision. Out of her derision she had come to have her cracked and dirty fingers and be standing in a field far to the south of her own point of origin. In her own homeland Gedda had been a member of a tribe called the Hill People who are known to do no farming and no bending in the field. They prefer to do collecting. They prefer crouching and hiding, they prefer soft walking and running, they prefer following and pursuing. They do very little dragging and hauling or even lifting and they never do any plowing. They prefer finding and catching and watching and plucking. Later it was said by them that Gedda had often mocked the farming people who lived around them as they gathered in the woods and set traps among the streams and rivers. It was said that out of her derision for the farmer people Gedda had come to be consigned to be one.

Gedda herself remembered how the fields had spread into their homeland like runaway water, overtaking forest land and seeping up the ferny mountains where her soft walking people increasingly felt as though they were no longer living, they were only hiding. Some of the farming people stoned them and some sought them for what they knew. More often the farming people approached them for salves, for potions and charms, for good luck signs and most especially for their songs and knitting. Gedda's mother Edda was especially called upon, and sometimes she went down to the fields to deliver her aids in trade for goods from the fields. The young woman Gedda was irritated by this and contemptuous of all of them even though her own relatives warned her not to be like that, her friends told her to hold in her sneers and lip curlings.

But Gedda could not resist going with her mother and showing her bad feelings. One day hands on hips she stood in her fine leather dress in the center of the farmers' field and told them they were not different from grubs burrowing in the underneath earth, nor different from the substance of the earth itself. Dirtlike and grubby she called them, saying, "You are like the little cold white grubs pushing their noses through the ground all day and all night. Clods without eyes!" She laughed at them and when she laughed her necklace jingled like an echo. And in her derision she wriggled her long white toes in the soil for them to watch and then she danced mockingly through the rows of tender plants, leaping and whirling among them.

"Gedda!" Her mother Edda was loud and angry in her reproachment. Already the usually so quiet farmers were roaring and standing taller with outrage for only special, sacred dancing should come near the young shoots. This special dancing was to encourage the domestication and affirm the pledge of the plants. The wild meadow dancing of Gedda could only turn their plantish minds again toward the wild mountains, forgetting their pledge and promise to bear domesticated food for the village of humans in return for concern and attention.

Be free again! Be free again! the young woman Gedda's heels and toes sang to the rows of green shoots and the bells on her ankles tinkled like silver brooks in the mountains.

One of the farmers lurched forward and grabbing her arm with silver bracelets stopped her bad dancing. Then he stared in his fascination at the tattooed lines on her face, the rolling swirls on her cheeks of significance.

"Grubby, dirty thing!" Gedda screamed into his face. "May your fields shrivel like dying caterpillars," she hollered running backwards lightfooted to the edge of the field. "May you eat dirt for your dinner," she called as he wiped away her curses in spit rolling down his face of disturbance.

Within a few days caterpillars appeared devouring the green shoots with delicacy and completeness. And the stout farmers remembering Gedda's dance of derision, went looking for her in a loose footed band. Banding together in anger the farmers formed clubs from the trees to help them in their search as they marched through the Hill tribe belongings, house upon thatched and daubled house. When darkness came they did not turn home instead enflaming their thoughts and also their clubs and did not pay attention to roofs and blankets catching fire from careless waving.

Carelessly waving their enflaming clubs they came on through more houses even those constructed half back into the hillsides searching for the dancing Gedda, and soon her mother Edda ran into the hill-dug house where Gedda sat tenderly playing with her tiny redhaired daughter Margedda.

"Gedda, oh my Gedda," the mother called with urgency and both hands waving, "you have to get out of here, you have to go away."

Crying she explained to her proud daughter what wriggling her long toes derisively in the dirt had wrought for all the people.

"You have misused your dancing," she said, "and now everyone will be ruined for years if we don't tell the farmer people you have left."

Standing in the doorway hands on hips Gedda could see flaming roofs and hear the panicked cries and heavy footed marching of the bands of farmers. Soon, she knew that lots of her own kinsmen would come to tell her to go away. She spit to ward away their anger but she could see from the smallness of the wad of spittle that it was too little and too late.

"I'll go," she said, remembering suddenly she had been wanting to travel and improve her dancing. Snatching the pouch and blanket her mother had wrapped for her to take while bending down her head in a gesture of caring farewell she received the heavy necklace Edda draped around her daughter's proud shoulders of clan remembrance and of station. Then as Gedda was leaving she reached down and grabbed the round chubby arms of her little redheaded daughter.

"Oh no, don't take her," Grandmother Edda cried.

"Oh yes," Gedda answered, "I'm taking her." And she began a loping run with much bending and some crouching over the back hill trails with three year old Margedda already dragging at the muscles of her baby-lugging arm.

Yet in her anger at the farmers she would keep going with all her bones and muscles aching as for months she trundled over the hilly countrysides and down the coastline looking for a place to stop and raise her daughter, and forget her anger. Only the anger kept her going for she was shocked to find that no one liked her. Once out of her homeland territory of the Hill people she found that no one looked like her nor spoke like her nor liked her.

Many people in the towns and villages she found were tall like her and many had white skin, a few also had red hair like her girl Margedda but no one at all was covered with lovely spiraled blue tattooes from head to foot like her or delicate flowers on her cheeks and circles within circles on her chest and hands such as the child Margedda. And no one liked them for it, some children even chunked stones in their direction and the people were not much interested in hiring Gedda for her songs, her sorcery or predictions let alone her dancing.

She did sell some bags of wind to sailors. She found sailors who would feed them, who would hide and clothe them and would ship them down along the warmer coastline. She found sailors who would feed her. But it wasn't for her dancing.

She Must Expect To Stay All Night

Blueberry Jon was still remembering Gedda's story and wondering if she would be happy to see him having reached her doorway by the time Ernesta's mother Donna had finished talking to Aunt Three in the common room of the Snake clan of transformation. Ernesta, half dozing in her shorter bed heard her mother rustling through a wicker basket for her cloak across the room. Most interesting of all night noises to Ernesta were the rustlings of her mother who so often went out to gather herbs on nights when they had reached their fullest meaning, the juices timed with the phases of the moon as well as by the season and the weather. Ernesta rolled wakefully with her calves twitching hearing Donna rummaging for heavier sandals and her thickest cloak. "She must be planning to stay out all night," Ernesta thought, with newly arriving tremors of anticipation that this time she herself might be invited.

Nearly disappearing inside her long cloak deep in the night Donna could slide her head down through its opening, squatting down and staying hidden in that frog-like position until something irresistible was happening. Donna wore no clothing underneath her cloak, since the power of plants would be increased if they were gathered by a naked human body with the two energies transferring magnetically at the moment of the gathering. Donna said her body energy 'fixed' a plant's power at the moment it was picked, keeping it alive in a new stream of particles and being as familiar as she was with the nighttime habits of plants as ever with their daytime selves.

Ernesta's eyes were huge as her mother leaned over her hissing the long-awaited invitation: "Ernesta, get up. I want you to come with me. This is the night." In a daze of good feelings Ernesta stood by her bed. "But what shall I wear," she wondered.

"Here. Take off everything and put this on." Donna handed her a thick garment, fresh, stiff and woolly smelling turning out to be a dark colored cloak exactly her size.

"Your Aunt Three made it for you with wool material Uncle Jon brought from his last sailing trip."

How full of forethought her aunts could be, Ernesta thought as she dressed for her new occasion of meeting the spirit mate who lived far in the hills of her mother's dreaming and in a welter of excitement.

As the two cloaked figures passed the back garden on their way up the road beside so many houses, even Gedda's on the outskirts where Blueberry Jon had currently taken off his shoes of tiredness and relief for being welcome, Aunt Two looked up from reaching into her lettuces.

"Don't forget to come back before dawn," she said, a reminder of Donna's known forgetfulness. Ernesta looked up at her mother with sympathy. She thought the aunts must believe her mother was stupid to forget where she was so often. Whereas she, the daughter and girl Ernesta, understood. She knew that her mother was not so much forgetful as she was plagued by an excess of ability to concentrate which once her concentration was fixed on something, didn't like to change places.

Past the turns in the road they walked, the two of them together, matching paces as they followed the winding road up out of the city on Gedda's end of town. Yellow candle light gleamed under the tattooed woman's door as it faced the hills to the east, the very last house on the road, abandoned by some women of the Tortoise clan who had built it, then outgrew it and built another further in toward the center of the city. Gedda had been given plaster to redo the small house for her own after the Tortoise clan adopted her.

Behind the glowing door, Blueberry Jon waited for Gedda to finish splashing herself with cold water from a basin and come into her bed. She had found the city from listening to the sailors talking on the riverboats carrying her southward from her point of origin. She had heard it was a warm city on a busy river where there were so many different kinds of people no one would really mind another. And she felt so hopeful as she disembarked on the sunny wharf to hear the jingling of so many kinds of bracelets and to see faces of such variety on so many different kinds of bodies.

No faces there had quite so much variety as her own however and because the staring of the people only made her angry she would have turned back to the ship and left the city altogether, even going back to her point of origin facing wrath from outraged farmers she had angered by her actions if not for current and more pressing actions of her daughter Margedda.

Through her current actions Margedda persuaded her mother to stay in this new place. For Margedda never caring for her mother's style of living while traveling had developed a raging fever along with a terrifying swollen belly and some sores along her arms and legs. Her eyes glittering the first day as though with fever then went dull with disinterest in living. She refused to eat or in any way open her mouth, not even talking or combatting which heightened the drama of her changed appearance.

Help Can Come From Unexpected Sobbing

After a day and half another of trying to keep Margedda on the docks and still keep contact with the sailors, Gedda gave up her thoughts of traveling, and when she finally was offered food and shelter and then complete adoption by the Tortoise clan, she gave up all her derision for the farmers, and became one. Clutching the heavy, furiously failing child she picked out the plumpest most prosperous looking woman selling market wares along the dock.

"Help my child," Gedda said in the language she had been learning from the sailors. Approaching the woman's brightly covered booth she fell headlong before her with the silent redhaired bundle. Unexpectedly sobbing Gedda continued, "I'll be good for anything to help you too. . ." She was trying to formulate a list of things she could do in exchange for food, shelter and medicine when the woman interrupted.

"First go wash that blue gunk off your face and then come back again and talk to me." the woman said, her chin chopping up and down as she was in fact Ernesta's most ferocious Aunt Two.

"This *is* my face," Gedda snapped, rising as she prepared to spit hissingly into the arrogant indifferent eyes. But Aunt Two had already turned her back to sell some garlics to a passing herdsman. Drying her face on Margedda's crusty blanket Gedda huddled at the edge of the dock in fury, glaring out of her person like a striped hill-born animal wounded in the bushes. Hunched and all but hissing was how Blueberry Jon had found her, when he came to fetch her after sunset.

Fortunately for Gedda, Aunt Two loved to meddle, and she loved to talk about new doings at the dock on the days when she had market chores to do, sitting under the awning all day waiting on customers to sell her sisters' wares.

"They are the strangest looking creatures," Aunt Two gossiped to her sisters all that evening in their big common room in the house they all had in the quarter of the Snake clan of transformation and balancing solutions.

"Pale as ghosts and painted just like pots." Aunt Two licked her fingers after dipping them into the tasty sauce Aunt One had just prepared to go with dinner. "She said she couldn't even wash it off. Some kind of permanent paint, I suppose. I wonder what it's made of?" Aunt Two loved experimenting with her pots and paints.

She told them how sick the young woman's child had been, and how strange looking with her red hair.

"Do you suppose it was caused by her illness," Aunt One wanted to know, as she put tiny neat stacks of tidbits on her plate.

"You mean the red hair?" Aunt Three said.

Their brother looked up from his plate. "The people in the north lands look like that," he said. "They live on islands."

"Maybe the hot sun does it then," said Aunt One.

"Very cold and wet," said Blueberry Jon. "There's hardly any sun."

"All bleached out then," Aunt Two decided.

"I wonder if the Tortoise clan would take them," Aunt Three said, heaping her plate for the second time of thoroughly relishing her own cooking.

"They might not be so eager to have something looking like her out there among the ripe plants but they do owe me a few favors," Aunt Two said. "I suppose I could introduce her, if someone will go down to get her. I have so much pity for the child, you know, though from their coloration I wouldn't expect either one to live past next week."

"Blue lines all over them," Aunt One said by way of explanation to her niece Ernesta, who sat beside her on the floor with her supper in a bowl. Aunt One was trying to make a picture in her mind to look at. "Blue lines like maps to everywhere."

"Like ordinary *pots* with maze designs," Aunt Two corrected. "Said you couldn't even wash it. Indelible."

"And will the barley raising people take them, this time of year?" Aunt Three wondered.

"As big as that clan is they always have room for more. They always need more food to feed the babies, and they always need more babies to help grow the food." Aunt One took tiny bites from her tiny stacks as though to prove that she had no such overabundant needs.

"Blue lines like maps to nowhere," Aunt One repeated to Ernesta as she scraped some of her leftover food into the girl's bowl.

Blueberry Jon left early, went to the dock and brought back the strange woman and her child. Gedda spent several nights sleeping in the Snake clan communal room, until the child's rash and fever cleared and she got warm enough to stop being so angry with her mother and then Aunt Two took them to the Tortoise clan, along with some medicine for Margedda.

And so Gedda had come out of her derision and in so doing had come to have cracked and dirty fingers and be often standing in a field far to the south of her point of origin, and missing everything for long moments. And though she had come so painfully to appreciate the green shoots and the fields and even the farmers, her daughter Margedda had not.

And if young Gedda had been a person who does not agree with her mother, her own daughter Margedda was also and even more so. Margedda as she grew from child to girl to budding woman had become so rebellious toward her mother and toward the farming clan of their adoption that everyone for blocks around them knew of it and Blueberry Jon who had become used to staying over with Gedda was now caught square in the middle.

None of this bothered the softly walking mother and daughter who passed Gedda's house on the road and on their way into the hills to a meeting with a spirit mate.

Schemings Of A Scheming Weed Are Complicated

If in the city the oak tree of such outlandish age has found a splendid method of exchange with animals and other creatures of mobility, high in the hills east of the city a scheming weed has not. Twisting its leaves in consternation out from a thorny smooth stem the weed has not found a satisfactory means of locomotion for its seeds and has been confined to one area.

Deep in the hills east of the city beyond the end of the road lives a meadow consisting mainly of tight grasses and some loose living nettles who have taken over in the middle. They together have been pressing the thin vines back into a grove of beech trees with shrubs interspersing on one side while pressing against a mound of lichen-covered alkaline rocky outcrops on the other. Whitish dirt in scattered pockets set among the outcropped rocks support a few seasonal dandelions, three sturdy rosemary bushes and one ambitious scheming weed who is a nightshade with a thornish woody stem and moth-chewed leaves.

The roots of the scheming weed are confined to a tiny pocket of crushed minerals with the remains of one rotten beechnut mixed in to help out. Every spring the nightshade has noticed the billowing spider babies who climb every stem of every plant by the hundreds and the dozens throwing their lightweight bodies into the wind in order to be carried miles like little seeds far from their mother spider plant.

Every fall the scheming weed has noticed the dandelions and puffweeds releasing their feathery lightweight seeds into the wind to be carried miles like little baby spiders away from their mother plant spider.

Heavy with her own barely rolling and uneaten berries, heavy with her seeds encased in round hardskinned berries, and busily scheming the weed every year lets down her round and heavy babies only to see them barely roll a few inches hoping for rain to wash them into some dirt and cover them. Hoping for the heaviest wind to blow them to a dirty place, hoping even for the ants to come to carry them home and bury them, so hoping every year a scheming weed lets down her heavy seeds of barely rolling motion.

Every year she has been dropping the gleaming black berries when the heavier winds of autumn shake her body and every year she has been watching as they roll among the rocks sticking in rocky places. And her seeds by falling hopefully onto the meadow yet unable to get underneath the soil which is so tightly locked into place by the webs of surface roots put out by the prolific grasses have led to the distress of the needy weed.

Lonely, watching most of her berries gobbled on the spot by field mice and meadow birds rarely has anyone bothered to carry one of them to a burrow where the seed might escape notice long enough to sprout if the burial were shallow enough to reach the air and light in time for growing. Lonely, she has felt some of her sprouts choking in the underground for lack of light, has seen another munched in the more succulent youth of its growth by a slobbering caterpillar who did not bother to wash the juices off its face afterwards wobbling past her. If it weren't her only sprout she wouldn't mind it, but the nightshade year upon year has been trying to leave the rocks with no success, and to produce some true companions with no success. This year she is the only nightshade plant left in all the meadow and there are no more pockets of alkaline soil in the rocks, and so more than ever she is scheming.

Wrapped In Cloaks
With Nothing For A Special Meeting

Wrapped in their long cloaks with nothing else, Donna took her daughter Ernesta on a deep night journey to gather herbs and meet the spirit mate who had caused the one to dream the other. They took baskets walking barefoot through the cool air past the Moon Temple full of sprouts in growing darkness, past the street where Margedda lived with Ernesta almost believing that the soft hoot sound she heard was Margedda's little owl stirring in its wicker box behind the door. Past the outskirts of the city itself they padded, past the charnel house platforms where Lillian's vulture-polished bones had days ago been removed with such sorrow and respect by Sonia, washed and dried and painted before their placement under her bed.

East of the city they climbed softly padding into the hills until the older woman led them from the ending road onto a rough rising path steeply cut by wild goats' hooves as they were tracing their own way higher and higher. Ernesta was surprised at how well she herself could sense the path with her feet although she also held the end of her mother's cloak bunched in one hand for assurance. After an hour of rapid climbing the cloak in front unexpectedly vanished into the side of a hill. Pawing the air and scraping a rock surface with her knuckles Ernesta for a moment nearly dropped her basket searching with her hands for her mother in the side of a hill.

"Where are you," she whispered, how could Donna be so good at disappearing as to terrify her daughter. Then she saw her mother's head framed in moonlight and a strong hand gripped her arm to pull her forward.

"In here," Donna said, and Ernesta's feet walked forward into the side of the hill that was turning out to be a cave. For a while they crouched resting and lighting a small lamp Donna had brought with her. The shallow golden light splayed out over the cave's inturning curving stony surface. Ernesta's staring eyes could see the walls were cut in many places with triangular formations painted thrillingly in red. She sucked in her breath and held it tight inside her chest to keep the excitement from making her talk too much and disturb her mother's silence. So much holiness collected in one place! she thought.

Tucked into one niche of the wall stood a fine gold statue of Mother Ana of the Snake clan of transformation; she was gold and plump with one great ancestor snake of changes girdling her waist. Donna put her lamp in front of Ana and began talking to her.

"Will you help us tonight, to find what we are looking for, won't you, First Mother? Would you like to do that? I will bring you fresh vegetables," she added, "though if you won't help us I might not feel like coming all the way here with them, I might be too sodden with the disappointment."

Slender flickers from the lamp jumped up then casting lights and shadows on Ana's chin and breasts and forehead who seemed to be nodding with understanding and encouragement. Ernesta reached her bold fingers out to the flame for a moment. "Thank you for helping me to meet my mother's spirit mate," she whispered. She trembled with desire and anticipation as she hunkered down next to her mother who had begun her swaying and enchanting.

East of the city and stuck on a small outcropping of limestone rocks the roots of a needy weed dig around in the shallow dirt held in the small hollow of a rock overlooking an overgrown grassy meadow, scheming for a release from confinement. Needing to make use of all her genius to find a good solution, the weed schemes on into the mother night.

The scheming weed has always found it satisfactory and relatively easy to send off his male portions being the part that travels most easily. Always it has been the cumbersome female parts, the womb with heavy fruits and seeds that have provided consternation and puzzle. Because dispersal of the so-important products of the womb are so complex and time consuming she is more often acting as a she than he.

Earlier in the summer he has begun straining to open his delicate flower petals tempting the passing night moths with appealing masculine parts of flower stem and powdered pollen. Tempting the mobility of insects has become a major occupation of the flower-bearing vegetables who must strain all their genius in order to carry themselves forward any distance. Closing his flowers at dawn as a shop owner closes a shop for business during the day to keep out the local insects who would simply waste the pollen in their own interest, the nightshade unfolded his petals to their most open position again at night to attract the far-flying white night moths of his persuasion. Irresistibly thrusting his pollen-covered male enticements out into the air the moths walked and felt all over them until their legs collected all the yellow goods and messages and so the flowers succeeded.

Long ago she had designed her seeds to be attractive to certain migratory birds, making sure they were heavy with liquid and thickly coated and colored, making sure the balance of sugar and tartness would be appealing. But the migratory birds no longer came here. She had not made the seeds lightweight on purpose to be blown around the meadow by the breezes. She had not made them stickery on purpose to cling to anyone's passing coat or paw. She had thought of trying to imitate the blackberries in their color but she had not correct ingredients for a method of softening and sweeting them so they would greedily be eaten by the fleeting local birds with seeds hardcoated to go sliding through the gullets and slender guts of birds to land down onto the ground somewhere far away from their scheming mother and her confinement.

Now it was too late for her to redesign the seeds so they would have some burs to cling to someone's fur and even becoming murderous like the driving foxtail. Burrowing their long pointed sheaths through fur and skin and the layers of tissue in the bodies of live animals the foxtail seeds are fond of lying in their hearts and lungs embedded til they die and lie down rotting to make fertile soil wherein the foxtail young will grow, and learn to drive again.

No, it was too late to make the seeds arrow-shaped, as it was too late also to construct a highly pressured capsule tightening as it dried hugging around the seeds to an exploding point when the pod burst, catapulting, spewing everyone in a grand loud shower across the surface of the meadow, or at least a ways out enough to land beyond the clean rock surfaces. And to leave their mother.

Scheming with distress for a solution to her problem, a nightshade dreams deep in the hills east of the city of an animal who will take an interest in her berries and carry them away to dirty places. She has one more plan, because there is a human who has shown an interest in her future in the past. Opportunities to make use of the mobility of animals had never been wasted by some other plants of her observation, so why shouldn't she be able to scheme successfully also. Anyone has a genius, a spirit double who speaks for the most lively pieces of oneself. The genius of the eager weed had been for several seasons reaching out to find the woman Donna's genius reaching back, taking an interest in her body as she was casting her sparkling purple berry eyes upon the woman as a lover would, showing the flowers and seeds and other assets, enticing the woman to get to know her better.

The woman Donna meanwhile on this night has been enchanting in a cave dedicated to Ana the Mother and has gone about this for so long that her daughter is leaning her head dozing against the wall. Ernesta has slid into a fitful, not very restful sleep in a welter of desire for adventure and knowledge.

She had not been asleep for more than a moment or so when a nightmare vision came to her and gripped her. She could see herself bending low on a strip of light shale river beach and knew she was back to the day of Lillian's death, ominously brilliant, trying to see something horrible and unbelievable that lay on the sand or in a pit on the sand. Trying to see it and not to see it at the same time.

She knew she didn't want to see it, but was drawn down to look anyway by the special feeling of horror that clutched her stomach in the nightmare. Suddenly her dream hand firmly determined began reaching out grabbing the object with a sense of relief that now that she was holding it she would no longer have to look at it or think about what it meant or what it had to do with Lillian, and with the bad bad fortune that was coming onto Sonia and her family and Ernesta's friend Jessi-ma. Now she ran away in long strides, clutching what she had picked, and running toward her grandmother, Mama Mundane.

"Look at it, Ernesta," the dream old woman said. And when she could no longer resist looking at it because the grandmother had called her, she saw it was a long simple grey feather with a color on it. The feather was very beautiful and glowing and valuable though it filled her with dread, sorrow and overwhelming trembling. The color as she peered more closely was a stain, a raspberry colored one. She woke in the cave with a jerk as her mother touched her, knocking her head against the hard stone wall with red ochre triangle formations. Her hands were cold and filmy with sweat or night dew. She didn't know where she was bursting into tears which her mother's slender fingers wiped away warmly as she listened to the content of the nightmare that her daughter told her.

"You cannot see clearly yet," she said. "You've been squinting lately too. We need to find something to help you with your eyesight." When Ernesta calmed down and remembered where the cave was and what they were doing there in the middle of the night she felt much better. Soon after they left Ana's hidden hillside cave as Donna led them through some pathless brush until their feet ached and finally they hoisted themselves up one

70

last mound of rocks where Donna knelt down in the bright moonlight of a meadow high in the hills and east of the city.

Dreaming In The Night
May Lead To Disappointment

"I want you to meet my old friend," she said and leaned over.

"This is my spirit mate, who was with me when I dreamed you into the purse of my belly. Here is why your eyes are black as berries and here is why you have such fine black hairs along your arms and a strong spine." She spoke to someone stringy in the ground beside her. "I want you to meet my daughter, and the joy of my life," she said.

Trembling with suspense Ernesta bent down into a strong alkali rock smell that made her wrinkle her nose, straining to see more clearly in the mute white-shadowed moonlight.

The spirit mate had the form of a plant about three feet tall with a twisted woody stem. A few thin hairs stood along her thorny branches, black as Ernesta's eyebrows and looking peculiar on a plant's body. Her leaves were notched like a nettle's, a mottled green, laced with holes of several shapes where insects had chewed chunks of flesh out of them. Dust had settled over everything.

Ernesta drew back in disappointment. She had hoped the spirit mate who had helped to dream her into her mother's belly would be a fine chrysanthemum flower at least, or perhaps an olive tree. She had even dared hope for something like the acacia trees in Aunt Two's garden.

Even a plain and simple stand of lettuce would have had more bearing in her eyes than this odorous bristle with motheaten spikey leaves, a poor disposition and no known use who was hardly a fine ancestor. Ernesta stiffened her strong spine with disgust, barely restrained from speaking sharply to the eager woman on the ground kneeling beside her. This was the first time she was ever tempted to share her aunts' opinions of their younger sister as having too whimsical a nature.

"Look, Ernesta," the kneeling woman murmured, not feeling any of Ernesta's feelings in her eagerness to make the introductions. She was fondling the unfriendly looking leaves and contorted woody spine. "Look at the remnants of the precious flowers. I wish you had seen them when they were blooming, they were so attractive. Just irresistible."

Reluctantly Ernesta stooped. At the ends of the brittle branches were drooping dried lumps of aging flower petals, delicate only when compared to the thorny body of the plant, drooping lumps because they had reached full bloom weeks ago, had given over and received their prizes, and no longer had anything left to offer. They were a grayish memory of purple. Under them were green berries in a cluster mixed with some of the roundest, blackest berries Ernesta had ever seen, in irregular clusters. With a start she wondered if this ungainly plant were the cause of her wandering eye, and her interest quickened, though not her affection.

"These are like your eyes," her mother said, "these are where they must have been created. These are the berries your eyes are as black and round and shiny as."

Ernesta stared fiercely at the staring-back eyes of the berries with neither of them blinking.

Then the girl and the woman took off their cloaks. Shivering in the late night air they first drank sips of a hot pepper drink Donna had brought along in her basket to keep them vivacious. The peppers bit into Ernesta's lip and mouth parts on the way down to her stomach so that she winced realizing that the taste certainly was vivacious and stopped her shivering.

She folded their two cloaks and set them piled on a rock while her mother chanted and beat on the ground all around the dark bush of her companionship, who kept herself covered in the darkness, her leaves blending with the shadows, not reflecting any moonlight, her berries the color of the night sky.

After a while the moon rose even higher and this helped them. Ernesta learned the words of some wild vegetable songs joining in making the chorus for her mother's singing. They could see how the leaves of the spirit mate lifted and bulged and shone under the pressure of their singing. They could see how the stem responded under the influence of their descriptive hands and body gestures. They could see how the black black berries gleamed more fiercely from the fierce vivacious gleaming of their own dark eyes.

The grown woman danced a long solitary dance of attention, paying special care to the leaves where she thought all the plant's attention would be concentrated in the coming autumn. Ernesta stomped and clapped keeping time to the chanting, trying to imitate her mother's firm hand and foot motions, the rhythmic descriptions of what she wanted the plant to become in her behalf.

72

Then Donna meticulously spit on the leaves, rubbing some of their stinking surface with her palms, leaning forward to rub her breasts and stomach on them and to chew on the tips with her lips and tongue. In a little while she fell to the ground moving hither and thither in grotesque positions, changing energies with the plant, who became more and more excited and eager for having the human do this.

Ernesta fanned them both with her hands and blew on them to add her own energy to the situation, knowing this was a form of transformation, this relationship between a human woman and an eerie vegetable. At the zenith of the moon's rise her mother crouched in a squatting position, duck-walking around the stem of the bush, dripping some drops which Ernesta could not see so clearly from between her legs. How different, Ernesta thought as she watched the drops soak into the alkaline dirt, from Aunt One's neat garden habits. Aunt One always sat on a jar in a corner of the garden by herself to make some acrid piss she needed for her basket dyes.

After a while Donna stopped the duck-walking and stood up. Then they walked around sprinkling the bush with water from a sprinkling jar they had brought packed in Ernesta's basket. Then they reached down and picked several of the berries, dropping them into a purse in Donna's basket.

"This is for increase," Donna chanted, and she said some other parting words of encouragement to the plant too which Ernesta did not understand. Then they put on their cloaks and left. At Ana's cave they stopped long enough to leave four of the plant's greener berries for Ana, and for retrieving their lamp.

"What kind of plant IS that," Ernesta said munching a chunk of bread as they padded softly back to the city on the wide road.

"I don't know. I only know the power has increased greatly since I saw her last, although she is still unhappy. I used to go up there all the time to visit, when you were a baby. The oracle told me, 'Watch for diamond leaves and berries dark as any lover's eyes you have ever seen. That plant will give you everything you need for your daughter.'" She paused. "'And it will demand everything you have from yourself,'" she finished. "When did the oracle tell you that?" Ernesta asked.

"When I was just a little older than you are. It took me years to find the proper bush but how happy I was then when I did! It gave me you!" She squeezed her daughter's shoulders. Ernesta wondered why nothing so exciting ever happened to her, only to other people, such as her mother and Aunt Three, who was related to an oak tree or her grandmother Mundane who went on journeys and could travel in her mind. She wondered if this relative dullness in herself was because, as her aunts had pointed out, she really didn't have much bearing in any situation. She wondered if the irregular placement of the plant's berries along her branches could have given her a wandering eye. She put the basket on her head for practice with her bearing.

"Everything happens to other people and not to me," she said grumpily, nearly dropping the basket which was overloaded on one side.

"So what," her mother said.

"I hate that plant."

"How could you hate her? You just met!" Donna sounded surprised.

"I do hate it. I think it's the ugliest thing I ever saw." She did not want to know what effect her strong feelings had on her mother, closing her eyes instead while pretending to practice her balance.

Deep in the hills, the scheming weed exulted that her berries were carried away by some humans, this was such a good sign. Now they would bury them in some lucrative, alkaline place with a little dirty mix, a little drop of water. Surely this was the year of the turning of her fortune, with no necessity of trying to dry her berries into lightheaded burs, of being jealous of those who elongate their seed casings into spearheads like the lying foxtails. Perhaps she needed no more internal trickery or further effort whatsoever, just the further enticement of gullible, bright-eyed dancing humans who would carry the seeds away to everywhere, to away from this stranded pile of rock.

Sitting Under The Old Oak Tree With Someone Else

"Smack." Ernesta woke foggily in her own bed with pebbles landing on her stomach, pebbles Jessi-ma was skimming through the narrow window. The day had been designated for the two of them to pay their first respects to the oak tree as Aunt Three had pinched them into promising. She flopped from her bed. Stopping only to pitch some of the pebbles back at Jessi-ma, who ducked awkwardly, Ernesta plodded outside. She could hardly remember her long journey of the night before and the reason she could be so tired.

In the pink and silver dawn they slid down the steps to the

sunken courtyard. Ernesta has noticed how far away the oak tree seems. This is a surprise for she had never realized just how close to her the oak tree had always seemed before. Now as she saw the great branches stretching far away into the sky remotely dreaming of other matters and the thick brown trunk flat and featureless as a person's face turned in the opposite direction from her own Ernesta shivered and began to understand the great extent of their transgression.

"Let's sit down here," she whispered, dropping cross-legged just within the outer limit of the shadow of the tree's crown. Jessi-ma lumped down beside her making a sour face.

Now that Ernesta knew that the oak tree and Aunt Three were related she felt truly sorry for having caused pain and damage. But Jessi-ma did not agree, she still considered the oak tree greedy for having drunk up all the water in the well and making her mother Sonia unhappy on top of all her other problems including her problems with a donkey. Contrarily her friend Jessi-ma had kept their appointment not because of piety or regret but rather because she liked the chance to sit on the ground in the early morning next to her friend Ernesta who had a warm cheery body and a face looking alert and interesting in the first rays of the sun even when she's had such small amount of sleep because of going night walking in the hills with her mother. Whereas Jessi-ma herself shriveled like a mop in the morning feeling cold, stupid and hating to wake up too quickly.

While Ernesta patiently chanted and thought out loud trying to make some contact with the oak tree, Jessi-ma drowsed through the meditative ritual with her head rubbing up and down against her friend's warm and moving shoulderblade.

Occasionally Ernesta shuddered watching the light rays standing among the leaves and limbs so much like hair, seeing for a few moments that the oak tree WAS Aunt Three, Aunt Three naked without her heavy red and white dress or bracelets, formidably naked with thick dark brown skin and light standing in her startling green hair.

While they were sitting somewhat entranced under the oak tree gradually it came clear to Ernesta that she was seeing a very particular something hanging in the air, a shimmering blob behind Jessi-ma's left shoulder, that she had seen several times before in recent times. To change the angle she moved around to the other side of her friend, chanted some more, then glancing from her wandering eye again saw the blob.

"What's that!" she shrieked, no longer entranced.

"What's what, what's what?" Jessi-ma jerked with great nervousness nearly falling over.

Deciding to be dramatic Ernesta gripped her friend's arm with pupils huge and her wandering eye not wandering. "Over your shoulder," she hissed. "Jessi-ma, there's a big white shadow behind you! It's always there! It's following you!"

Jessi-ma craned her long neck over her own shoulder. She sat down. "Oh I know it," she said. She yawned twice rapidly looking so uncomfortable.

"What *is* it," Ernesta demanded to know. "Now look. It's bobbing up and down."

"Oh I know it is." Jessi-ma had a sorrowful expression and was plucking at her fingers. Then she looked intently into Ernesta's dark shiny eyes. "You have to promise to be like a sister to me from now on," she said.

"I'm not sure I want a sister," Ernesta pulled her face back being shaken by the proposal. "Why do you want me to be your sister all of a sudden."

Jessi-ma pulled harder on her long thumbs. "Because my mother told me not to talk about this to anyone except close relatives like her and Jon Lilly."

"Oh all right," Ernesta said after understanding this reasoning. "I'll be your sister. Does that mean I can stay over at your house sometime?" She leaned closer with her arm lying completely along Jessi-ma's arm, in the opposite direction. "Can I?"

Jessi-ma spoke in a tiny voice almost directly into Ernesta's mouth. "That's my Aunt Lillian who died while we were at the river and no one knows why it happened, and it's brought nothing but bad attention to my mother. Now everywhere I go, Aunt Lillian's light shade goes. She just keeps hanging in the air around me, and she will until something is known about what happened. That's what my mother says. I'm afraid everyone can see her. It's very shameful." Tears slid down Jessi-ma's brown face.

Ernesta stared at the misty shaking shadow over her friend's shoulder. "Why is she doing that?"

Jessi-ma looked her in the face. "She just has no easy resting, because of things that happened." Her sudden eyes met Ernesta's. "*You know.*" And Ernesta being tired and disappointed from her night journey and very nervous over her recurring nightmares and the bobbing blob over her friend's shoulder, felt that she was losing whatever bearing she ever did have.

Conversations Can Be Thumping
In A Hum Drum Society

On the morning of the first day of the midsummer festival Ernesta found all her grown relatives in Aunt Two's kitchen at sunrise, getting ready for the special days of licentious solemnity.

"Fell down the bank and broke her head open," Aunt Two was saying in her serious gravelly voice. "Now that doesn't make any sense at all. It's completely out of place for that to have happened." She was voicing a suspicion shared by many in the city, that Lillian's death needed a thorough investigation, which it was getting through the office of the gossips.

"Everything has a place," Aunt One argued. "Everything has to have a place or it can't exist at all." With the flat of her hand she patted the table. "This has a place, it has a where that it is. Otherwise, it could not be here. So with everything." She nodded to Ernesta.

But Aunt Two was not interested in philosophy. She was disturbed especially since a friend from the Spider Society had told her that nothing in the dead woman's chart of stars or palm or any other divination had foretold the happening of her violent death. This was casting shame upon the family, and affecting Sonia's ability to function as a member of the Bee clan.

"She was such a careful person," Aunt Two went on, whumping hard at the bread dough she was vigorously kneading, "always measuring everything. I can't imagine why she would fall down the river bank like that and kill herself." Her hands snapped and twisted in the dough.

"Caddis," Aunt Three said, Caddis being Aunt Two's name, "Caddis, if you beat the bread like that people may try to build a wall with it."

Aunt Two was named Caddis after the fly, because the first sound out of her mouth at birth had been a buzzing burble on account of some mucous caught in her throat and since she was also a breach birth needing turning their mother Mundane had said that she would always cause trouble like a caddis fly. Aunt One was named Gladys after a flower since Mama Mundane was sentimental about her first child and Aunt Three was named Lattice for the sturdy wooden supports built for vines in the gardens.

The fourth sister had been born much later after Jon and when their mother Mundane no longer had interest in interconnected names, so she called her last child "Donna" by which she meant, "Maybe this one will be a gentlemannered lady." Donna's three older sisters and one older brother Blueberry Jon never considered that she quite filled out her name but they loved her well enough and were still waiting.

"It's possible," Gladys the eldest said thoughtfully, "that the diviners simply overlooked something in Lillian's chart." But she bit her lip after that. Aunt One enjoyed believing emphatically in everything Spider Society women said. She said their divinations were about changes and believing emphatically in them helped to strengthen her understanding that everything always changes.

Aunt Three, who did not believe or disbelieve in Spider Society computations, having developed a system of her own, said, "Yes, they could have made a mathematical error from the very beginning and if so they should be called upon in the council meeting to account for it, and to explain the nature of Lillian's death to us."

Ernesta wriggled wanting to enter into the conversation as it was making her very anxious. "We found . . ." she began speaking.

"Why the woman was already thirty three, she should know what she's doing," Aunt Two gravelled on, pounding the mound of dough with her fist. "I heard from Sonia she was making plans for another baby. Though she hadn't started it yet," she added, catching Aunt Three's eye. They both believed that Bee clan women had too many babies in spite of the natural fact that Sonia and Lillian had only one apiece whereas their own mother, Mundane, had produced five.

"We found—" Ernesta started again even though she couldn't find a place in the conversation. Her aunts had gone off into a long name count of Bee clan children, in order of their appearance from their mother's wombs.

Donna, who had been patiently washing pots in the doorway stood up slowly watching her older sisters rattle names off on their fingers with an impatient frown creasing the fine black hairs on her forehead.

"What did you find, Ernesta?" she asked in a sharp almostwhisper and with expert timing dropped a large old stoneware pot on the floor. In the space of silence following the crash Ernesta's voice boomed out with plenty of room to express itself.

"We found birds."

"What bird was that?" Aunt One asked, whirling in attention to her niece, while Aunt Two shrieked, "Donna, a broken pot so early in the morning and on festival day," before Donna held up the intact vessel for her older sister's inspection. "It's only bruised," she said.

"We found one of Lillian's doves," Ernesta was explaining to Aunt Three, "Jessi-ma recognized the feathers."

"Where did you find the sacred doves," Aunt Three wanted to know. "Here in town? Sonia says they've been missing for days."

"Did you give them to Sonia?" Aunt One asked. "She needs them for her measuring."

"What are you talking about!" Aunt Two was so irritated, having somehow managed to miss the essence of the news.

"Doves," Donna said.

"Lillian's," Aunt One said helpfully.

"Lillian's little measuring birdies," Aunt Three said. She looked calmly at her neice. "And you should give them back to Sonia as soon as you can if you haven't already."

Ernesta bit her lip feeling ground shifting under her feet of reality. "We lost it in the river when we fell in."

"Oh really," Aunt Two said with her eyes rolling as if this were the wierdest story she had ever heard. "You drowned the sacred birds?" Not believing for a moment that such a thing was possible.

"That was the day they saw the mother lion," Aunt One put in. "Perhaps she captured their imaginations."

"Yes, they. . ." Ernesta was swallowing knowing she had too much to tell to tell any of it yet. "The feathers had blood on them." She shut her eyes as the dream feeling of dread flooded her and she was about to begin floating and trembling. She could hear one of the women gasping.

"Oh dear me," Aunt One said, "poor, poor Lillian. First her own death and now her birds too." She wiped tears from her own cheeks. "She must have clutched the dear things when she fell stumbling down the murdering rocks."

"And squashed them against her chest?" Aunt Two's voice was biting at her sister. "I want to talk to you about this, Ernesta, and I mean *thoroughly.*"

"Were the doves down among some rocks?" Aunt Three asked in her friendliest manner.

"No, it was. . ." Ernesta didn't want to say the rest of it, especially not the nightmare part that had horrified her and left her with a taste of minerals in her mouth. How could she describe any of it anyway? Donna had her back turned now drying pots while humming to herself when Ernesta glanced toward her for support. Her mother seemed completely preoccupied, thinking about her snakes or her charms or her scheming spirit mate. Ernesta's eye wandered out of control with her confusion. She gave up talking.

"No, yes. I don't really know where we found anything, it was just someplace down by the river."

Aunt Three narrowed her eyes suspiciously and then was caught back into a heated discussion concerning how Jon Lilly would fare now without Lillian when everyone knew how his Aunt Sonia favored her own daughter Jessi-ma and would hardly do anything without her.

"I never favored any of mine," Aunt Two said, "and they have done splendidly, bless Ana."

"We all took care of them," Aunt One responded. "Bless all of us. But who will favor Jon Lilly and give him the attention he needs?"

"Jessi-ma loves Jon Lilly," Ernesta said protectively. "She takes good care of him."

"Yes, that may be so," Aunt Three conceded.

"That Jessi-ma is the clumsiest girl I ever saw," Aunt Two began whereupon Ernesta prepared to slide out of the room before she had to hear a lecture on the merits of Jessi-ma's physical character, but just then the bells of early singers out on the street reminded them that they had to hustle along to get on with preparations for the noonday procession.

Aunt Three began cooking everyone some eggs using her four minute boiling song, keeping the time with her big toe smacking the ground at the same time that she tore up some of yesterday's bread. At the last measure of the song's time she poised over the eggs in their boiling jar and on the last notes she began dipping them out of the water, rinsing them in a cold jug of well water to stop their cooking.

In the middle of the eggs' song and not disharmoniously with it if you like to think in two kinds of time at once Aunt Two began a twenty five minute baking song for the thick barley mealcakes she had lined in the baking oven just outside the doorway for the special occasion of a festival. She kept time lightly with her strong fingers on the bottom of a pan. Shortly she remembered something else demanding her attention so she handed the pan to Ernesta who took up the rhythm and made up some verses of her own. Aunt Two then went off into another room still singing verses which would tell her when the cakes were probably done.

"Go and get me some onions from the storeroom when you're finished singing," Aunt One told Ernesta who was hardly listening, she was busy making music.

Almost all of the work of the city was done to music, much of the most tedious grinding or threshing work was done using various part harmonies and rhythms that could keep everyone's interest in what they were doing as well as allow some people to move at a different pace than others. Already Ernesta had noticed that she herself likes the slower rhythms, while Aunt Two for instance loves the rapid ones. Aunt Two uses a lot of energy, liking the feeling that she is getting everything done as quickly as possible and that there is always more to do and complain about and look forward to. Looking forward has given Aunt Two's face a sharp, forward pointing feature.

In addition to singing, humming and drumming out rhythms for the work, dancing was something else the people love to do for many kinds of standing up activities. Aunt Two often dances at her potter's work, the movement of her hips suggesting to her fingertips certain shapes her thumbs alone would not have imagined, as well keeping her back from being too strained after hours of tight bending or her feet from swelling. She didn't do her dancing for these or any other reasons though, but just because she knew inside to do it.

Thus it was that many of the city's people spent much of their work day humming and drumming for the purpose of the keeping of different kinds of time and for the physical expression of rhythmic emotions, and they were known for having an extremely hum drum society.

It was certainly a hum drum society, it was so hum drum, ho hum, dum dedum, dum deedle deedle tweedle dum, humming and drumming, every good time was a clap trap. By the time they had measured the moon a thousand times and carved it out on antler bones they knew what hour it was and when the baby would be born, ho hum. By the times they had measured the moving sun and tested their time with a may pole they knew what days to plant the grain. Barley dance wheat dance beet dance corn dance, rattle rattle, millet dance rice dance rattle rattle, corn dance rattle, you *will* grow high, you *will* grow high. Humming and drumming. Every clap is a time trap in a slap happy ho hum, ho down, ho derry derry down, ho hum drum dromedary dum dum ho, ho down dance. By the time they had measured the moving stars they knew how round the world is and how to get from one place to another. They had caught time and kept time, measuring universal time in their temple buildings in the precise alignment of minerals and stones with points along the horizon, keeping everyday time in their hands and hips and feet and nodding heads. It was a very very ordinary hum drum society with time clap space clap energy.

How Cooking Took A Long Time To Learn

Ernesta can tell that cooking takes a long time to learn because lately she has been spending so much of her time watching her aunts cutting up onions. Sitting next to each one in turn night upon night or in the middle of the day she has seen their peculiarities. She has noticed that although the little pungent piles of cut up onions are similar as they sit stacked near the bowls or hot pans ready to be swept away into the recipe, nevertheless they have their serious differences. She has noticed that these serious differences have to do with the philosophical meanings of the onions, and this depends entirely on which aunt has done the cutting.

Aunt One's white piles of cut up onions are often soggy with water drops and have great potential for stinging the eyes. Aunt One says onions have such potential for stinging the eyes that she always cuts them holding them in a bowl under some water so they can't get out to her and sting her. She slices them first in half making a crisscross pattern on the flat half of an onion she then cuts across horizontally, causing a dozen or so neat little squares of white flesh to fall into the bottom of the bowl of water at a time.

Aunt Two says there is only one way to cut up onions and that anyone knows this, and she herself knows it the best. She says the onions might sting some people's eyes and this shouldn't bother anyone least of all her. She prefers a chopping method of approach, first cutting the onion into slices while holding its round body down with the other hand and then holding one end of the knife down with her same holding hand while the cutting hand rapidly slaps the blade up and down with a swift swiveling motion that reduces the onion to hundreds of parts of itself in a little minute. Her piles of onions are always rapidly moving, sometimes so rapidly that it is nearly impossible to see them, and she sweeps them rapidly also, sweeping them into the bowl or the hot pan of waiting oil to get them all at once into the recipe.

Aunt Three says there is every way to cut up an onion and it really doesn't matter which one anyone uses. She says they do not sting a person and are the world's most wondrous vegetable. Sometimes she just puts the whole onion or two halves of an onion into the recipe without cutting anything at all, or she might sit carving large chunks from the whole, or other times she once in a while meticulously chops them into tiny bits in something of a flurry. Parts of Aunt Three's onions sometimes end up on the floor, under furniture or even up her wide sleeves and never do make it to the recipe in time for dinner. Her piles do not sting the eyes much nor do they move rapidly. They do tend to lie around in odd places occasionally turning grey or causing a slipping sensation if someone steps on one of them.

What Ernesta loves best is to be sent into one of the storerooms hung with ropes of onions woven together into a braid by their long dried stems,, gleaming and wrapped in their tight crisp golden skins with the remnants of their roots curled against their bottoms like little old beards.

Ernesta can see how cooking took a long time to learn from the heavy work of rolling barrels and jars up from the cellars and onto the wagons being done now by her grown cousins. Lifting the packed containers in their striped robes and weathered, friendly faces the men are sweating even in the early morning. Deep in the barrels are fish who were smoked before their packing in layers of salt. Ernesta remembers those days of salt and herring with her nose wrinkling every time she thinks about preservation, the strings of onions and garlics hung to dry in knobby bundles and the piles of peppers and apricots spread out on racks for weeks were no one can walk and she must fan the flies away for days waiting for them to shrivel and be preserved.

Ernesta's nose wrinkles even more recalling vinegar days, the pleasant in the beginning and then increasingly uncomfortable smell of the cucumbers, fish, pork, hardboiled eggs, onions, bits of melon and wild fruits pickled and pickled and pickled in vinegar and spices, brine and rock salt until everyone's hands were pickled too, shrivelling from the minerals of the preparations and everyone's eyes too had watered from the gasses and the smoke and the concentrations of acids and odors, and everyone's hands had wrinkled and everyone's nose had wrinkled as though these too were preserved. Once out of the storeroom however and back in the fresh morning air her nose unclenched and when she came back into the kitchen with the rope of onions she had been sent to fetch the time had come for her to go to her mother's room to get dressed for the festival and for her mother to fix her hair.

Ernesta's Head Forms Its Own World

Ernesta's head forms its own world; coils out on springs that make it a bush, a growth of its own kind. Dirty, it merely darkens or greys; wet, a thousand eyes look out. Wet, it catches the water and rolls the drops into a thousand lights or phosphorescent insects. Oiled, Ernesta's hair catches the blue black mineral colors of the world and reflects them to each other; every hair a mirror for every other. Anything lives in Ernesta's hair, everything loves it there; leaves, fluff, bits of string move in as if the hairs themselves invited them. Birds had been known to take things from Ernesta's hair for their own purposes, and almost everyone at some time wanted to put their hands into it, to play it like water turned into thin strands of musical wire, to want feeling like that, in Ernesta's hair. All of it moves in one piece, a bouncing motion; combed all the way out it stayed there; left to its own devices it coiled deeper and deeper into itself as though to go back into her head. Often she ran a belt around the crown of it, just off her forehead, letting the main bulk of the bush push up out of the top like a loaf of lava rock.

On the morning of the first day of the festival Donna washed Ernesta's hair for her, holding a mirror so she could see how the round water eyes sparkled out like thousands of stars from between the hairs all over her head. Then, even though Donna is a slender small person and Ernesta has grown to be so tall lately, Donna grabbed her and lurched outside holding her upside down laughing and shaking her so that water flew everywhere and they could see how the drops of it fell and then stayed in perfect gleaming globes in the dust under their feet. Then Donna set Ernesta down top side up on the rug in their room, and rubbed oil into her hair, all over her face and down her arms. The oil had been soaked in saffron petals.

"Phew," Ernesta said, "that smells too strong."

"Not for a festival," Donna said. "Don't you want everyone to know that you're there?"

Ernesta thought they would not have any trouble doing that. Her mother began spreading a green powder around Ernesta's eyes, who scraped some of it off examining it on the end of one finger.

"Don't rub that," Donna warned. "It might get into your eye." People often spread the powdered green malachite around their eyes in the summer for it not only kept flies away and kept the ambitious creatures from walking on children's eyeballs, it also prevented eye infections. Ernesta had a habit of rubbing her wandering eye if she became self-conscious for any reason and so often in the summer she had a greenish streak down one cheek.

Donna hung two silver earrings from the perpetual holes in Ernesta's ears while finishing painting her with slender white and red stripes on her cheeks, nose and chin.

"See how you look?" She flashed the mirror as Ernesta laughed in delight.

"I'm a green-eyed zebra."

"You're a fire-dragon child."

Aunt Two appeared in the doorway, her hands dripping suds from washing her own hair and that of the other aunts. She waved one hand with suds flying. "Zebras don't drag their stripes on the ground," she said. Ernesta hitched up her skirts, which were pleated and made with yards of brightly dyed material.

Then She Was Ready For A Procession

Donna then covered Ernesta's hair loosely with a wide dark red scarf with black designs. Her pleated skirts were made of yards of brightly dyed material, a festival dress being heavier and more decorated than everyday dresses by far.

Aunt Two said the decorations were lost on Ernesta who would drag or snag the silver filigree as easily as she would if it were plainer weave, but Aunt Three had worked hours on the pleats and hem decorations anyway. To Ernesta they seemed unnecessarily and excitingly solid. She loved the designs of snakes and quarter moons in silver and black on a deep red background.

She was also entrusted with silver family rings for her fingers and ears, part of a collection the aunts had gotten from their missing mother Mundane, who thought that children should begin wearing metal early to attract the better quality of mineral spirit. After she had put on her best sandals, her own mother Donna tied tiny bells to each of Ernesta's ankles so she would have incentive to pick up her feet and perhaps improve her dancing and her balance. Then she was ready for the procession.

Aunt One leaned down to hand her a stick of smoking incense and a little bundle of flowers to be carrying in addition to the cart of small children to be pushing. As she was waiting for everyone to begin walking in procession Ernesta was thinking about her three aunts, wondering what did it mean to be a full Snake clan woman, did it mean to have some bearing. And what was it to have bearing. Did it mean to walk the way a pregnant woman began to, in her seventh month. Aunt Two said that by the time Ernesta had learned to balance even the lightest, roundest water jar upon her head she would have all the bearing she could stand.

By midmorning the Snake clan had gathered in the streets for the procession. The men, two of them Mundane's elderly brothers, three of them Aunt Two's and Aunt Three's grown men sons, were carrying sacks of fuel they had gathered. Ernesta had also helped do this yesterday after her visit to the oak tree of her remorsefulness. She loaded two neighbor Snake children into a wooden cart of pulling them during the procession. The men pushed carts piled with tent cloth to set up booths later in the market, and stacks of branches and dung for fuel. The women gathered behind carts of steaming food for lunch and gifts to outlanders and townspeople as well as bunches of flowers and presents for Ana to be given at the great house of the Tortoise clan. The Tortoise was the clan of great provision and midsummer being the festival of plenty, that is where the procession was all going.

As they began walking Ernesta's uncle Blueberry Jon moved to a place beside her with his chest and face oiled and his eyes smiling. He was pushing a two wheeled cart with two things in it, one was his sack of fuel and the other to Ernesta's surprise was Aunt One's basket. She hadn't known that Aunt One was taking her newly finished tall basket to the festival and she wondered what it might come home so full of. Two people had had to lift the basket into the cart empty and maybe five more would have to take it out full. In its newmade colors the basket looked as though it were dressed in procession finery.

The four Snake sisters of Ernesta's family went down the street in a straight across row as did other women in their finery and with skirts and bare chests, except for Aunt One who never bared her chest for anyone. When they weren't taking their turns pushing the food carts they walked with their arms bent at the elbows and their hands with the palm open to the world, a gesture for the festival. Their skirts were heavy and pleated and a deep deep red of the aunts' own making.

The breasts of Aunt Two and Aunt Three and their sister

Donna were tremulous and shaking with the excitement of the festival. Their nipples were swollen on this day of procession as they had been swollen at the more vital times of their lives. The women wore dark green around their eyes and silver on their foreheads in heavy metal bands. They wore red and white stripes on their cheeks which were pendulous and shaking, and silver around their sturdy necks. Delicate silver lightly pounded into the intricate shapes of flowers hung down between their breasts, flowers of acacia trees for attracting the magnetism of the moon and menstruation hung on the younger, thinner necks and down the flatter, younger breasts, while flowers and finished fruits of trees and plentifulness hung on the older necks and bobbed in the deep older valleys of the older breasts.

They began moving and pushing, waving and walking along the street slowly on a route that would eventually lead to a festival. Passing in a grand procession they were rumbling the earth with their great many feet while underneath the city of the ants rocked in their travels and were disturbing. Cracks in the tunnel wall overhead threatened to break apart while chunks fell blocking some doorways completely as the parade of large overhead animals stomped and crashed on its way to the festival.

Running everywhere they waved clambering in their disturbance and struggled to remove the blocking boulders clearing away channels of necessity and firm passage. They tried not to worry too much about the walls cracking. Guards posted above waved vigorously reporting the passage of a large-bodied procession of groups of cart-pulling humans and ran up and down in the entrance sounding more alarms than usual.

Over the heads of the ants in their shakey tunnels, down into the large courtyard with its drying out well where days ago Ernesta had pulled Jessi-ma up from the bottom, and past the oak tree still building a woody callus around her wounds moved the gradually dancing procession on its way to the festival. However, first they must stop to pick up something, first they must halt, gather and mill at the doorway of the stopover place, the doorway to the Moon Temple.

Here in the temple dedicated to the moon Ernesta's mother Donna is often to be found entrancing herself if not others and being a charming woman without too many human friends. Here at the temple of the moon Ernesta could see heavy wooden doors set back between the columns leading to a plant nursery where she had been a few times, but today the women of the Snake clan in procession are only concerned with the main hall. Passing between the brightly painted columns, a few at a time the Snake clan sisters in particular passed into a large hall while the men and the larger children such as Ernesta waited outside with the carts waving their hands over the food to chase away flies and tempting odors.

Odors create flies, Ernesta has decided as she watches the relationship. As she waits for her aunts and mother to return to lead the proceeding of the Snake clan she can see the courtyard with the oak tree, she can see the water well behind her, she can see the sunstruck shadows on the ground near the stable. She cannot hear the donkey chewing in the stable, she cannot hear the ants and beetles chewing in the oak tree, she cannot hear herself chewing for she is not yet chewing.

A Fly Is Born With Little To Do

In the middle of the morning of a midsummer festival a fly has been born with little to do. Several hundred feet from a human procession which has been forming and now is waiting a fly is drying himself off inside a stable where it is not unusual for many creatures to be born with great irregularity and abundance. While the leaves of an oak tree may be born with regularity, and even ants and beetles may be born with regularity, this is not so true of creatures born inside a stable.

Wiping his face with new found feet and waiting for his wings to dry a copper green fly has begun another phase of life inside a stable in a stiffening pile of dung produced by a proud donkey who had several days before lost and won a noisy argument with a woman of the Bee clan. This same donkey had returned to the stable thirsty, dusty and bad tempered and had at the last moment stepped into the pile of dung burying the fly mother's new laid pocket of eggs down deep, deep inside the pile and making the first struggle of the pallid maggot difficult though still possible.

With a wriggly determination and willful movement the maggot had emerged from the donkey pile and rolled forward down its long blind body to the shadows of the stable floor joining the stable wall. Now days later from the woody shadows he has emerged transfigured from a wriggly determined and willful maggot to a brilliant fly with green and blue armored heavy coat and light transparent drying wings, learning to walk around and wash his face and after a while dive into the welcoming waves of hot midsummer air.

Elsewhere in the stable other creatures have also been recently born of no concern to the fly and in addition of no concern is a girl squatting with prominent hair and reaching the fingers of one human hand into a hole in the straw pile nearby to where a donkey is impatiently standing swatting its tail and occasionally shitting.

She was squatting, wearing a plain white work dress of the Tortoise clan, a dress she did not like not even with the yellow trim. She thought it was very dull and much preferred bright red and orange or even blue, however plain white with narrow yellow trim is how the Tortoise clan approached its festival dressing.

"My mother is so interested in clothes," she thought. "You'd think she could do something about this."

She did not remember at that moment the first years of their living in the city of Mundane that her mother Gedda had hidden at home or out in the countryside as long as possible during festivals covering her skin with long sleeves and heavy makeup so the fewest possible numbers of people would notice her tattoos of origin and strangeness. Only on later festival occasions has Gedda come to know the people of the Tortoise clan well enough to have gotten to be proud of her own place in the procession, of her white festival dress and often of her own origin.

Margedda stuck a copper comb deeper into the tower of her hair, a comb she had taken for this special occasion although here she was not going to the festival instead crouching in the stable where a fly has just now been born of a cocoon at the opposite wall and an unseen tall white chested owl sleeps in the shade of the overhead rafters. Deep under the straw where Margedda's fingers probe a mama mouse watches with brittle black eyes of her very own. She now has nine babies left of thirteen in this second litter to watch over and they had recently begun twittering revealing their positions to the ears of a waiting raftered owl under the straw.

Coming to her maturity only a few months ago, on both occasions the mama mouse had three men mice in the stable to choose from at the time of the mating. Two of these had been so attracted to fighting and chasing each other that she ignored them altogether, mating a variety of times instead with the more placid excitedly squealing third one.

Inside the stable where a copper green fly has recently emerged is Margedda a heavy set rapidly maturing girl with a round face and little eyes which no one at first notices because of her labyrinthian hair being so prominent. She has thrust the fingers of one wriggling hand deep into a hole in the straw and her tiny round eyes are closely watching the hooves of a restless donkey coming closer to her.

She is more concerned with what she is doing than with anything gathering outside in a courtyard and after noticing her reddish towering hair anyone would then notice that she has a small slatted birdcage hung from the wrist of her one free hand lifted high in the air as she is squatting. Anyone would see next that inside the tan slatted box that hangs from her thick and sturdy wrist is a fluffy small gray ball of owl, fluffy with unhappiness and hunger, with eyes clamped tightly shut so you cannot see their color or their expression. For this fluffy unhappy reason Margedda searches deep in the straw for mouse babies and is not attending the festival, in fact has disappeared from the watchful control of her mother Gedda.

Two Who Watch Out For Each Other Are Related

If a fly is created by odors it is also true that what is created creates in its own turn. Once a form is created it creates other forms and not just those like itself, often it creates other forms unlike itself in order to give itself limits, company and composition. As the bright eyes of a mama mouse watch from the mounds of straw on the floor of the stable, so a white chested owl dreams on a rafter near the roof of the stable. The two are related especially in the time they spend thinking about each other. The mama mouse thinks about the owl dreaming on its rafter above herself and her large family about thirty percent of the time, more thought than she often has time to give to her grown children although they will soon number in dozens. Since the owl thinks about the mouse and her children about seventy per cent of the time, together they are thinking about each other one hundred per cent of the time.

Living together as they so often do in the stable, the owl sits working on a beam near the ceiling while the mouse works below gathering goods into collections keeping them stored in a number of places. The two watch out for each other. The owl watches out of her huge flat eyes below her for the least motion or displaced shadow and the mouse watches out of her shiny round eyes above her for the similar motions, and she also watches the floor for any changes in the shadows of intent dropping. While the two were watching out so closely for each other they have forgotten to watch for a third entity who has appeared in the form of an immense, chubby determined stalking person named Margedda.

Trying to be unlike her own mother Margedda was determined never to cover her tattoos or be happy with a plain white dress of effort and gratitude, and never to go stalking in the woods or wild meadows for secret joy and not for mushrooms as her mother did. Instead she would stalk crouching in the stable, and she determined as she did this never to like farming as her mother had finally learned to like farming, bending and stooping, squatting and hauling, but rather to be a wild dancer and a gatherer of dreams and predictions. And today she would squat in order to be a gatherer of mice and other delicacies to take care of the baby owl her mother's lover Jon had brought her from the river.

"His mother is obviously dead," Blueberry Jon had said. "This little baby needs a patient person to take care of him." And for this task of patient care she must be wily. And she must grow up to be a wily woman.

For her part the mama mouse has already grown up to be a wily woman. The little present-minded children that she had trained ran around the edges of the objects in the stable as she herself did growing large and thickly furred while the little absent-minded children she forgot or decided not to train ran across the middle of the designated spaces directly one by one into the course of the owl's shadow of intent and rapidly dropping flight and nails and beak and stomach.

Because of her habits of trembling without moving the mouse has taught the owl to do a great deal of sitting and of dreaming it would not otherwise be doing. Because the mama mouse has habits of working at night the owl has been given plenty of night vision and silent, rapidly dropping flight in order to fall down on her from above. Falling down on a mouse from above is something the owl has practiced a great deal involving air currents and the precision of foot muscle releasing and gravitational diving. And because of this dropping flight of owls the mouse keeps always to the edges of the objects of her environment in the stable or anywhere, moving always in geometric lines as though drawing pictures of a space by running all around its parameters. For their part the owls have learned to think of other things extensively with their big eyes open for otherwise the waiting is all too boring. Waiting for a mouse to move within a given space so you can suddenly drop down on it from above is boring, even apparently paralysing unless you are excellent at finding other things to ponder.

For a mouse to have so many babies at a time as she loves to do she must have someone to give some of them over to and for this reason her kind have thought up the family of owls and dreamed them into existence. With their bright mouse eyes gleaming and jerking they dreamed and thought them up, with their noses pointed into a circle of each other around the scattered grain pile, the sharp whiskered noses of the mama mice and the imitative smaller noses of the children mice and the jowlfaced noses of the men mice. They thought them up, the few birds who do not live at all like mice at the scattered grain pile but who rather live on the succulent bodies of mice and who constantly ponder the smell and the feel and the possible every movement of mice.

Though most birds live on grain and fruits and twitter and play and tremble and live somewhat like mice a few birds do not do this, they do not twitter or quiver but perch and hover for long periods, sitting in the rafters or the tree limbs hour upon hour of their lives worshipping mice and pondering the subjects related to waiting for mice and how and just exactly when to drop down from above onto the sweet grainy bodies of mice. They do not do much more than this, and because of it the mice can produce plenty of hot little pink children knowing there will never be too many, and knowing that now there can also be great feathered creatures with large dreaming eyes who can never be disconnected from mice. For their part owls give a mouse more than one thing at a time to think about, so it is never boring to be a mouse. It is very exciting to be a mouse, so exciting she trembles and quivers continually from having different possible events to think about and different places to go that she might not come back from.

Smelling And Feeling
Are Not The Same As Drinking

Standing on the floor of the stable with all eight lenses of his eyes the drying fly is beginning to see in all directions, and everything is beginning to be interesting to imagine taking off and landing on. In particular dark shiny surfaces that might be pools of liquid substance are interesting to imagine and for his first landing the fly has decided on the large visible eye of a donkey.

Taking off however shortly he has found that the surface of a donkey's eye is not good for a landing, being guarded by heavy blinking, and moreover is not good in any case for drinking, being more solidly constructed and less giving than its first appearance. Knocked away by the lashes blinking back to the floor at least the fly feels he has made his first imaginative landing.

Not learning from the first disappointment is one of the fly's primary characteristics, so that he must try to land on the donkey's eye forty one more times before attempting some other imagining. Launching his new body into the heavily holding air he has been waved away vigorously from the face of the young girl with the prominent hair using one free hand that had been a moment before groping for mice and has zoomed up out of the stable door into the hot air over the street.

There are four major streets in the city altogether just as there are four clans and four great houses. The street over which the fly is now maneuvering leads from the stables of the Lion clan past the now quiet steamy baths for humans past many connected houses with shuttered windows to a busy bakery with open doorways tended by people wearing white dresses with yellow trim from the big farming Tortoise clan, the clan of provision.

In preparation for the festival smells from the bakery suggest warm puddles of edible matter toward which the fly buzzes in a zig zag course with occasional pauses. Thick with smells of hot wet grain, people in the doorways of the bakery are guarding these with fans like giant lashes waving that are frightening to a young fly not so used to being batted about. Trying one hundred and twenty three times to get into the bakery the fly is too recent in his body to make full use of his physical knowledge of aerial acrobatics necessary to bypass fans that long ago his ancestors had arranged for his inheritance.

Spiraling high into the sky for a change of air the fly can see if he is looking that there are four wider streets in the city altogether and four large freestanding buildings among the close cluster of living buildings attached each to the other. The city is united into four clans, all of them are of different numbers. The proportions of the numbers of people in each clan are that the Tortoise clan is the largest with more than half of the population; next largest is the Lion clan of animal keeping and responsibility; then the much smaller Bee clan of architects and measurement; and smallest of all is the Snake clan of healing and herbology. The fly does not see the relative numbers of the clans from high in the air. What he does see is a great deal of milling activity in front of the Snake clan temple of the moon, so stopping to rest only twice he can make a perfectly zig zag course over the roofs to where an active procession is finally proceeding in search of a warm puddle.

Finding a variety of people in long and short red skirts pushing carts of covered smells and with warm brown pools for eyes is very exciting to a young fly. To his misfortune the carts are protected by the same fanning motions as the bakery, slapping fanning motions meant to demolish his body rather than simply send him away. Furthermore circling everyone's eyes is a layer of repulsive green malachite powder. While he is resting in disappointment on a broad woman's shoulder, the woman who a second ago was marching along talking with hands floating in the air before her is now whirling and suddenly smacking the fly with a hard broad finger across his face.

Spinning over and over through the air the disoriented fly realizes that much of the vision is dimming on the right side where one of his bright new multi-sided eyes is injured. Lurching now in an ugly unformed zig zag the fly lunges for the sheltering hair of a rectangular shaped girl who is imitating older women in a procession while pushing a cart with two small children and not watching out for what gets into her hair. Finding a shiny black coil of protection under the red bandana the fly crouches in the shadow of a silver headpiece keeping quiet and resting, dizzy from all the adventures of entering a new body.

Meanwhile the procession is passing a distracted woman in a white dress with yellow trim who is anxiously calling "Margedda, Margedda!" and after a while the procession is passing out of the courtyard with the oak tree and onto a street that leads past the stable.

A Procession Proceeds To What Is Best Loved

Ernesta was amazed when the Snake clan sisters emerged from their moon temple in special red dresses. She knew they had gone in to get the wooden statue of Ana but she didn't know she would love to see the image so much when she saw it. The women had dressed the wooden Ana in festival clothing to match their own and in silver jewelry. Over her head arched a crescent of the moon and round her waist curled the great snake of their clan. Snakes and crescents ran round the trim of her skirt as they did round the trim of Ernesta's, and beyond that there was no comparison.

Ana's wooden face bore no comparison to their own human faces for hers was fixed as though in all time, fixed in a stare of great entranced comprehension and endless wonder to the young eyes of Ernesta looking for balance and bearing. Here was balance and bearing, borne and balanced on wooden stakes high on the shoulders of the aunts and her mother as they proceeded to lead the procession to the festival of midsummer.

Ana, shaped like the women themselves with their upraised arms and high faces, was heavy for them to carry. They must rest the butt of the wooden carrying stakes on their thighs at times for a brace. Like them her skirts wound around in thick pleats, like them silver flowers hung down between her breasts; she too was oiled and brown and painted on her cheeks.

Walking behind her they proceeded along the street to the main temple of the city, and Ernesta realized how large the city was on this day as she could tell by the tiredness in her arms and the amount of sweat everyone began producing. Her arms grew so tired from pushing the cart with two little children that she began to wonder why everyone loved the festival before finally they reached the first entrance pillars of the great house of the Tortoise clan, the House of the Rising Sun.

A throng of townspeople and many newly arriving outlanders and distant relatives stood around outside the great clay building. Ernesta was proud of how well dressed and good looking the Snake clan appeared in their red dresses and her well oiled uncle and the great uncles and grown cousins in their bracelets and fine leg wrappings. She was glad they had gathered together to walk between the pillars of the great temple of the sun, the gates of Ana as they were called, the stomach, the great container, the house of Ana.

Donna and Aunt Three went ahead to carry the moon image of Ana between the great legs, the pillars, and now everyone followed, the other aunts with their arms raised, the more Snake women, the painted women with skirts hanging and red and wound round with pleats, the bread and grain carrying Tortoise clan, the Lion clan with young lambs clutched in their arms; the children with their flowers and beads, the musicians carrying drums and flutes and the men with their fuel stacked in their arms and their sacks and their oiled skin and their gifted eyes.

Ernesta could not take her eyes from all the festival. She could not take her eyes in particular from Donna and her own three aunts. If ever she was aware of them day by day she was seven times more keenly aware of them now at festival times for their reminders: the resolve of their faces, the openness of their hands pushing forward, the forward motion of their great hips under the thick red cloth; the heavy silver weighting down their ears and necks as it weighted down hers, wrapped around their waists in belts, wrapped around their wrists and upper arms and ankles and fingers setting off the deep brown of their skins.

Altogether they reminded her of something she was often forgetting in her everyday habits, they reminded her of what was ahead and behind in time as well as what was already here. All around her inside the great hall of the great sun temple the white walls had been painted over with many colors and pictures; she saw the tree hung with all kinds of fruits and birds, cows with their horns decorated and sheaves of grain rising over everything. At the back the painting of Ana with sun rays beaming out from behind her looked somewhat like Donna, since she had been used as a model for the repainting that took place this winter. Ernesta was pleased to look at the painting and then look at her mother. She thought Donna looked much livelier and more fun than Ana, though they were both lovely, and of course, as she could hear Aunt Two saying with emphasis, Ana was a great basket of plentifulness, and a great empty basket of need, such being the nature of transformation.

Last year Ernesta remembered that the wall painting of the older Ana had round, drooping down breasts more like Aunt Three's. This year she had narrow sloping pears like Donna's. Ernesta did not know what kind of breasts she would have when she finally had more than her fast growing nubbins.

Turning the two carted children over to the care of their own Snake mothers, Ernesta had to hurry to catch the procession winding around the great hall of Ana in the sun temple. Over the heads and shoulders of the people around her she could no longer see her aunts although she did still see the tall head of the wooden Ana that Donna was carrying. She could not see the row of chairs at one end of the hall near the wall painting of Ana until she had caught up with her uncle who was not only walking now he was drumming and humming.

As they approached the chairs she could see that the center one was a birthing chair, with round holes in the lap of the seat, ringed with ivory and gold. The feet of all the chairs were carved with the paws of the lions of Mundane, and two wooden mother goats with heavy bagging breasts arched their bodies up on their hind legs to form the backs of the chairs. The round hole, Aunt Three had explained to her last year, was for the babe's head to come through after it left the body of Ana the mother, who was Ana of fortune, "whatever is given," to the Tortoise clan, Ma-Ana as they called her. On the chair with crescent horns over the top and snake's heads for the arms, she saw her mother set the wooden Ana from their own Snake temple onto their own Snake clan chair, next to the central birthing chair. Ernesta thought Ana looked more lovely sitting in the beautiful chair in her red dress than anything.

Suddenly someone pinched her arm and she jumped into the air, whirling around to see her laughing friend Jessi-ma looking very alert in the black and yellow face paint of the Bee clan.

"Let's get away from all these adults," Jessi-ma whispered. "I'm sick to death of walking in a circle. Let's go sit together."

Shocked by her friend's impatience Ernesta let Jessi-ma pull her by the arm to a sitting down circle of children from various clans who were hiding behind some lattice screens keeping away from the tiring procession. Hardly had she settled into a first relaxed giggle when Aunt Three appeared looming over them and beckoning not only herself, Jessi-ma too must come to a central position in the Sun temple and sit with the aunts while the fires were made and the bread loaves broken.

Squashed between Aunt Three's great girth and many layers of dress and Jessi-ma's lethal elbows Ernesta sweated noticing there were hearths all around the walls of the long chamber where she could see men kneeling while others unloaded the sacks of fuel. She thought she saw her Uncle Jon drumming among them.

The men knelt to start their fires in the traditional older way of rubbing a stick in a groove with the instrument of a bow, and the women were noisy with raunchy sex joking while they did this and Ernesta and Jessi-ma were embarrassed at not understanding all of it and thought it took them forever. The men twirled their sticks rapidly grunting and looking at each other as the women sat ribaldly remarking with glistening eyes until the early wisps of smoke rose and the people shouted. Some of the men had bulges under their tunics by the time they finished, and they kept their eyes away from each other for as Aunt Two said the festival days were primarily days of women, a time of bringing all of one's presents to Ana, and soon the women would begin gathering the presents that had been brought to them.

From the corner of her eye Ernesta could see that Jessi-ma was imitating Aunt Three's posture behind her back and she gurgled with suppressed giggles that went back down her throat and up her nose of snorting. Aunt Three pinched her when she snorted and Jessi-ma pinched her when she did not so that between them she imagined this could be a very bruising day.

Ernesta also saw that while she herself and Jessi-ma were present and while in the crowd she had seen the shining black hair and fiercely handsome face of Fran-keen and the smaller bodied Dee who between them had led a lamb in as a gift to the temple, nowhere had she yet seen Margedda. And she wondered what she could be doing and why had Gedda been out on the street near the stable calling her.

Some Mice Are Born Over And Over Again

Inside the stable a village of born over again mice lies mainly sleeping in their nests, young and grown ones mixed together with their furry bodies touching. In the newest nest a pile of furless pink infants lie mixed together in a pyramid formation.

A mama mouse whose alert eyes peer from the straw has nests and gathered stashes everywhere in the stable. She has found by staying near one gathering place of floor all kinds of usable objects will fall from the bodies of passing animals and humans. What she likes to gather in her stashes are feathers, bits of bone and leather, things dropped by the humans such as old biscuits, string and shiny pins and beads, even a heavy metal ring that took so much long neck stretching to carry.

All these usable objects she put in several places of storage along with large chunks of vegetable greens growing on stalks around the stable door and most of all the continual grains that so often dribble from the perpetually chewing mouths of donkeys who live in the stable. Her grown sons from the first litter live in their own bachelor nests or sleep in the daytime with their sisters. Her daughter mice have nests of their own or sometimes come to sleep with her and her newest born infants.

For herself the mama mouse is exceptional at digging, at hollowing, at hiding and at finding. She is very good at squealing. She is somewhat good at climbing and very good at looking after her children, at cleaning and at storing. She is extremely good at shredding. She is not at all so good at weaving, at pounding, at pouncing or at growling. In her village inside the stable she likes to make a lot of paths, she likes to have a lot of nests to sleep in and a lot of storage. She does not care so much for open spaces except on mating nights when she loves to run wild and dancing in the open where she can be certain to be chased and where she can make certain that the mate chasing has enough running enthusiasm to be advantageous to future mice.

The mama mouse was a careful self-contained individual who enjoyed washing her face while sitting in the early morning sunshine and running up the walls to find interesting high perches. She loved to eat the greens that grew outside the door of the stable. She was never so foolish about what to bring home for storage as her brother mouse who ambitiously attempted one night to drag away a donkey by its hock, and who was mashed under the hay for the enormity of his vision. The mama mouse lived for a period of two years and three months, and bore an average of eight babies every two months following her own two-month childhood, totalling ninety-six new mice of whom fifty-four were females, eleven of those living to have babies and each of them producing a number of daughters though only one lived as long as their original mother did.

By the end of her life the mama mouse had been already responsible for contributing 2,916 of her own kind to the world, some two hundred fifty or more pounds of mice, most of whom had made a wealth of living for the various barn owls, shrews, voles and moles, hawks, frogs, snakes, ants, wasps, beetles, cats and weasels who pass through stables and other mousely places. Many of those she fed depend so thoroughly on her provision that her habits have completely formed their body shapes, eyesights, hearings, sleeping patterns, body movements, stances, attention spans, habitats, digestions, nervous systems, states of mind, and relative positions in the world. In return they gave her their undivided attention and plenty of reason for living.

Of this her second litter, thirteen babies had been born. One was immediately dead which she pushed out efficiently along with the turds, uneaten scraps and other trash. The rest of the new babies pleased her immensely not so much yet as individuals as a moving warm conglomerate with pretty pointed pink faces sucking milk from her breasts and twittering with cries that she left only after the second day and then only for the water she could extract from a melon rind dropped by a passing human.

The new babies were five days old when Margedda's fingers found them, folded all around themselves to form a ball with a labyrinthian middle in a similarly round house of straw and shredded apron left hanging over a rail by a stable hand from the Lion clan, to judge by its blue color. The blue fibers mixed attractively with the straw bundle surrounding the twelve who lay in a softly padded hollow with their big sister sleeping curled around them. The sister mouse who was half grown and covered with bright straw-colored fur did not squeal but ran out of the house when Margedda's monstrous hand lifted the outside layer of shredded hay with her big fingers reaching in to gather three of the stretching clean warm babies.

"It's only me, the human owl," she whispered, carefully replacing the nest with its curled outer sheath and topping hay. As she reached her fingers holding one pink naked infant toward the little triangle of owl beak showing through bedraggled fluffy facial feathers she remembered that Blueberry Jon had said he thought the mother owl might chew up the baby's food before feeding her. Margedda's own face recoiled in horror at this possibility, and she was greatly relieved when the little beak opened and the little mouth closed over her offering. "That's a good baby," she murmured, offering a second helping. When the owl did not accept the third naked mouse she wondered if she had been too hasty in taking three at one time.

"Margedda, Margedda," suddenly she could hear her mother calling her along the street outside the stable. She could tell it was her mother not only because her name was being publically called and who besides her mother ever called her name? In addition, she could tell because her mother Gedda had a way of pronouncing words that differed from everyone else in the city, differed from Blueberry Jon's words and even differed from her daughter Margedda's words.

She jerked to her feet with the birdcage bobbing against her arm. Gedda would not appreciate her long disappearance and the search she had to make to find her daughter. She would not appreciate, Margedda felt certain, her crouching in a stable in her festival dress hunting for mice. Most of all, she would not appreciate the precious pink mouse infant clutched in her palm like a piece of fig candy, nor were there any pockets or secret places in the ceremonial dress.

"I'm keeping this for you until later," Margedda whispered fiercely to the startled ball of owl clinging to the side of the slatted box, and then she popped the warm little body into her mouth where it lay quietly sleeping between her tongue and cheek.

How Cooking Took A Long Time To Learn

"The bread of Ana," Ernesta heard someone say and someone else handed her a bread cake. This had been made, she knew, by the Tortoise clan in their public bakery ovens, the dough mixed and endlessly mixed with great paddles in ceramic troughs to be poured into bread molds six inches long shaped into Ana with crescent horns coming from her head, bread the shape of Ana who had made so much variety of life possible, to remind them that the earth is quiet until someone knows to turn it over as the wind and rain turn it over; that grain is inedible grass until someone knows to swell and tend and harvest its seeds and how to dance to them and talk to them and tell them about human problems of digestion and chewing and desirability of texture and cooking.

In her Ana-shaped cake she knew the powers of Ana were being personified and remembered in the millions of women on the earth stooping over their fires and their fields and their wild meadows who had accumulated and passed on the shared knowledge of how and why to make bread; how and why to control small pieces of fire, how and why to grow the grain heads, and to soften them, grind them, mix them, form them, bake them in the heat. All this reminded them that bread is not a free form occurence but is a collective labor, a cooperation between themselves, the earth and sky, a willful body of knowledge they called Ana.

Ernesta began to think of such things as she chewed the first dark sweet bite of her bread cake, having strong feelings when she looked at the figure with her arms raised bent at the elbow and her tiny bread breasts bared in the position of veneration and nourishment she had seen her mother and her aunts do so many times.

Ernesta decided to eat her Ana cake from the feet upward so she would take the longest time to kill her great body and her face, though sneaking looks at Jessi-ma next to her in her paint and mass of black and yellow Bee clan robes she saw her friend begin with the hands first, then the head; then one breast. She also saw when Jessi-ma dropped her entire cake on the floor, snatching it back quickly to wipe it on her robe hoping no one would notice. And when she met her eyes the giggles welled up again and she had to turn away or choke on her joke with Jessi-ma instead of paying attention to the bread cake of Ana.

As Ernesta bit into the belly of the bread cake she saw across the room sitting with the Tortoise clan women Dee a girl who had been with them when they spent the day recently at the river, and she watched her as she stuffed all of her cake into her mouth at once, then pulled some of it out sticky with saliva and not a bit self conscious that she had so grossly overreached herself. She was standing nearly naked, a white and yellow tortoise painted on her stomach with sun rays coming off the shell and the nose pointed in an upward direction, toward the north of her mouth. In her nakedness she looked much younger than she really was.

The adults, Ernesta noticed, chewed their cakes carefully, wiping their fingers on the insides of their clothing, their faces intent with strong feelings and memories, and she tried to imitate their motions as she chewed the remainder of Ana's head.

In a while there was some chanting while the room filled with the heavy smell of smoking incense. People began standing and moving to the fires for the offerings. Her mother Donna was already bending over a small flame with a long handled silver skillet in one hand. Smiling in understanding into Ernesta's watching eyes Donna took a pouch from her belt, drawing open the strings and taking from it five greenish black seeds she had gathered from her spirit mate during the midnight trek she and her daughter had gone on so recently.

So many other things had happened Ernesta had nearly forgotten her meeting with the hairy weed of midnight, and her mother's promise, as she pulled the seeds from their sticky flower pods, "I'll take care of these." Now here she was keeping her promise, arranging the five plump seeds in the long handled offering skillet held over the fire of Ana.

Ernesta wondered just how pleased the scheming weed would be to see her seeds hopping and frying and turning blacker and blacker putting off charcoal odors in the skillet of her mother's loving attention. Certainly they were turning blacker than they ever would have turned ripening on the bush of their origination, and smelling far differently besides.

Ernesta herself was not so concerned with these matters, she was more interested in going outside to a major festival gathering where people were preparing for the dancing. In the center of the courtyard of the Sun temple the men had built the largest fire of all, a blaze surrounded by watching people of all the clans plus outlanders. Ernesta saw that her uncle Blueberry Jon and another man were carrying Aunt One's basket, and she became very excited wondering what they would fill it with, would they fill it with bread of Ana, and would they now be eating cakes every day of the year, or would they fill it with food from the carts standing all around steaming and creating flies and people fanning.

Aunt One stepped near the fire while everyone grew silent.

"I wish my basket to be an idea of baskets," Aunt One said, and so saying she helped the men place the tall basket in the center of the largest fire the men had made in front of the temple of Ana, with all the people watching who could see through the crowd of shoulders. To Ernesta's complete amazement Aunt One filled her basket with fire while everyone watched as it blazed out in a flame so hot that the whole basket caught fire all at one time. When this happened the exact shape and structure of the thousands of fibers and wickers and all the different colors and pattern of cranes and snakes woven into the basket were outlined in brilliant white flame, like an idea shell of the basket's entire self.

This idea shell burned out of the basket and into the eyes and the memory of all the onlookers. All the people watching through the crowd of shoulders saw the basket burn into their own memories as the appropriate size and shape of baskets. From this event on whenever anyone in the city went to make a basket or describe one out loud or brag about or hold their arms in the shape of one, Aunt One's tall burning basket was the idea that came to mind.

The consequence of this is that the size of the people's baskets grew larger as so did their expectations since much more material substance was required to fill the new size than the older smaller sizes. More material substance came into the possession of the people since they had now more storage in the form of larger baskets and the town increasingly materialized with objects and substances unbeknownst before. Aunt One was given credit for these increased material matters of the city at the speeches each year on midsummer's eve and asked to rise and sing her basketmaking song with fervor which she did. Thereafter Aunt One's basket burning was remembered as the most significant event of this particular year's midsummer festival.

Ernesta wondered what all this had to do with cooking. Was cooking the same as ripening on the limb. Was burning in the fire the same as cooking. Was shaping into a form the same as making. Was producing the same as mothering. Was receiving the same as worshipping. Was eating the same as valuing. Was looking the same as eating.

All these questions about cooking passed through Ernesta's mind as she ate the Ana bread and then as she watched Donna's fingers crumble ashes of the scheming weed's precious seeds and then as she watched huge-eyed while Aunt One's idea basket blazed into the minds of the people.

Pitching A Tent Is Rising And Falling

"Ernesta," she is hearing someone calling and turning her head she has spotted Jessi-ma trying to reach her through the crowd of people leaving while spilling out the temple and toward the market for the afternoon of everyone trading and talking before the mass saga of dances will begin.

"Let's get a tent of our own," her friend was already urging in breathless puffs as she reached her side.

"How shall we do that? " Ernesta instantly imagined a lot of sewing under Aunt One's malingering supervision.

"You shall borrow it from one of your aunts," Jessi-ma has never been short on ideas regarding Ernesta and her aunts. Ernesta groaned and rolled her eyes, however when they reached the Snake clan row of tents at the south end of the wide market place Aunt Three was more than willing to lend her a small tent that wasn't being used, in addition to some lunch wrapped in large dried leaves that weren't being used.

The two girls walked with the orange and black striped cloth mounding in front of Ernesta's eyes as she carried her side of it with her back humped against the weight. Skinny crooked tent stakes jutted out from Jessi-ma's bony body of leadership in dangerous extensions of her person.

Jon Lilly skipped up to them as they passed the Bee clan exhibit of jugglers warming up for the show they were giving tomorrow afternoon. The juggling show would be a paltry replacement for the Bee clan's long awaited ceremony of releasing of the measuring doves at the site of the new temple, which now could not take place in the absence of Lillian and the two sacred birds. Jon Lilly was already practicing his juggling with smooth stones plucked along his way. Grownups avoided walking near the flesh-bruising children of the Bee clan, while Ernesta wondered if heavy bearing was similar to bearing and balance or simply misuse of them.

Everywhere groups of bearded shepherds and other outlanders laughed scratching their wind-thickened faces, Ernesta's own older cousins among them. Those who had been raised in the city joined in the gathering choruses of singers and drummers or formed comic circle dances with each other waiting for city women to approach them or call them over to the market tents to trade for their wool, leather and other countryside goods.

The marketplace was rapidly becoming another small town, a brighter one of multi-colored striped tents, stalls and umbrellas. People coming in wagons from the outlandish places everywhere displayed their trades and crafts, wares, goods and wiles.

Local shepherds stood bargaining the wool and sheepskins remaining from their obligations to their sisters and mothers, exchanging for the tingling spices, mystifying numbers of healing herbs, chart divinations and ceramic wares offered by the women and the exotic polished metal knives and older stone tools made by the famous Arrow Society of men. Scientific seers juggled golden balls high in the air to advertise their skillful hands and travellers unrolled astrological and geological maps and charts which local Lion clan navigators compared with their own for imagination and accuracy.

The three children stopped to watch the jugglers for a while and were joined by Dee and two boys from the Tortoise clan, and then Fran-keen and two of her sisters. Soon all these children were following the mound of orange and black cloth as it bobbed along on top of Ernesta who had an exact spot in mind. When she reached it she dropped her burden and called to Jessi-ma to drop hers. Tent stakes wavered in all directions as they began the assemblage.

Crowded under the billowing cloth the children found that solid objects take their own time settling into place. First the tent poles must fall over to the west and then to the south. Then Fran-keen and Ernesta must decide which of them should place the stakes and who should hit them with a flat topped rock. Then they must stop to wipe spit off their faces from the hot word discussion and then they must have a more active spit discussion.

Then first the bright striped cloth body of the tent must flap short in the breeze and then it must bunch up in a lump at the top. Then Dee and Margedda must decide which of them can pull cloth the hardest and longest without breaking any fingernails and Jon Lilly must stop digging holes in the wrong place and must stop moving the tent-bracing rocks to sit his small body down on.

Next before they even notice they have all been distracted by some drummers who began playing on the other side of a long row of market tents. Following Dee who has run out first to involve herself they join her swaying near the drummers with her belly extended to show off the lines of the drawing of a tortoise painted on it. Having gotten the painting done to her on her first birthday she had not forgotten the joy of this attention and now for every festival and special occasion insisted on having her older sisters paint her with a new outline of tortoise on her stomach.

Dee was standing now very near the drummers, and Ernesta saw one of them lean over to lay her head for a second on Dee's chest, beginning a rhythm which imitated her heartbeat. A second drummer broke the rhythm in half and another multiplied it by two and a third. Then the tambourine players and hummers began a song about the wind playing sexily with itself by rattling dry seeds in preparation for harvest, while some of the men who were flute players stepped up to take the part of the wind itself.

Eighteen young women of the Tortoise clan, Dee's sisters among them, stepped forward to begin a Tortoise clan dance of formal statement to the earth in behalf of the high hope of harvest and to entreat patient endurance for the dry crops now struggling to hold up their heads in the fields outside the city.

Jessi-ma hung her arms down over Ernesta's shoulder liking the feeling of her fingers dangling. She especially liked to watch dancing envying the swaying motions. This was a dance of increasing expectations as the tambourines in particular played by the older men and women were voicing both their moist grainy hopes and their dry grainy fears.

Being graceful was a part of belonging to the Tortoise clan of provision for whom grace meant returning to Ana some of what she has offered and for them Ana is Ana the earth and a planter and harvester of renewal, as for the Lion clan she is Ana of animals of companionship, terror and satisfaction, as for the Snake clan she is Ana the dreadful transformer and for the Bee clan she is both Ana the explosive creator and Ana the orderly constructor who wears a city on the statue of her head.

In a gesture of grace the dancers sprinkled pearls of shiny grain all around them. Ernesta watched seeing the grains were as pretty as insects, wondering if that's what having bearing means, to dance a gesture of returning what has been given, and did Dee have that quality secretly though she didn't appear to, grinning with bread crumbs stuck to her face and thrusting her stomach out childishly behind the drummers, imitating the dance. After a few minutes the women drummers turned the drumming over to a group of young men from the Tortoise clan who had time to practice and perfect the delicacy of their drumming muscles, and who would keep the rhythm going for as long as the dancers continued though this might be for the duration of the festival.

Tired now of watching an event that would continue so

relentlessly, Ernesta led her friends back to their own almost existing tent. By the time everything was balanced evenly and they were sitting close together in privacy and still not too hungry everyone was apparently ready for Ernesta's story and bored with Jessi-ma's joking to help the work go faster, and tired of Jon Lilly practicing his rocky juggling in their faces.

However as Ernesta arranged her face to begin her story telling they were distracted once again with heads turning to peer out the flap for what was passing of such interest. First, whiskers and tufts of black fur thrusting beyond reddish ears and a collar with a braided leather chain, then the entire body of a nearly wild reed cat from the marshes straining at his leash, trying to poke a way inside the tent.

Then, a tattooed hand holding the chain, and a boldly pictured face with self-controlled grey eyes peering through the folds of tent. Ernesta and Jessi-ma recognized Gedda, the woman from the wild islands to the north who was the lover of Ernesta's uncle.

"Have you seen my daughter," the woman asked in accents too thick for Dee, who giggled rudely as Ernesta said, "No, we haven't seen her all day." And Jessi-ma added helpfully, "but we haven't looked."

"I don't think we cheered her up," Ernesta said when Gedda's face was gone. Once again she gathered her resources to begin her story, when suddenly the tent bubbled up at the rear and began rising. Soon feet appeared, and then a dusty white linen dress with yellow trim, a tubby belly, then a slatted box with something feathered wadded in the bottom, and finally Margedda's grinning face.

"Margedda!" Jessi-ma shrieked. "Your mother was just here looking for you."

"Shhhut your mouth," Margedda screamed, falling on Jessi-ma and sticking her gummy palm over the astonished girl's mouth. "It happens I am not looking for her." Her voice was muffled. No one asked about this or the personal fight between the mother and the daughter. Instead they scootched their bodies together until there was room for Margedda's larger one.

And while Ernesta cleared her throat restlessly to begin her story, first the others must admire Margedda's ball of owl and poke their fingers at it, then Dee must begin screaming with laughter when Margedda opened her mouth to reveal a hairless pink baby mouse lying sleeping on the side of her tongue. Then nothing would do but that they must all watch while Margedda fed the warm-bodied mouse to the scruffy round owl, who swallowed eagerly, and then they must croon to the baby.

Then Dee had to show Margedda the fly collection she kept in a shallow box and was willing to trade for a favor. Then the fly trapped in Ernesta's hair moved restlessly so she must scratch her head and when Jon Lilly and Fran-keen began clamoring for lunch after watching the owl eat Ernesta had to walk outside the tent for a while to regain any amount of balanced feeling.

"Is this what bearing is all about," she whispered fiercely to the tent stakes, "waiting and waiting and waiting for your part to begin?" And getting no answer she kicked fiercely in the dirt.

They had settled into quiet munching and swallowing when she came back in and sat down in front of all of them.

"LISTEN, NOW." she said with all her patience exploding. "THIS IS IMPORTANT." Seeing their eyes tied to hers in ever expanding knots, she lowered her tone dramatically. "We are going to remember the day we met the lion." And to her amazement, they were completely ready, and she guided them into the story.

Telling Stories Is One Way Of Recalling

She pictured the day for them, how the road felt under their feet, how the river had looked shiny as brass. She reminded them that the five girls had all been sent to the river to gather reeds by her own Aunt One and other weavers who needed them for their wicker baskets, and that most of the morning they had wandered every which where finding out what they each most liked to do. And while she was talking to them, refreshing their memories, she found she was remembering her own.

They had gotten so hot they thought they would die of it. Ernesta had spotted the sandy beach leading to a shallow pool partially cut off from the rest of the river by a bank of white sand with trees draping into the water. She had plunged into the cool water skirt and all, taking the cloth off under the water and throwing it in a wet wad on the shore.

"Watch for crocodiles," Margedda called. Crocodiles were her favorite subject lately because she was eager to meet one. She folded her own skirt neatly, and Ernesta's too after shaking it first.

"They sit all day with their mouths open like this," Margedda continued. She stiffened in the sand while the others undressed doing a lengthy open jawed imitation.

"There are no crocodiles around here," Jessi-ma said with authority. "My mother says they live in the delta near Celeste." She was an authority on the metropolis of Celeste because many of her mother's people still lived there, her aunt and mother having been sent to this northern countryside of Mundane to do some continental engineering. She stripped off her thin skirt and raced to the edge of the pool, then stopped, thrashing one foot around in the water without getting in.

"Come on, Jessi-ma," Fran-keen urged. Her own sturdy deep brown body spun through the air in a ball and vanished briefly underneath the surface. She came up blowing a long spew into the air. Dee paddled by spewing too. They were rolling their eyes to the side secretly examining Margedda's lighter skin and blue patterns of spiral tattoos.

Jessi-ma watched the two spewing for a while commenting on the shape of the arcs they were creating in the air: "Fran-keen's is the highest but Dee gets more water in her mouth." She herself liked arcs and arches better than any other shape, she thought, and she was still standing with one foot in the water when Margedda stopped being a crocodile and asked her, "What's the matter? Why don't you get into the water?"

"I don't know. I just can't swim."

"Everybody can swim," Margedda said flatly.

"No, not me. I'm just too clumsy." Jessi-ma sat down, gathering stones around her to begin building a narrow play wall.

"She's listening to us," Margedda jerked her head in Ernesta's direction.

"She is?"

"She's heard everything we've said."

"How do you know?"

"Because I've noticed that she listens to everything. Haven't you noticed?"

"But you don't even know her," Jessi-ma began to be jealous of her friendship.

"Yes I do, I've known her since we were little babies, practically. She listens," Margedda said, shifting her weight in the hot sand. "She's one of those Snake clan people."

"You're just jealous," Jessi-ma said, "because you're not one." When Margedda flipped sand at her she flipped sand back and then moved to the other corner of the beach cove, again compiling building stones. She began to build another wall.

"It's true," Ernesta thought as she floated out past the spewers. "I do listen to everything. I watch a lot too." She wondered what this meant. Did it mean she was nosey, or was this part of bearing, to bear a lot of information?

"Remember how we built the raft," Margedda interrupted her reveries and for a moment she was brought back to the tent and to the story she was telling. Ernesta remembered the raft very well since it had been her own idea, though Jessi-ma and then Fran-keen had actually engineered it. They had found the rough runner vines and tied endless numbers of them together, Jessi-ma making the most complicated knots any of them had ever seen.

"This is a regular sailor's knot," she had explained. Knots were sacred to the Bee clan, who kept models of them to pass down as toys for their Bee clan engineering children. "And this one is for an ordinary halter and then if you want a sling to carry heavy stuff, you do this. . ." Her long brown fingers rapidly twisted the cords into a multitude of useful shapes.

"Wait, show me that one again." Fran-keen knew some sailor and animal halter knots and wanted to know more.

"Come on," Ernesta hustled them impatiently. "All we have to do is tie these two floats together." She had found the pigskin floats tied up along the shore. Traveling herders and a few people who chronically camped in the stands of trees and brush woods used them as rafts to cross the river. Each pigskin, blown full of air and with the leg parts tied and caulked, would float a full grown person.

Two pigskins tied together, Ernesta had figured, would be plenty for the four of them to hang onto in the water, while Jessi-ma could sit on high and dry top.

Ernesta and Fran-keen dived under the skins tying them together in a netlike sling from the vine-rope as Jessi-ma payed it out to them from the bank. They all marvelled at the glistening reddish brown raft when it was completed, including a flat bark seat tied onto the top.

. Jessi-ma was ecstatic. "We're going to Celeste in style," she said. Going to Celeste was Jessi-ma's idea of an appropriate adventure since she had heard so much about it from her mother, whose own mother still lived there, and most of the other girls thought the trip sounded feasible and even easy the way Jessi-ma described it. None of them realized that the famous metropolis was on another river altogether, not on their river.

Margedda had not wanted to go with them, Ernesta remembered. She had closed her eyes, squinched up her face and predicted, "The raft is going to sink."

But Margedda had come with them because Ernesta stared

at her with her wandering eye tearing off to the left and said, "Margedda, you can't stay here by yourself, a crocodile will get you."

"Don't be an ass," Margedda said. "I *am* the crocodile." Then she had waded in, grabbed a leg of the pigskin and come along.

At first it seemed simple to tow the raft upstream. Both Fran-keen and Ernesta had strong swimming shoulders while Margedda's broad body floated effortlessly in front of her big kicking feet. Dee, though she was the youngest, paddled a relentless course. And Jessi-ma sang to them from the top of the raft, to give them courage and enjoyment.

Then it seemed more complex as the current pushed like young goats against them driving them further into the main course of the river, tricky with undercurrents and cross streams. Ernesta could feel them being rapidly sucked into cold, fast running water. Soon even with a sweating Jessi-ma leaning far off her perch to splash hands in the water with them, Ernesta knew they would be pulled across the river unless something happened to stop them.

They were tired now. Fran-keen hung to the net of vines with one hand, the other clutching her knife. It was her most prized possession, a yellow bone carved handle set with sharp blue shells along the cutting edge and a long thong looped through the bored hole in the handle, so she could loop it around her wrist. She was sorry she had brought it. Jessi-ma took it from her, leaning far far over.

"I'll hold it for you," she panted. Her arms were not so used to paddling.

Almost immediately the knife squirted from her hand and skidded across the wet pigskin with Jessi-ma lunging after. The cutting edge caught under the tying vine as Jessi-ma grabbed it, her rushing momentum carrying her straight overboard headfirst.

"Oh no!" someone yelled and then Ernesta heard her own voice call, "Jessi-ma".

The double pigskins lurched and one made a blabby hissing noise as they separated from each other. Ernesta found her hand holding a piece of loosely floating vine realizing in horror that Jessi-ma had cut some of the vitals as she went on her way. One pigskin began to collapse.

"I told you, I told you, I told you." Margedda yelled. "Go for the shore, the raft is sinking." She dived under the water.

Ernesta saw Fran-keen unravelling Dee from a tangle of vines as they both swam toward the riverbank where they had first launched the raft. She saw a ribbon of smoke rise from the shore. Alone now in the water both Ernesta's eyes bugged out over the glistening river until at last Jessi-ma's garbling face surfaced. She still clutched the knife in one hand, thrashing it and herself around and around. The remaining pigskin bobbed in the distance, headed for the opposite shore as Ernesta maneuvered to get close to the thrashing and dangerous arms.

"Jessi-ma, hold still," she shouted fiercely but Jessi-ma would not. She began clutching Ernesta down under the water with the top of her head knocking against Ernesta's chin. Her head hurt and her face was anxiously furrowed as she saw the formless thrashing under the water. Ernesta was suddenly furious with Jessi-ma's continual drowning. She reached under the water grabbing Jessi-ma's hair pulling her head back. Behind her Margedda suddenly appeared.

"Oh, there you are," she said and Ernesta rested for a second while Margedda began slapping at Jessi-ma trying to get a grip on her slippery skin, then getting the flailing arms down and the head up out of the water and the knife pressed flat and harmless against Jessi-ma's chest all at the same time. Margedda could not unravel the bone knife from the panicky fingers as the three bobbed uneasily in the water.

"Take her other arm," Ernesta gasped, and between them they floated and kicked and bobbed and slapped Jessi-ma toward the shore.

Rattlings On A Stony Shore
Of Not Yet Understanding

She lay as though petrified for several minutes while they batted and shook water out of their own ears, and then she relaxed grinning up at them from a prone position on the shale beach they had dragged her to.

"I'm getting better, aren't I."

"Better at what?" Ernesta looked down at her, wondering how such a skinny body could have been so strong as nearly to drown both of them.

"Better at not drowning." Jessi-ma sat up picking pebbles from between her toes. Ernesta and Margedda stared into each other's gleaming eyes, not knowing what to say to that.

The three had landed at a different spot than the other two.

And after they had recovered their breath and dried off the first they discovered about the cove was that they couldn't easily leave it. A shale cliff backed up the beach with three crumbling sheets of stone too steep to climb. Thick brush grew at the bottom while above them on the bluff a huge dead tree towered into the blue sky. Exploring these bushes Ernesta found something intriguing, a black wing of a bird spread in the top of a bush. She picked it up.

"What's that," Jessi-ma just behind her asked. She took it from Ernesta's hand, then jumped and wiped her palm on her bare leg.

"Oooh," she said, "this thing has fresh blood on it." Margedda took it in hand curiously.

"Maybe that death bird dropped it," Jessi-ma said. High above they saw the black dot of a buzzard passing over.

They leaped nervously as some droppings of shale clattered down behind them from the cliff side.

"This place is weird," Margedda said, while Jessi-ma began to shudder. She took some steps toward the place where the clattering shale had landed, and picked something up.

"Someone lost a sandal down here."

"Let's see," Margedda said.

Suddenly Jessi-ma's eyes rolled. "Let's get out of here," she whispered. And without knowing why they felt so panicked they all ran down to the water.

"How can we do this?" Margedda started to question, thinking of the tumult of the ride in.

"We'll float her to the next cove." Ernesta was certain. She grabbed their arms.

"What *was* that thing I felt," Jessi-ma said.

"It doesn't matter," Margedda said, already neck deep in water.

"Get in, Jessi-ma." Ernesta pushed Jessi-ma protesting into the water where they floated her without slapping around the corner and downstream to another low getting-out place.

Dee yelled to them immediately from further down the bank as they scrambled onto the sand. She appeared soon with Frankeen and a bundle of cloth.

"We walked back up to where we got in and found all our clothes. What happened to you?"

Margedda and Ernesta didn't speak as they dressed, and Jessi-ma's trembling voice joked weakly.

"I don't know what's the matter with them. First they pull me out of the water and then they push me back in." She told how they had kept her from drowning and then gave Fran-keen back her knife.

"Let's go home," Margedda suggested.

"What about the reeds we're supposed to pick?" Dee asked.

"Oh no," Ernesta groaned. "I forgot about them." Grumpily they followed Ernesta as she walked along the river trying to get to the most marshy place. And along the way they found something else of interest, a campfire still smoldering.

"Mmm, let's get warm," Dee said holding her hands over the embers.

"We're already warm," the sweating Jessi-ma reminded her. Then she reached down and picked up another bird wing exactly like the one they had found earlier.

"Look at this!" she said uneasily. "What's going on?—these look like Bee clan birds." But none of the rest of them knew what Bee clan birds were supposed to look like.

"Doves!" Jessi-ma exploded. "Measuring doves Aunt Lillian brought from Celeste just for the festival."

"I thought doves were white," Margedda said.

Jessi-ma looked directly into Ernesta's wandering eye. "You might understand if you came with me to meet some of the rulers of the city," she said, and when Ernesta's expression did not change, she snorted as though she didn't care any more.

"Oh never mind." Jessi-ma spit on stones in irritation and they walked on to the marsh land where they picked reeds in a frantic realization of the end of the day. After that they met the mama lion and went for a third dip in the river, fortunately so shallow at this marshy point no one had to carry Jessi-ma.

"That lion was the least of it," Ernesta thought as she ended the story of the facts of the day.

"What I want to know is," Jessi-ma said, pulling out a dried bird wing from the purse she lately had begun wearing over her shoulder, "we know that Aunt Lillian took the two sacred doves down to the river and no one has seen them since. Why did the wing have fresh blood on it?"

"Because someone killed it," Margedda is combing her own tangled red hair as she says this. Dee and Jon Lilly are shrieking and giggling over the idea of blood so that one of the jugglers pokes his head in to say they can't hear their own drums for the racket. Awake now in the light-struck nest of Ernesta's coiled hair the fly is washing his face, rubbing one furry claw over the myriad lenses of his enormous eyes and healing the injured one.

"And why," Ernesta continues when the noise subsides,

"why is it only the wings we found—where is the rest of the bird?"

"Someone ate it," Margedda says popping a tidbit of cooked meat from their lunch into the little owl's gaping beak.

And they shrieked and left the story at that. Dee began laughing.

Ernesta asked Dee why she was giggling so hard and Dee said, "Not everyone pops their eye out like you do and it looks funny."

Jessi-ma laughed too at this. "I like when the eye does that too, I think she looks like a pretty frog."

Ernesta jumped on Jessi-ma then and rolled around with her, Jon Lilly scrambling in between them. The fly lost his balance in Ernesta's hair from the jostling and fell out into the air. Scrambling for balance he was soon chased by the avid hands of Dee who wanted to put him into her box and trade him for one of Margedda's hairpins.

Only sharp buzzy spinning and upward spiraling released the fly from this threat of sudden boxing and carried him outside into the winds of the festival. There he quickly smelled his way to the public bakery only a few tent rows away and in front of it he began finding the subject of his destiny.

Out on the street near a puddle of stimulation are a number of flies circling, among flies circling is certain to gather increasing attention. If a number of male flies are circling, a female fly will find this of interest. The fly does not explain how he knows this, how he knows it for certain. But everything in him understands how to circle, his left wing knows how to shorten the stroke and his right wing to lengthen. Watching the number of circlers he is drawn to them, and to the idea of special selection. She will arrive, she will notice the circling and she will pick one, and that is the one who continues.

Trembling after sleeping and waking and washing now he is all eager, he is anxious to be one of those who circles and circles, not any longer standing and washing, not searching and smelling, not walking and probing and endlessly looking, no longer magnetized by puddles, reflections and odors. He understands the culmination of his life, his long egg life, his longer maggot life and now his all day long fly life, he understands the culmination of all this effort to be about circling.

To be one among one's fellows, following and leading, turning and diving, maintaining and angling, steadying and displaying, planing and repeating. Because she just might be choosing, she would certainly be arriving, she would probably be noticing, she would definitely be attracted to the dancers of the circling.

And when she is arriving, they must be circling, they must be precisely whirling. It just might be himself that she will be choosing for continuing, especially if he is most precisely whirling. Now he is joining, he is no longer buzzing, now he is turning, now again he is turning, he is joining and no longer puzzling or seeking, he is very happy to be turning and following and leading with his fellows in their circling.

It Is Not So Easy To See The Rulers Of A City

"Who are the rulers of the city," Ernesta asked her aunts early the next morning, before they left for the steamroom of the women's bathhouse to steam themselves in preparation for the second day of the festival, and they laughed and entered into an intense conversation regarding the fairness of the barter between the Snake clan at the market and some people who lived a day and a half up the river.

Ernesta had waited up late until her mother came home from the street dancing the night before having met up with a sailor friend of her former acquaintance, and asked her the similar question.

"The rulers of this city? I suppose you mean the gossips," Donna had said with lilting laughter, still Ernesta was not satisfied. She thought that knowing the rulers of the city would give her another idea about the nature of balance and bearing.

"I could introduce you to them," Jessi-ma said when the two met in front of Ernesta's house to decide what to do on the second day of festival. They were still too young to go to the women's bathhouse on a ritual occasion and the planned ceremony of the releasing of doves could not happen because of the absence of Jessi-ma's aunt Lillian in her death, to say nothing of the disappearance of the pair of doves themselves. Since the two girls had witnessed the replacement show of jugglers rehearsing at length the afternoon before, they were bored to go see them again.

"I can show you most of the rulers of the city, my mother and my aunt Lillian have told me a lot about them and where they live."

So following Jessi-ma's loping lead they were walking past the oak tree in her sunken courtyard of no activity on a day when many were concentrated in another portion of the city.

"Well," Jessi-ma says, waving her arm.

Ernesta is looking anxious. "Are we going to the Moon Temple?"

"Why?"

"Because my aunts will be there, they are stopping by to see my mother and they might give me some more chores to do this morning."

"Then let's go over to the bakery. I'm hungry and it takes a lot of energy to see all the rulers in one day."

The bakery was a central place for news as well as sentences Ernesta did not exactly understand, such as, "Cottonroot works to root out little unwanted tufts of cotton better than acacia leaf." In the yard outside the two friends squatted in the shade eating cakes, sipping hot honey tea and listening to the gossips. A clatch of gathered women from the Tortoise clan kept commentary on the state of health, love, work, trade and the general quality of life in the city and the countryside.

Jessi-ma's face heated up when her mother Sonia was named as someone responsible for the altered schedule of the festival.

"She couldn't find anything of her sister's doves except a wing nor come up with any measuring birds of her own as substitutes and so the initial work on the new temple has been indefinitely suspended."

"After all that talk and planning and sending of emissaries, taxes and whatall."

"Such an incompleted business," another gossip said furtively, giving sly sideways expressions with her mouth and eyes. Ernesta felt her own heat rising and was about to speak in behalf of Jessi-ma's family when the entire group was distracted by the appearance of a stocky blue-lined woman in the Tortoise clan formal dress. As though her skin alone didn't distinguish her, Margedda's mother Gedda was nearly dragging a willful reed cat on a leather chain leash.

"What wonderful earrings!" Jessi-ma exclaimed. Concentrating, Ernesta recognized that the reed cat's gold earrings were some her uncle Blueberry Jon had recently won in a gambling game the Snake clan like to play this time of year.

"Now here's one who can't keep track of her own child," said the furtive woman in a loud whisper.

"Tries to keep her daughter cooped up in the house like a sick chicken, no wonder she runs off."

"Have you seen that redhaired girl? There's something very

117

peculiar about her, I don't really blame the mother."

Dauntless, Gedda strode finely into their midst, tying the cat's line to a post very near the furtive woman's foot.

"I've never met a mother in this place yet," she said loudly and with a heavy accent, "who didn't think she could raise my child better than I can." And on this truthful statement she stomped stiff-backed into the smokey bakery. The half-wild cat yawned elaborately at the closely watching faces, then growled roundly in his throat when the surrounding gossips wiggled their fingers at him.

"Poor Margedda, she must be somewhere hunting baby mice. Why don't we go look for her in the stable." Ernesta was watching a green grasshopper stand on the furtive woman's sandal close to the premeditating paws of the grumpy wildcat.

"It's the simplicity of fate," one of the gossips said, "that Gedda should have had a daughter like Margedda, and then can't get along with her. They chose each other to fight with. It makes them more strongly defined."

What do they mean they chose each other?" Jessi-ma asked Ernesta.

"Before Margedda entered Gedda's dream womb," Ernesta said, "they knew each other in time before."

"What do they mean by *fate*?" Jessi-ma said as Ernesta tugged on her elbow attentively.

"Oh, you know."

"No, I mean really."

Ernesta wrinkled her forehead impatiently. "See that grasshopper? It's that grasshopper's big fat fate to be eaten by somebody. Otherwise it wouldn't taste so good to so many creatures. But it's too skinny and too early in the season for my aunts to roast it, so it's going to be snapped up by Gedda's cat unless we catch it for Margedda."

"I thought you wanted to see the rulers of the city?" Jessi-ma asked, but she also clamped her fingers over the long-bodied insect as Ernesta dragged a stick of distraction in front of the sharp-eared reed cat.

"Ooh, this is a wriggly one," Jessi-ma said, trotting a meandering course away from the bakery.

"Are you sure it's really still in there?" Ernesta said, stopping her with one outstretched arm to peer breathlessly into her clenched hand. Instantly the grasshopper zipped between the netlike fingers, arcing past Ernesta's examining eye into a gutter at the corner of the street.

"Actually, maybe it's our fate to follow the grasshopper that we're talking about. And it's our fate today to see the rulers of the city."

"I see it," Ernesta says, looking down the wooden grating.

"Get off," Jessi-ma says, pulling at the grate and pushing away Ernesta's implanted foot of solidity and resistance. Throwing the slatted frame to one side, she wriggles past the clinging grasshopper down into the gutter, slick as a weasel.

"We're going down there?" Ernesta now has a wrinkled face of unpleasantry.

"Sometimes," her companion replies in muffled tones, "to see the rulers of the city you have to go through channels."

Rather than be left behind Ernesta is soon squirming shoulders and hips through a narrow space. In a moment they are standing in a tunnel lined with clay-smirched tiles leading under the city's buildings in a downward slope where far down the tunnel they can see smears of light from other grates set at street level.

"This set of tunnels rules the irrigation water of the city by telling it where to go and how much at a time," Jessi-ma explains, "and it rules and directs the runoff, so during overabundant rains these tunnels keep the streets above us from flooding water into the houses."

"I didn't expect rulers to be so dirty," Ernesta says.

"There's the grasshopper," Jessi-ma says, "it just flew past my face. There it is." She lurches forward.

"I don't see anything." Skeptically Ernesta clutches at the air and walls to maintain her balance, Jessi-ma a dimly moving shape in front of her. She wonders how long it will take them to suffocate in the dry trashy air.

"Be quiet," Jessi-ma hissed. Then she rocked the walls of the tunnel with her own bellowing voice, "Haloo? Haloo? Grasshopper! We're trying to help you!"

"Liar," Ernesta muttered, stumbling after.

"We are, we're helping it explore its fate," her friend insisted. "And it's helping us. Hey, where are you going?" She stopped at a grate set in the side wall.

"What's happening?" Ernesta nearly shrieked, bumping into her solid form at the same time sneezing a nose full of dust with one hand clasping a clammy spider web. "Oh yarg."

"In here." Jessi-ma fumbled with the grate's wooden hook, then flung it open and lifted herself through on her crawling muscled stomach.

Following close behind Ernesta saw a ring of serene female faces meditating so deeply within themselves they did not flick an eyebrow as Jessi-ma poured out of the wall with bony arms waving, dress torn and plaster dust raining from each elbow.

Giggling and scuffling her feet Jessi-ma skittered across the tiled and polished floor of what they both realized must be the women's oracular bathhouse, and heedless of the gradually turning gazes, she flung herself into the shallow pool of barely rippling water with steam slipping in a moderate haze of tranquility around the women who sat dreaming and only occasionally deliberately shaping their incoming thoughts. Ernesta had never seen such serenity on so many faces at once.

"She can't swim! She can't swim!" Ernesta decided panic was the best solution to Jessi-ma's rude breach of peacefulness. With drama she skittered after her friend to the edge of the pool, as if in a dream herself, so far was this event from her imagining of how she might enter the women's oracular bathhouse, cooly and with graceful bearing, not this elbow-waving shrieking skittering.

When Jessi-ma's sopping hand clutching the shiny green grasshopper stuck up in front of her face she grabbed the bony elbow fiercely dragging her doubling over laughing companion out of the room without looking back at the residue of disruption they had left on the faces of the women or the residue of oily dust and leaves they had left on the face of the water.

Reaching the dark vestibule leading outside, they heard the familiar voices of Sonia and Aunt Three sharply discussing in one of the massage rooms off the main bath room, with the serenity of the air shaking as though something heavy footed was passing by. Ernesta felt Jessi-ma's hand on her shoulder shooting electric tension through her and for an instant breaking their merriment before the embarrassment of what they had just done again attracted them irresistibly.

Outside in the little garden attached to the bathhouse their bodies hung together laughing and leaning on the wall stamping their feet occasionally to shake the laughing all the way down so it wouldn't stay gathered in their ribs and nauseate them.

Persons Of Moderate Cubits Make Harmonious Rulers

"Come on, Jessi-ma," Ernesta said standing in the bathhouse garden with her hands jammed on her hips looking exactly like Aunt Two. "Let's take the grasshopper over to Margedda's house."

120

Jessi-ma had taken her dress off to dry in the sun slashing through the latticed roof of beams above them. "Put your clothes in the bushes. I'm not going through the streets dripping wet."

"Are you afraid your mother will find you in here?"

"No, Sonia and your aunt are probably rubbing each other down with olive oil while they have their discussion. That's usually what they do."

"They don't sound as though they're enjoying themselves much today." Ernesta picked at one ragged toenail while her two sandals dripped dry in the sand beside her. Toenails, she had found, could be stripped with the fingers provided your aim was good and you didn't tear them too close to the quick.

"What do you think they are arguing about?"

Jessi-ma looked extremely troubled, her face puckering into sorrow.

"Your aunt says the gossips say my aunt Lillian was murdered and my mother doesn't want to believe it."

"Murdered?" Ernesta jolted in horror and then shuddered. "How was she murdered?" She believed it instantly.

"The gossips say somebody knocked her on the head with a rock, that she couldn't have just fallen down and hit herself."

"Who could have done that, Jessi-ma? That's awful." She reached a hand out side ways to touch her friend but Jessi-ma ducked away, skinning her face on the side of the plastered wall.

"Ow. See what you made me do?"

"I didn't do that. That was fate. Come on, everything's dry enough. Let's go see Margedda."

"Don't you want to see some more rulers? Or were those oracles too much for you?" And so challenged, Ernesta let Jessi-ma lead her into the small stellar temple of the Bee clan to look at her mother's hat and palms.

"This is not just any hat," Jessi-ma explained, "this is a measuring hat. My mother Sonia was to have worn it today at the ceremony of the release of the doves. My uncle Jad would have sighted through the troughs in the top of the hat to ceremonially display the lay out of the foundations of the new temple, and I was to have held the measuring rope."

Tears hung trembling on Jessi-ma's long lashes as she ran her hands over the painted wooden and reed structures of the two cubit high hat. Jessi-ma practiced her own cubit measurement of elbow to outstretched middle finger tip and was only a little short of the two cubits her uncle measured with his arm.

"This is because the women of the Bee clan are so tall and long boned," she said. "My uncle was chosen for moderate everyday cubits because he is a medium sized person. My mother practiced carrying heavy objects on her head all year so she would be strong enough to bear the weight of this particular hat on this particular day."

The cumbersome hat, Ernesta noticed, was a stylized statue of Ana with specially executed geometric angles and sighting troughs. This was Ana of measurement and surety, a major figure of the Bee clan. Surely, she thought, anyone who could wear this heavy measuring instrument would have to have bearing and balance. She began to admire Jessi-ma's mother Sonia, and her aunt Lillian, for the two of them had shipped the hat all the way from Celeste for the purpose of formally marking the foundation for the new temple in the cleared area near the river that cuts through the plain of Mundane.

"What about the palms," Ernesta said, looking for potted trees in the small temple but there were none. Jessi-ma held up wooden carvings of two human palms, one larger than the other.

"These are standard measures, one is royal and the other is everyday. We use them to measure length and breadth and the size of piles of grain for taxes to send to Celeste."

Ernesta hadn't known that Jessi-ma's family was so connected to the southern metropolis, her own family was completely connected to the city of their own foundation, called "Mundane" in memory of her grandmother's ancestor, the first Mama Mundane.

Next to the hat was a coiled rope for field measuring and a standardized ivory cubit model of the elbow to finger length of a Celestial ruler of long ago, whose arm measurement had been reproduced for 1400 years as a standard tool of Bee clan measurings.

Then Jessi-ma explained to Ernesta how the temple they were in itself was used for measuring, how the line-up of the columns allowed the evening star light to shine in, landing on a crystal stone face caligraphed to mark zodiac events.

"To rule the sequences of stellar time," she said. The line up of another set of columns allowed sunlight to beam in to a special stones marking winter and summer solstices. "To rule the year," she said.

Ernesta began to understand why Aunt Three said that in all of Mundane's world, the Bee clan were the greatest rulers. They had built temples for keeping time for the other clans as well as for their own, and the new planned temple would coordinate time keeping with temples located at other places on the surface of the earth.

"They never stop measuring," Ernesta thought. "They measure everything with everything else."

She thought this as Jessi-ma was showing her the large dovecotes in the temple courtyard, where big breasted birds with red eyes cooed and shoved their curved beaks down into their own feathers. Some were white as sand and a few were charcoal black.

"Two of these were to have gone flying over the sea to beautiful Celeste today, the two who disappeared with Aunt Lillian."

"The bloody wings!" Ernesta said.

"Yes, they disappeared into bloody wings, two black doves who would have flown home and the Bee clan members in Celeste would measure the distance from there to here in kilometers of time and distance by comparing the difference in flight time between their arrivals." More tears clung to her eyelashes.

"I used to feed them," she wept. "They stood with their little orange feet in my hand."

"I've never seen measuring doves before," Ernesta said. "Would they fly at night, too?"

"Not really," Jessi-ma said.

Ernesta was anxious to leave the timekeeping building since it made her friend so sad and it made her so unaccountably uneasy.

"Let's take the grasshopper to Margedda," she insisted and so they left on their way to Margedda's house.

"I didn't get to show you the Bee dancers," Jessi-ma complained.

"*Bee* dancers or Bee *clan* dancers?" Ernesta wondered.

"Bees dancing *and* Bee clan dancing. We learned Bee clan dancing from the dancing of Bees so it's always a dance of measurement. The Bees ask: How far to the flowers? How many, which direction, what wind velocity, what obstacles? These are Bee dance questions and answers. Our dancing is about geometry and the questions of Bees as applied to human wonderment. We don't use dancing to tell stories as much as other clans do. I only wish I could do the Bee dance better so I didn't shame my mother in front of our relatives."

Rulers Of Some Cities May Be Found
Nearly Anywhere

As they passed the stable on their way to Margedda's mother's house, Ernesta felt an inside tug urging her to go looking in the stable and there crouching on the straw-littered floor near the feet of an indifferent donkey was Margedda.

"Are you still in here?"

"Ssshhh. Don't startle the diviners," Margedda said. She was holding a covered basket with a flat bottom.

"What's in there?" Jessi-ma hissed through the darkness inside the stable striking her eyes.

Reluctantly and swiftly, Margedda uncovered the top of the basket a crack enough for them to catch a musky smell and a glimmer of fast moving fur.

"Did you see them?"

"No," Ernesta said, "you just gave us a whiff."

"I'll tell you, then. Inside here," and she displayed the basket importantly, "are seven mice big enough to have fur. They are all sleeping now."

"What are you doing with them," Jessi-ma said, "your owl isn't big enough to eat mice with fur is it? We brought you a grass hopper."

"I left the owl home today. Would you take the grasshopper over there and feed her for me? I'm only borrowing these mice from their mother to practice my divination."

"More rulers of the city," Jessi-ma said quickly, sweeping Ernesta out of the stable before she could ask for a demonstration of the divination.

"Don't you have some rulers, too?" she asked as they crossed the courtyard where the oak tree glinted her leaves in the late afternoon sun, and Ernesta bowed her body to the oak tree in a gesture of recognition of how much she owed the tree, and all trees.

"The Snake clan acknowledges the oak tree as our ancestor. I guess you could call her a ruler. We speak to her as a meditative oracle. And my mother is also an oracle. She sits in the Moon Temple sometimes while people come to ask her questions. When she doesn't want to see anyone she stays out in the hills with the black eyed plant who helped my mother dream me into physicality."

"Don't your aunts use any rulers?" Jessi-ma asked.

"Oh well, of course, there's my aunt One's baskets, she uses them to store things and also to magnify people's minds. I can also show you my second aunt's rulers."

She led Jessi-ma over the back wall of the Snake clan court yard and out to a storeroom behind the garden, a storeroom filled with every kind of pot imaginable.

"Oh these are pretty good rulers," Jessi-ma said. She was examining a pot for distillation with its special compartments for hot coals and specific measures of liquid.

"Not only these small ones," Ernesta said, "look." She led Jessi-ma into a tall round room next door. "This whole room is a pot. This pot is used to redistribute grain after we get it in carts from the Tortoise clan. See the marks on the wall, that's how we know how much each family gets."

"How much is that?" Jessi-ma asked.

"Aunt One's sons take the grain from this mark to this mark, and Aunt Two's take the next marking all the way to my mother and I who take this one. After the harvest you won't be able to see any of the marks again until distribution day."

Then nothing would do but that Ernesta must take Jessi-ma into Aunt Two's pot storeroom to see all of her kinds of pots including those she had inherited from her own aunts and great grandmother Mundane.

Jessi-ma admired all the containers with their differentiated shapes and functions for holding chicken feet slops, oil, beer and herbal refinements, as well the jars that served as chamber pots, sinks, open fire cookery, ladles, pitchers, grinding machines, baby bottles, lamps, trays, warming pans, portable stoves, double boilers, laundry tubs and mortars and pestles. She especially liked the cow-shaped one with four chambers for each of the four elements, used for distillation.

"I'm tired of carrying this grasshopper," she suddenly complained, revealing to Ernesta the sweat slick insect with limp antennae. "My fingers are cramping."

"Stick it here," Ernesta opened a lidded jar and they dropped the grasshopper down into it.

"Let's take it to Margedda now." Jessi-ma seemed altogether exhausted, and her eyes were swollen as though she would like most to cry over something and couldn't think what. "Let's run it over to Margedda's house without stopping for anything in the world."

Arriving puffing and sweating they banged on the door and

immediately a woman opened it for them.

"Hello, Gedda," Ernesta said respectfully. "Is Margedda home? We brought something for her."

Gedda scowled at mention of her wayward daughter who was so seldom home let alone helpful. Nervously Jessi-ma peeked into the jar as a guarantee of the grasshopper's presence and the longbodied insect took the opportunity to leap in a great arc past the tipped lid and the watching human face landing directly in front of a medium sized cat on the end of a leather leash held by Gedda who reached with one paw and fastened the grasshopper to the earth.

"Oh no," Jessi-ma said and her disbelieving expression as the grasshopper shell began crunching under the reed cat's teeth caused Ernesta to whoop even as she led her friend away from Gedda's grouchy face and Margedda's fruitless doorway.

Once out of the woman's hearing Ernesta said, "She's probably still in the stable anyhow, chasing those poor mice around for divination practice." She was laughing but not Jessi-ma, who said dourly, "That was fate, wasn't it? I wonder how it works."

"My aunt Two calls this 'Fate of Decision'," Ernesta said. "That grasshopper made up its mind nobody was going to eat it except the reed cat, and so it was. Shall I walk you halfway to your house?"

But Jessi-ma said, "No, my mother told me to spend the night with you. She wants to concentrate completely on the rain-dance tonight, because," and here she scratched the side of her face hard, "if it doesn't rain soon some of us in the Bee clan are going to be in big trouble."

Deep Underground
Some Ants Are Waiting Eventfully

As two human girls are walking overhead on their way to the house of one of them, deep underground the ants are settling into the dry dirt tunnels of their existence, turning their long bodies around the corners and into the chambers of their construction. Lining and lying, curling and coiling, they settle and rest while in his own chamber of constriction a large ungrown beetle too sleeps waiting for the transformation that would tell the more meaning of his larval existence.

Above ground the humans have all day moved restlessly,

some processioning, dancing and playing, some consorting with each other among bushes and some talking in disgruntled voices of the disruption of the festival by the absence of some of the more important expected ceremonies of temple dedication. Along the course of her walking one tall woman of the Bee clan in particular has noticed the talking not so much as talking as that the talking falls into silence whenever she herself arrives in its vicinity. Nevertheless she continues the course of her walking in order to reach the house of a number of sisters of the Snake clan where her own daughter has already gathered.

As the ants settle into their lining and lying, Jessi-ma joined by her cousin Jon Lilly are eating with Ernesta and her cousins, a long spicy dinner especially appreciated by the two older girls after their day of looking for the rulers of the city. Before they had finished Sonia arrived to be let in at the gate in her multicolored nighttime dancing dress rather than the brilliant blue robe of her daytime procession.

"Come play snakebones with us," Aunt Three invited her to the aunts' favorite gambling game with snake backbones as they often did like throwing on special occasions.

Tonight they were playing with the many handmade pins of their possession as exchanges. Aunt Two currently had the most of them, a row of twenty five pins. Some were straight and made of beaten copper, gold or silver with designs and bulbous heads and bodies. Many were crooked or geometrically shaped with inlaid shining stones and one had a snake's head with eyes of two rubies. Some others were made of ivory or hard wood with pictures of elephants and figures tediously carved and traded from people south and west of Mundane. Some were from materials made in the city and all had equal value in the game and because they were all pins to hold the clothes onto a person's body.

The aunts swore that if you stared at the snake pin's ruby eyes long enough you would see their mother Mundane's face, as she had made the pin requiring such close work it had absorbed the imprint of her features. Ernesta had sometimes tried the staring and in fact had inevitably seen her grandmother's unsmiling concentrated face. "She is watching me," she thought.

All the aunts and Sonia were sitting on pillows thrown on the floor of the aunts sitting and eating room in a circle with bowls of roasted pistachios and sweet millet cakes, drinking mugs of Aunt One's barley beer which she had broken open a keg of for the festival. The adults had finished eating bowls of

Aunt One's spicy goat meat stew cooked outside in a recipe on the roof.

Sonia stripped all the pins out of her clothing and hair to join the game. Some of hers were made of carved bone and very old, since the Bee clan prowls around in ancient places often finding useful objects to bring home. Some people find them disrespectful in this respect.

"You're going to lose three pins on this throw, Lattice," Aunt Two predicted. "My tailbone, your bellybutton and Sonia's nipple." Lattice was Aunt Three's other name. They liked to rename the pins during the game, sometimes by the names of all the men or women they could remember bringing home with them during festivals, then by the names of all the cousins in the Snake medicine clan, and now by all the variations in the parts of their various bodies, made more visible because their clothing had no pins to hold it together.

While the game was playing, Donna was in the many blanketed sleeping room next to this sitting room playing with a vivid young man passing through town on his way south. They did not speak the same language which neither of them minded as they were mainly speaking body language. She had been attracted to his beautiful stretched ears decorated with large oddsized holes each the size of a thumbnail. He had been wearing a multicolored cotton robe when he arrived and now he was not wearing anything except a string around his waist and some pouches.

Ernesta and Jessi-ma took turns peeking through the beaded curtains of her mother's doorway for a while to see what the two of them were doing together in there and then came back to watching the rattling snakebone game. The two girls had some bones to make a game of their own.

As a whimsical woman, the mother of Ernesta loved to go to festivals with the most outlandish young men she could find, especially men who had never been near a city, drum and flute players who knew nothing of formal city habits or of sciences, who roared and laughed and trilled as lightly as she did. She would take them into her room where they would paint each other rich colors and play different kinds of mating games, imitating birds, butterflies and small mammals from deep in the hills. Ernesta now could hear the formal patter of bare feet and strange warbling calls coming from the room where Donna and her sometime lover had fun with each other imitating ceremonies invented eons ago by some randy ancestor of the wild grouse.

As the two girls peered through the curtains with interesting giggly eyes they were amazed that heavy human flesh could be so feathery light while bouncing about with heads and elbows bobbing as the color sparkles off the roundly moving buttocks and twisting backs.

"What are they doing in there," Aunt Two asked as Ernesta sat down again to watch the aunts.

"Imitating birds, I guess," she said. She was closely examining the symbols carved onto the thickest parts of the snake backbones Jessi-ma had rolled trying to decipher them. Ernesta always was given an old wooden set of Mundane's bones to play with and the markers were nearly worn away. The snakebones used by the aunts had been newly imported from Jessi-ma's Celestial Bee clan homeland and were made of ivory.

"Donna truly belongs out in the wild bush somewhere," Aunt One said. "She grew up here in town just like the rest of us but her spirit blew out into the hills like a dandelion."

Aunt Two nodded, frowning while wiping her greasy hands on a dishcloth.

"Your move, Caddis," Aunt Three said.

"Well, they look just like peahens," Aunt One said, leaning back to the beaded curtains and doing a little peeking of her own.

Aunt Two frowned more deeply as the roll of her bones showed a clear dispersal of her jewelry in Aunt Three's direction.

"A snake is going east," Aunt Three read. She was sitting east of her middle sister. She picked up the pin with rubies glaring out of it. "You've had this snake pin for years haven't you? Didn't Mama give it directly to you?"

"Yes," Aunt Two said, "I suppose I haven't been wearing it enough lately. Nothing tires a pin more than lack of use, especially Mama's pins."

Aunt Three laughed and pinned the glaring snake onto her belt. "She's been watching you all these years she's been gone, hasn't she."

"Not just me, all of us," Aunt Two replied. "I see her often, with big yellow eyes."

Ernesta shuddered at the description that reminded her of the mama lion's eyes, and turned her attention to the wooden gambling bones.

"Does anyone want to go to the raindance with me?" Sonia asked. She didn't want to talk about Snake clan ancestors, and had never met Mama Mundane, who had wandered off on a journey before Sonia, Lillian and their children had joined the other architects of the Bee clan in the town of Mundane's world.

Ernesta was surprised that Aunt Three who had seemed so

tired a moment ago, now got full of energy, and sparkling eyes. Sonia had been watching Aunt Three, who had been watching her back, and Ernesta noticed that their lips were very full and they had bad nerves. They kept dropping their snakebones and losing their places with the predictions.

She and Jessi-ma hadn't known there would be a raindance tonight but before they knew what to think, Aunt Three and Sonia were up and out of the door, Aunt Three carrying her middle sized drum with her.

A raindance was a configuration of women dancing out in the open in a special place and making dew together, so that Ana of the clouds would get so excited she would pour down her juices, which often happened. While the women danced other women and some specially chosen roundhouse men stood around in a circle surrounding and protecting them from the view of outsiders, beating drums and timbrels. Everyone shouted lusty provocative invocations to Ana of the clouds and some people went off together into the bushes.

Aunt Three liked to do this making dew together especially with Sonia, and Ana loved all of it never failing to respond and even if she didn't shake down some dew of her own the very first night she almost always managed to thunder.

A Mixture Of Cats And Birds Is Like Pots Flying

As Sonia and Aunt Three have been making their way out to the hills to the special place set aside for raindancing they are gradually joined by other sultry members of the Spider Society, talking rapidly preparing for the drumming and moving that will shake Ana's juices out of the clouds. As the road winds along up and out of the city, past the last small household of a member of the Tortoise clan, they can hear the sound of harsh shouting from inside some walls inhabited by a farming woman who is presently more than just annoyed with her daughter Margedda.

Watching from a stool in the household corner, Ernesta's uncle Blueberry Jon can see that Gedda is more than just annoyed with her daughter Margedda for the veins along her neck are protruding more than he has ever seen them, and he has seen them do a great deal of protruding.

All evening in Margedda's house the new wild cat that her mother had brought home sat glowering on one side of the fire place while Margedda crouched glaring back on the other. There was no fire, but the two generated more than enough heat between them, more than had been generated all day at the Festival that Margedda hadn't even bothered to attend as her mother firmly said more than once to her.

For her part Margedda had been more than shocked to find someone living in her very house who had ambitions toward eating her little owl and had gone without her supper or any social amenities, refusing even to cross over to the kitchen portion of the bigger general family room where the large cat was sitting alternately hissing and washing his spotted sides and feet.

Her mother Gedda being equally stubborn had refused to cross the short length of the room with a bowl of food for her. They were having another mother-daughter fight which Blueberry Jon had come to call "There they were being Gedda and More-Gedda" when he described his in-the-middle-situation to his large-eared sisters of the Snake clan homestead.

If there was joy, sorrow and high activity in many households, and more of all these qualities among the sultry people making their way into the hills for a raindance, there were not so many of these things in one household, the house of a woman Gedda adopted into the Tortoise clan after more than a year of desperate travel. The Tortoise clan of farming and provision has many different kinds of people being the largest clan in the city with only one kind of behavior.

One of these people is Gedda who has given up her northern woodish people and their mushroom gathering eccentricities, she has given up staying up all night and going walking for two weeks at a time especially during harvest, and she has given up a love of dancing among trees and of wild mice in favor of a captured reed river cat who is now causing trouble in her own household. Being given to loneliness and other ailments of displacement Gedda had thought for a long time that she would find solace in her daughter as she got older but she instead is finding only aggravation.

She had produced for herself a terrible daughter in Margedda, a robust daughter with small eyes, great wads of bright red hair, huge ambitions and not much agility with farming, who hated everything to do with orderly rows of planted foods and stooping endlessly over the planting and the weeding and the harvest and the preservation, and who had no respect for the fragility of stored foods, staying away from the festival of ceremony and committment and then bringing home mice, mice to invade the fields and grain bins and display to the neighbors that

Gedda was not a serious farming woman who deserved a place in the clan and her own household with its own fire and a place for her daughter and a place for a man of her choice.

Grimly Gedda told these lengthy things to her daughter and grimly Margedda shut her ears and mouth to them clutching her little owl cage to her chest and holding a pink baby mouse quietly under her tongue until owl feeding time.

Only occasionally had Blueberry Jon and Gedda quarreled between each other over the several years they had been keeping company, and she had never asked him to leave for more than a few days to give her some peace or because there was another man she thought she liked there for a week or so but now the two had become close companions and coordinated in their misunderstandings. They liked now to sit quietly together talking about their past times without doing much explaining. Lately they haven't done too much of this quiet talking because of so much quarreling between the mother and the daughter.

To counter the owl and the mice who she knows the Tortoise people do not like Gedda has now brought home a cat of sorts, not the sort of cat Blueberry Jon had heard people were beginning to keep with much ado in the metropolis of the southland but a wildish river reed cat with strong musk smells and untrustworthy habits. Already Blueberry Jon can feel he does not like this cat who makes him uneasy by staring at him for long minutes and giving him no privacy.

Blueberry Jon likes best to play his flute and ruminate, he says that Margedda's bad temper and the cat are the same amount of distraction. Gedda says she has brought home the cat which she likes and that will look good in new gold earrings and whose presence is Margedda's responsibility because without the threat of escaping mice they would not need a cat at home in the first place. She refuses to discuss the matter further, she says now, although she does make some groaning noises of inner suffering, pressing her hand to various spots on her body.

Blueberry Jon is sighing and lifting his wooden flute expertly to his lips. "I wish it would rain so everything on earth would melt and when it all reformed everyone would feel like singing," he was saying, the sentence trilling and spilling out of his instrument in elongated notes rather than words.

Women Together
Are Often More Than Making Dew

Somewhat out of town and low in the hills a group of human dancers moves rapidly in time to the rhythms of the rain and wind, enticing the natural forces to visit the parched landscape of their adoring. Some of the members of the Spider Society have brought some feather dolls depicting Ana of the clouds and some of the thunder gods just to be sure somebody out there beyond the human sphere of influence would be interested in listening to the rhythms. In their songs they are using precise repetition of description and enticement and in their bodies they use imitation of the rain and the shaking and the sparkling and the wanting and the roaring of making dew together. Water sparkles down their faces and their breasts bobbling and weaving in the evening light as the drummers walk the muscles of their hands across the stretched skins of drums and entered into descriptions of the gathering of clouds and thunders.

Of all the dancers of the night the one with the most enjoyment was Lattice, Ernesta's Aunt Three, who loved being with Sonia, and the one with the most desperation was Sonia, who as a water bearing woman bore Bee clan responsibility for the gradual drying up of the wells and waterways surrounding the city. She danced more lustily than anyone and sweated more, she swung her beaded skirts the most and rattled the clicking pod branches gathered from the click branch tree most frequently. She had the most bells at her ankles and she stamped her feet the most and flashed her eyes at the other dancers and particularly at the third sister of her desiring of the Snake clan.

Soon some of the other dancers began to pace themselves, as midnight approached with the stars turning in their mazing courses overhead, soon everyone began noticing that while everyone had slowed to pace themselves not Aunt Three and Sonia, who were if anything going faster and faster as though to turn the stars faster and faster in their dew-drenched courses, collecting clouds in the greatest billows ever gathered. And the other dancers and the drummers noticed this, and looked at each other about it, every little once in a while.

Not doing much dancing except high in her branches in anticipation the greens of the oak tree in the center of the city rustled with the warning wind of the coming of a storm before her great brown beam of self swelled darkly as the first water of Ana's dew began dripping down the huge parched grooves of her thickened skin. She stiffened her leaves with absorption of the new moisture, lifting them with swelling pleasure to the cooler temperature she loved best. Droop and despair of posture began to leave her in these first moments along with the gathered dust and abandoned spiderwebs choking her greenery. Also the falling drops began to drown or at least wash away a percentage of the insects in their several phases who had brought themselves into her care lately and who had been flourishing in numbers too frequent for the oak tree to easily bear.

Turning to touch every leaf to the rain her multiple senses faced upwards. Wafting from below she detected the musky waves from the earth she herself had helped to make with all her residues and sheddings as they thickly mixed with water to give off their lusty summer gasses.

Wafting the lusty gasses high into the air everywhere the drops of dew gathered and fell. Sitting in a doorway of great dissension the reed cat twitched his whiskers as he smelled it; the ball of peaked owl clutched to the Margedda's sleeping chest twitched her pointed beak as she smelled it. Donna's well-kept snakes with their flat tongues coiled deep in slatted baskets in the House of the Moon smelled it, they snapped out their tongues to ask some further questions; all the people of the city smelled it, older men and women waking from their dozes smelled remembering the other welcome summers that the smell was well worth talking about.

The smell of Ana's water coming down raised everyone's senses reminding them of how fine it is to let your dew come down, to roll the entire earth between your legs, to be so large that you could cradle the ball of Ana's earth, roll it down your stomach and rock it between your legs until your own waters came down and the musky gasses rose anew the way they were now, glistening down the fleshy folds and crevices of the oak tree's body, soaking into the waiting mouth of the earth's dust, shining on the smooth and sensual stones, Ana's water coming down to more than match the musky waters of the dancers.

If to most of the creatures in the city Ana's lusty gasses were wondrous to some creatures the lusty rain gas was a warning smell, causing them to crouch closer into their nests or stuff more leaves into the doorways of their holes and havens. Some people of the Tortoise clan ran out to shut storage doors and some women pulled laundry suddenly inside from the roofs of drying and laying out. Outdoor human sleepers in the market-place crawled under their wagons in excited anticipation. As the water filtered into the dryest, oldest cracks of gardens and yards, thousands of insect bodies crept out to look for higher ground. Potato bugs, gray armored beetles, trap door spiders, long milli-pedes rubbed body to body in their rush to escape the much too insistent sensual dew that everywhere rushed them through their lives in ever greater sweeps of water. Some were clinging to sticks or folding up their legs going into a leafy trance of rush-ing with the currents, while those who knew how to trap air stayed beneath the water releasing pleasant little bubbles all the next day from under their bodies at the bottoms of the puddles.

Sometime after midnight walking down the road a middle sized man with broad shoulders is swinging a blanket roll pack with a disgruntled face and sharp unmeasured motions. From his waist swings on golden cords of long attraction a wooden flute carved from a single river reed carefully marked along the way with special carvings of significance.

Face downward he is walking angrily and sadly simultane-ously in recent memory of the warm place of companionship and understanding he is leaving.

Always he has tried to be amiable with the difficult foreign born woman Gedda and always until this night he has succeed-ed. Now because of a controversy between her and her growing daughter over mice he is having to abandon the hearth where he had been made welcome by her warm and sturdy arms and daily providing of bowls of prepared food, company and dense satisfying blanket rolls under her Tortoise clan roof.

However on this night scarcely had he begun playing his flutesong as a comfort to himself and to the tension of the house-hold situation when Gedda had begun so bitterly accusing him of enticing full grown mice into the house with his long flute playing of which she herself had already spotted two or three. Scarcely had he begun describing his complete misunderstand-ing of her description of him as someone who entices mice when his belongings begin flying out into the night air through the rapidly widening doorway of the house he had been sharing with this accusing woman month upon month for several years and only when his packets of smoking herbs and very best apothe-cary mixing bowl is flying through the air as well does he run to catch them gathering up the stuff of his belongings and be-ginning his walk down the road with gruff words of retaliation and no return intentions.

Now as he has been walking his grumbling is including a

further understanding from remembrance of the past that he has heard the woman Gedda describe the wondrous mouse and rat pipers of her northern village childhood people, special men musicians who could lead rodents by the hundreds from the fields with the ever entreating songs of their flutes and as Jon Mundane thought of this he began to feel some better about himself and his accomplishment of possible enticements.

"Perhaps I've turned into a flute player with some special rodent connections, and perhaps the Tortoise clan will sometime find a use for them." And as he is walking further and further down the road from Gedda's arms and body he is beginning to wonder about other arms and other bodies and the likely place he could be going.

The first most likely place he could be going is to his mother Mundane's house inhabited by his four sisters. Since especially his three older sisters and certainly the middle of the three will make too much fun of him for living with the tattooed woman Gedda, as she has enjoyed doing ever since the day he moved his belongings into Gedda's house he is not too anxious to end his roadway footsteps in her kitchen.

Since the second most likely place he can be going is the roundhouse for the fellows this is the place that he now begins to think about as he is walking, and feeling the first few pelts of water he looks up astonished that the stars have vanished.

"It's going to rain!" he thinks and unexpectedly his heart is lighter, not so filled with loss and sorrow.

"It's going to rain," the drums are singing low in the hills above the walking man as Lattice Mundane and Sonia of the Bee clan fall sweating onto each other's shoulders after their exultant effort to gather the clouds and milk them onto their city of need. After her efforts in particular Sonia loves the Snake woman's arms of comfort and encompassment.

"Perhaps the fear and sorrow of my water bearing situation will turn into joy now for a while," Sonia says.

"It's going to rain," down lower in the city near the courtyard of a recently washing oak tree Aunt Two is saying as she yanks the covers off the sleeping Ernesta and her friend Jessima who lie dreaming on the rooftop outside a main room of the Snake clan where earlier some sisters had been playing snakebones, not the divination form of this game, the simpler gambling form of it.

The two girls had gone to sleep close together until later Ernesta moved to the edge of the blankets to avoid the sharp jabs of Jessi-ma's too-bony elbow and now they are startled to see

Aunt Two's sleepy face with lightening lighting up the sky over the city all around them.

Water drops were falling rapidly enough to wetly coat the blankets as the two bedraggling girls stumbled into the interior, turning back in excitement to peer outside at more lightning and increasing water downfall.

Jessi-ma stuck her hand outside and then suddenly bolted back out on the roof to dance around, calling, "Rain, rain, more, more! Oh Ernesta, this is what the Bee clan has been waiting all summer for!"

They both ran back out onto the second story roof to dance in the spattering rain and celebrate the lightning as Aunt Two and Aunt One stood happily swaying and clapping out rhythms in the doorway and in imitation of the clapping Ana's thighs were doing to the clouds. So excited were the girls by the efforts of pouring water they couldn't resist washing each other's hair and faces in it. And then Jessi-ma did a special personal dance too near the edge of the roof so that Ernesta had to catch her by one arm to pull her back while both aunts made exclamatory noises.

Beyond the edge of the roof in the streets below they began to see other members of the Snake and nearby Lion clans climbing out of their houses to dance in the rain on their roofs or in the streets. They joined in this wild dance of the excited humans, a dance of looking down at their own feet while jiggling hands in the air as though ringing tambourines of celebration for the rain, and then holding chins high up toward the draining sky, closing their eyes for the brimming and the swimming of the rain, the rain, the rain, for the dripping and the dropping and the slipping and the slopping and the flipping and the flopping of the rain, for the rushing and the gushing, the flirting and the spurting, the breaking and the shaking, the streaming and the creaming of the rain, the rain, for the hissing and the pissing, the bawling and the falling of the rain, the rain, the rain, the rain!

Withering Roots Have An Awesome Effect

The warning smell of the water had not formed into a path much sooner before the body of the water formed a path down into the labyrinthian chambers of the city of ants underground in the courtyard underneath the oak tree.

Ordinarily the ants are protected from a heavy flood because even though their current mound of effortful living is located in a low spot under the branches of the oak tree where not much water could expect to stream in torrents, access to the entrance of the mound from a crease in the soil is blocked by the lumping up of one of the oak tree's roots, one special one that swept up for a yard or so out of the earth leaving a space underneath its elbow which had been blocked by a a great clod of earth held in place by some root hairs for as long as the ants had been living there.

Unfortunately during recent events the oak tree had allowed these particular root hairs to wither in order to rush some necessary cells to the site of her burn wound, located at the end of the great root in the bottom of an old well many yards away from the site of the ants mound. This loosening of the root hairs weakened the hold of the clod in its wedged place, so that it easily dissolved itself away in the first torrent of ground water from the rain rapidly becoming a soft stream of pliant creamy mud instead of a hard protective clod.

This creamy event opened the way for a clear path of water to rush overcoming the natural boundaries of the sloping mound and slicing a stream directly into the entrance leading below the ground. This stream is not only gutting a furrow through a once intricate intact mound, now it is pouring forceful rushes of water into the labyrinthian chambers below.

At this forceful pouring in every direction alarms went off with the first alarm sweeping all the way down the front tunnel nearly drowning in a burst of water at the first turn before grabbing the ceiling for support. By tuning into her outraged antennae wavings a night worker rearranging some larvae became herself an alarm, rushing first toward the entrance only to be swept back by the twisting water whence before anyone could detect her wavings the front chambers flooded halfway to the ceiling with the formerly sleeping workers and other alarms half floating and half pulling their bodies along the ceilings, trying to straighten their soggy antennae enough to spread information back to the precious inner sanctuaries.

Cleverly designed for deep sleeping by his mother, the beetle larva did not share in the wavering panic of the ants, floating instead neatly and complacently on top of the new cushion surface that was filling the chambers rapidly of the labyrinth, and in this complacent floating he was joined by the eggs and larvae of the ants themselves. As for the queen and her attendants they were more than jostled, they were nearly saturated, drowned and bloated.

The water itself was doing more than forward rushing, it was doing channel reformation and then when its own weight increased it was doing wall and floor collapsing, and then when the major force of its rushing began waning, it was doing disastrous seeping. In this way the water reached to every chamber that the ants had built in their city of rooms and channels.

Some alarms by reaching the bottom chambers just before the seeping water did began an evacuation of the city through its back tunnel. This tunnel emerging as it did under a rock shelf far from the oak tree and in the shelter of a wall of the human city, though it did not keep them from the heavy drops of water, did keep them from the rushing walls of water that could carry them so far from any semblance of orderly procession. Not far from this wall however and all over the courtyard where the oak tree stood night and day the water began rising, covering the surface that had formerly been hard, dry and passable for the feet of ants and others in their daily labors.

Carrying eggs and larva in their mandibles the barely awakened workers marched wavering ahead of these rising waters with their round and oblong white treasures.

Past the wavering lines of workers as they wound their bobbing routes through chinks of clay and stone walls of retention and definition built by humans, flowed the rising waters sweeping leavings of the oak tree and sloshing against the heavy legs of a solitary human on his way to the roundhouse and too aware of rainwater gushing into his face to pay the slightest attention to their rapid nighttime procession.

Arriving Is Not Inevitably Coming Home

At first as Blueberry Jon began walking he had not remembered too many pictures about his past life in the roundhouse with his fellows, he had been too busy remembering hot emotional occurences with his friend the woman Gedda and her daughter in her house at the outskirts of town.

However as he shifted his bedroll to the back of his neck and shoved his flute inside his robe to protect it from the first film of water that filtered from the sky he began remembering how the other men looked and smelled inside a roundhouse of fellows gathered around a common fire, how their muscles gleamed as they reached for tools and how they would say sentences of memory such as the very most excellent way to chip a flint ax head or the way to check if a spoor belonged to a simple game animal or a more complexly dangerous one. He remembered then that the men would sometimes reach over with a bit of food to shove into each others mouths, and this feeding each other in a comradely fashion he began to look forward to on his arrival into that warm company.

And as the water sheets lashed more quickly onto his face and arms he stepped in wider arcs noticing already an accumulation of unpleasant mud on his lower parts and began to look forward to his arrival at the brotherly roundhouse with increasing eagerness. Although he was passing now the complex of buildings that made up the housing of the clan of Snakes, and he knew he could stop at his mother's house and be made welcome in her absence by his sisters he did not do so, he instead began planning how he would feel entering the roundhouse, stooping slightly under his bedroll and fresh from a disappointment with a woman he had long been living with, to look into the eager welcoming faces of his story-telling fellows.

Outside in the courtyards around him some people were dancing to celebrate the rain and he joined them for a moment, whirling around with his bedroll and feeling joyful.

Above him and now behind him as he passed by his own niece and her friend were raindancing too on the roof where they had formerly been sleeping.

Presently, Ernesta said, "Ow, this isn't rain, this is rocks," and to their surprise little rocks stung them from the sky.

"Come back in," Aunt Two said, who frowned with worry once again peering over the edge of the roof at her garden. "This is hail."

The inside of the house seemed intolerably small and dull now compared to the great outside glitter and gleam, and the two girls were too giggly to sleep especially after Jessi-ma dumped water from the blankets all over Ernesta who was too excited to wonder how her mother and her companion were doing out in the Moon Temple where they had gone for the rest of the night before the man lover returned to his comrades of the Lion clan, or to wonder if Aunt Three and Sonia would find their way home before morning or would they spend the entire night at the rain dance of effectiveness and higher and higher spirits. Ernesta did not think of her uncle Jon at all.

Through the small door of a stone roundhouse located near the center of the city of Mundane and not far from a stable of interest to owls watching and in the same courtyard as the bakery of social gathering a man is stooping to enter.

Warm firelight that had been glowing from the doorway of attraction to him for several walking moments is now momentarily blocked as his stooping body enters the roundhouse of companionship and comfort.

However to his surprise no companionship is immediately occurring once inside the roundhouse where many familiar men's faces peer back at him as he is straightening and lowering his blanket roll. Though he recognizes several there are few greetings of nodding or smiling in a grim circle of silence that surrounds two half-grown boys of the Lion clan who are sitting on a central bench and holding their shoulders in rounded positions above their necks with lowered faces toward the mundane earth.

"Welcome, Jon Mundane," someone said on his left, someone who was holding some feathers unaccountably in one hand. "Perhaps you want to get dry and have something to eat before you hear about this." He gestured the feathers at the two lowered headed boys.

"No, go on ahead with your story," Jon said with a face of disappointment.

"These boys appear to have eaten the two sacred doves of the Bee clan," the man said, and Jon realized the speaking man was wearing the clothing of a Bee clan man himself.

Solemnly Jon sat down on the bench between two older men of his acquaintance to hear the remainder of the story. He touched the thigh of one of them and smelled the smell of chewing herbs, wishing one of them would reach over to put a little wad of food into his lips and that they would begin talking about the best way to sharpen a flint knife or remake its handle in the old fashioned way, and to ask when any one had last gone out hunting with spears and axes and close comradeship in the old fashioned way, as they had before the city became such a metropolis of storage and commerce and fancy temple measurement of architecture. While the Bee clan man stepped forward angrily continuing to talk, Jon wondered how soon he himself would begin to feel at home here in the roundhouse and the unfamiliar company of men.

When Everything Looks Different
There Is Difference

Ernesta woke to a landscape that had completely changed from anything she has seen before. For one thing, Jessi-ma's elbow and groggy face stuck up out of the blanket next to her, unlike other mornings. For another and more importantly when she looked out over the roof overlooking the courtyard, the smoothness of the new mud and the sparkling of many residual puddles was a different landscape from yesterday.

What was most different she did not begin to notice until later in the day when her strangely silent aunts shepherded both girls and Jon Lilly into the temple meeting hall where increasing numbers of not very cheery looking members of the Tortoise clan stood in clumps of complaining words and harsh gestures.

Ernesta soon noticed that there were two sides to an argument in which the farmer clan were bitterly accusing the Bee clan of bringing about and encouraging a hail stone storm that bashed several of their crops while members of the Bee clan bitterly accused two half-grown boys of the Lion clan of murdering their high priestess of architecture and eating the sacred doves of measurement and reassurance.

Though no one was talking very loudly anyone could tell that everyone was increasingly unhappy, especially Jessi-ma was very unhappy who went to stand by her bitterly talking mother Sonia glaring alternately into the faces of the Tortoise clan of empty handed farmers and the Lion clan of frightened sacred dove-eaters. By noon Aunt Two announced that the afternoon closing ceremony and procession that usually ended the festival would be replaced by a formal cursing ceremony. Sonia shuddered when she heard this, clutching the shoulders of her daughter Jessi-ma.

To her horror and to Jessi-ma's and Ernesta's by afternoon the formal cursing ceremony had begun with Sonia at the center of it. Nothing but bad luck had been happening since her appearance, the formal cursers said from behind their masks, and most of them, Ernesta noticed, were about the size and shape of the stolid Tortoise clan. Uneasily she also noticed that Aunt Two was absent from the group gathered to hear the masked speakers.

142

Too little water and now clearly too much and some of it in the form of hail that had bashed the crops to some extent irreparably the speakers said and they began to curse and revile the entire Bee clan with its heady ideas and cosmopolitan outlook on how to do things, and its incessant desire to do architecture. Where is your architecture now the masked persons sneered, dead by the river with one of their own as prime suspect in it.

"What?" Sonia leapt up for the first time aware that she was under suspicion for her sister's death simply because of her clear and current incompetence as a water bearing woman, first not doing enough and then in the heat of the rain dance doing entirely too much.

The cursing continued involving the persons of all the Bee clan and their origins in a distant metropolis and their attraction to measuring pigeons and larger than usual buildings they claimed would help everyone in the city measure time with the stars, when clearly they had forgotten to keep track of simpler Mundane necessities such as water.

"Is it about time, then?" the masked ones asked of the listeners in the ceremony. "Is it really about time?"

"If it is about time, then it is time for you to listen to the meaning of our cursing, and learn something very simple about time, that your sense of it is completely out of balance." And with this the Bee clan altogether left the ceremony.

"What does it mean," Ernesta asked, yanking on Jessi-ma's sleeve as she walked away with her arm through her mother Sonia's arm and her other hand in Jon Lilly's. "Why are you so unspeaking, where are you going, what is the meaning?"

But they neither answered nor turned to her, in their anger they continued walking to their home where they began packing.

"We can't get along with these unimaginery people, I can't let you grow up here," Sonia said to her tall daughter.

Through the evening they continued packing while the Lion clan reluctantly prepared the animals and messages to ships to take them, and a caravan of several families adding up to nearly one third of the Bee clan set out in the outrage of self-exile down to the dock at the river before midnight through the mud left by the rain without looking back or waving.

If there was no waving going on in a human procession of exile, however there was a great deal of waving going on in another procession, one that consisted of some ants attempting to construct a new city when their old one collapsed at the foot of the oak tree under the weight of falling water. Waving messages and directions they packed the last of their treasures from the place of their former living and prepared to expand their new tunnels and storage chambers.

Having brought the large beetle larva with them in their lengthy carrying they had set him down with remainders of their treasures in a temporary room of hasty construction when to their continually waving consternation he began thrashing through the skin of his former and rapidly shape changing container, ripping through a seam that split to reveal the back and sides of a dark brown full sized beetle of unexpected proportions and voracious behavior. Stepping heedless on the little rubbery eggs of vulnerability, squishing the ants' most precious dominion, and then clacking his long mandibles formidably the slick-shelled newborn beetle soon sent ants in hordes of great disturbance streaming back outside into the mud and stones of recent arduous moving.

At first the ants believed their heaviest carriers would be able to get under the new crushing beetle burden lifting him back up the tunnel and carrying him outside but this became a slippery problem of logistics that had no solution. As a smooth skinned larva the beetle had been an amicable burden who easily slid along the slopes of tunnels however as a barbed and multi-legged many-clawed young giant thrasher he stuck to every surface and came nowhere near to being lifted let alone carried, slid and shifted.

Next the ants believed their most paralysing stingers could work their long needles underneath the sheathed protective plated covering of the newborn they themselves had recently been feeding never noticing that in his eternal eating he had become enormous and increasingly capable of withstanding everything they could think of to get rid of him. Unable to get a foothold on his hardly armored surface after watching the beetle flatly squash a number of their own eggs and other babies, an army of ants decided most deliberately to fail to move him by flooding the outside of their newfound place with warning signals of consternation and no more entry.

Soon everyone had gotten the message that the moving was not finished and once again they began lugging the masses of unborn probabilities in their jaws as leader ants took them in columns to yet another place far from falling water, far from the oak tree and far from the foibles of their own storage methods of feeding a larva and then not having time to eat it before it was born into a full grown thrashing beetle of mammoth proportions

144

and endless appetite. Up the surface of a wall went the leader ants taking the long busy columns into places they had never explored much before, deep and high into the inner spaces of the walls built for personal habitation in the cities of the humans.

A Certain Disappearing Act
Can Also Be Some Transformation

And it seemed then to Ernesta in the aftermath of the rain that everyone in her world was disappearing for not only had Jessima and her cousin and her mother Sonia vanished into a boat bound for a warmer climate with no explanation but her uncle Jon reported that Margedda had run away from home and was nowhere to be found and certainly not in the stable of her earlier loitering. Then a few days later in addition Ernesta's own mother Donna was not in her room or in the Moon Temple nor had anyone thought to keep much track of her comings and her goings for some time since the festival ended with such frustration for everyone in the human city.

When Donna had not come home to her bed and breakfast for several days the aunts gathered to do some divination with their snakebones on a throw rug in the room Aunt One shared with Aunt Two now that the two oldest sisters had no children left living at home.

The divinatory snakebones gave information and direction of disaster on the first throw onto the throw rug from Aunt One's hand.

"I think I know just where to go to look for her," Aunt Two said grimly as the three aunts dressed wearing their everyday cottons rather than the thicker imported printed linens of festival times and they began walking dreadfully out into the hills high outside the city with a trembling Ernesta leading them to find first the cave of Ana of her remembrance with its remnants of burnt seed offerings and then on to the path to the high meadow with the alkali outcroppings and rampant grasses and the spiny almost familiar figure of the ever waiting greedy weed outlined against the lighter color of the soil.

An extremely still and formerly human corpse that was rapidly becoming the previous place of earthly existence for the woman Donna lay underneath the shadow of the weed curled convulsively somewhat chewed here and there by smaller creatures of biting ambition. When her relatives had stopped the screaming, exclaiming and heavy breathing of turning the deadened limbs this way and that in identification and realization, Aunt Three said hoarsely that clearly the spirit of her youngest sister had merged with the spirit of the wild plant of her desiring and through her sobs Ernesta understood that the greedy weed had eaten her mother entirely and for its own purposes and she was furious.

When Aunt One reached and pulled the plant entirely out of the ground in one lurch she felt a tiny satisfaction on her surface floating over the deepening pain of being so completely dissatisfied in losing her sister.

Clutching the weed in one hand Aunt One led them stumbling back to the center of the city while the other two heavy burdened aunts carried down the body of Donna, laying her in the sitting room, washing and unwrapping her carefully from her pretty clothing and then weeping and chanting while taking her out to the platform at the east end of the city to offer her up to the birds of the sky.

Before long watchful black dots again appeared against the endless blue and would again appear as they had in the past and would again and again in their meticulous task of cleaning the city of its recently dead humans.

Ernesta was not pleased when the aunts took the rapidly withering greedy weed into the yard outside the window overlooking her bed blankets and stuck the shriveling dry roots into the ground. Drooping more deeply than any creature she had ever seen the plant responded to the new shocking environment by losing nearly everything of ownership, dropping old seed pods, dried flowers and every single leaf onto the ground beneath itself exactly as Ernesta felt she was doing, shedding everything except her very skin in the act of proceeding through this transformation period of her life.

Thus Coming To Appreciate The Gift Of A Stick

The gift of a stick to grow outside her window did not please the mourning Ernesta who watched Aunt Two water its skinny frame with resentful eyes. If the people of the Tortoise clan had recently cursed the family of Jessi-ma who had then chosen to leave the city of Mundane for self-examination in exile she herself now cursed the slender body of the greedy weed for having stolen her own mother.

"Ugly ugly ugly dumb ugly," muttering tersely to the barely living plant whose body trembled in the earth against every breeze of her offended hand. Snapping the spine of it back and forth she wondered how much more pressure would spring its little anchor roots out of the earth's necessary clutch altogether.

Adding to her difficulty and discomfort when the aunts heard from their brother was the news that Margedda had been found living at the edges of the outmost fields in a disheveled condition from eating seeds and mice while consorting only with her owl in its slatted box they went all three on a short trip mysteriously at night and when they returned Margedda was half carried stumbling along with them.

Ernesta in her sullen temper hadn't been invited to attend the finding woke to their excited auntly voices deep in murmuring over a large feverish bundle with some red hair protruding. Later that day she was visited by Fran-keen of the Lion clan who told her that she and Dee had first found Margedda and had been stealing food out into the fields for her in her hiding.

All night and all the next day after being carried to the house of the Snake clan Margedda thrashed and sweated in her inner visions accompanied by gnashing of the teeth and groaning.

"Next she's going to move in here," Ernesta thought, "and take up all the space with her mice and owls and her big body. Now she's going to try to be my friend like Jessi-ma, and I don't want her to." She remembered that it was Margedda's mother's Tortoise clan who had driven away her Bee clan friends with insults and accusations. She glared at the ground when she thought this, a part of the ground that increasingly had regular columns of moving ants which she was too angry to notice. Sitting on a less ant-marching part of the ground next to the slender stick of wavering needy weed she confided her inmost fears and furies until feeling somewhat more like breathing she decided it was time to ask her grandmother to come back to her. Holding the small bead necklace Mama Mundane had given her the day she went on her journey Ernesta held a picture of her returning grandmother in her mind and began asking the old woman to return and help her with her increasingly troubling life.

Intimately the weed too heard this information so when Aunt Three emerged from the interior of the Snake clan house saying "Ernesta we are worried that the strength of Margedda's convulsions will ruin her thoughts instead of enhancing them," Ernesta found a picture-thought containing a solution immediately entering her own mind.

"I know a solution," she said.

"A solution will do fine," said Aunt Three. "I'll get Caddis to make it."

"My mother always said the ripest berries of this greedy little weed right here were food for the mind." Taking the woven straw pouch on its string from around her neck she opened it taking two wizened black berries out to drop them rolling into Aunt Three's waiting palm.

For her solution Aunt Two has decided to powder them finely and mix them with pleasing rosewater to balance the violence of their taste, and then Aunt One has poured them drop by drop into Margedda's moaning throat.

When two hours later Margedda opened her blue eyes speaking lucidly they credited Ernesta and the black berries for coming up with a solution.

"Let's give a proper name to the newest member of the Snake clan," Aunt One said soon after this. At first Ernesta thought they meant Margedda until following the meaningful procession of aunts into the yard she found herself looking down at the brittle stick of transplanted weed the Snake clan women had surrounded.

"Too much lust for unity," Aunt Two said. "There is too much transformation going on when a woman becomes completely merged with her spirit mate."

"Was this a Fateful Decision?" Ernesta asked.

"Yes," Aunt One answered. "Before she was born as a human being your mother decided to marry this plant and no one else." "Too much desire for unity," Aunt Two went on, "and between such unlike beings. And who knows what is really in this plant's mind."

"I do," Ernesta surprised herself by saying, as they all looked at her.

"What is a proper name, then?" Gladys asked while Aunt Three looked down at the quivering slender brown stickish body and said, "For the beauty of our lost sister who united with its spirit, 'Belladonna,'" and everyone agreed that was a proper name.

They had each brought a present for the plant and when Ernesta knelt to leave hers and to whisper the plant's new human name, "Belladonna," she also said, "Thank you for clearing Margedda's troubled mind." Then she noticed little black dots along its two remaining limbs after they split in a fork from the trunk.

"Oh look, she's sick, she has smallpox," she said, surprised that she felt sorry.

"No, she's not sick. She's optimistic, and going to leaf out again soon," Aunt Two said. "Those are bud dots."

Ernesta began to cry as she watered the shortly budding stick patting more soil up around the bed of roots, realizing that what she felt was not hatred or disgust but passionate love. She knew that Margedda would live with them for a while in the Snake clan and that she herself wouldn't get her feelings for Margedda confused with her feelings for the lost Jessi-ma. She knew that Belladonna would always talk to her and give her solutions to other people's problems and that she would often get the plant confused with her disappearing mother. And she knew that her grandmother Mama Mundane would return to the city of her naming soon to help her granddaughter through this hard time of going through losses in order to become a woman of purpose and bearing.

Walking Along A Path One Of Many

Along a path leading to several other paths leading to far apart cities and villages and wild places an old woman is walking. Although she can move very quickly on occasion she doesn't choose to. Holding a silver headed walking stick in one hand she leaves interesting footprints, two flat sandal marks with a round hole to one side on some occasions and when she is dragging the stick she leaves two flat sandal marks followed by a long snake shaped groove in the dust.

When she first began her journey and when she said her name was Mundane this attracted traveling companions who had heard of the city named for her ancestor grandmother Mundane, but when she got too far away from home for people to recognize the name of her city she changed her name to whatever large city was nearby and got more traveling companions which she liked to have in this way. Her two most continual companions were her own two grandsons one of whom was strongly carrying her goods and services on his shoulders and wanting to see the world with her, while the other limped along with one perpetually twisted foot and no capacity for carrying though with a very precise sense of direction. She had borrowed the two from her elder daughter Gladys, who is their mother.

Mundane would have completed her journey away from home and been back two years sooner than she was going to be except that she had developed such a great love of touching everything along the way.

Rarely had anyone ever met anyone so essentially mundane as Mundane when she was a traveling sightseer. Mundane could not refrain from touching, rubbing, feeling, smelling and even tasting so many objects in her path, from shiny pebble to matte dull twig, and some days almost every donkey neck and woman's skirt and little sticky blob of children's hand. She felt the cloth of people's passing clothing and smelled the gasses in dust raised by their passing sandals. She rubbed her shoulders on the house walls and stamped her naked feet in the tops of passing streams and rain puddles. Mundane nibbled the cakes and vegetables and spiced meat dishes of vendors and housekeepers and the ears of passing infants. She pinched and poked, inhaled and swallowed the material world to such an extent it was said this is one reason why she is such an avid sightseer who makes predictions from what she has witnessed.

However so much continual dawdling in her own Mundane mind left her traveling companions irritated and continually trying to decide whether to wait until she finished touching everything or to go ahead without her.

To gather the walking companions that she likes to have Mundane spread out a net of continual talking as she went along. Recently as she made her meticulous way back to her city of origin her net of continual talking had gathered several including two women from far to the east where she had once been given the gift of a small pink and brown pig and a woven straw packet filled with grains of rice, then three people furious that they had been exiled from their village, then six determined travelers who had always wanted to visit the city on the delta of the river because their own people once came from there, then one mountain herdsman with a rope of pack animals loaded with boxes full of wild bees, two itinerant spell casters, three stranded seamen whose ship had sunk in a storm, eight woman with their babies whose men had been killed and whose village had been burned by sudden wild raiders and who were continually mourning, and an old woman in a hot bearskin robe with blue eyes and blue tattoos who was looking for her daughter and her redhaired granddaughter.

In the course of her five year walking journey Mama Mundane had become in her body spryer, quicker, cleaner and dirtier than she ever had been in her life. In addition the coiled white hair on her head was exposed to so many severe changes of weather and opportunity for adventure it became for a time completely straight. After a while she stopped trying to do anything about this letting her hair hang out from her head like a white broom.

Walking along her path on this particular day surrounded by traveling companions and with one of her grandsons leading her now much larger fat pink and brown spotted pig Mundane's attention was caught by some ribbons hung from a tree branch up a slope where she climbed with her fingers out waiting to feel them.

Knowing she was a Snake woman and that she made her way through the world giving healing and divinatory advice to others and because of her increased age her companions had much more patience with her than they otherwise would have. They noticed the snake fang necklace she wore around her neck while traveling and knowing also that she had added a new set of fangs delivered to her by the snake people for every year of her long life and they were impressed at her gatherings. They knew that she had ways of traveling other than merely walking and so they were not in a hurry to make her angry. They sat waiting and talking while she went feeling and fingering.

Only after days of extreme impatience would they leave her, and sometimes this was done secretly, sometimes they came formally saying "Snake grandmother, we're leaving your fine company. Please don't harm us."

The Gift Of A Stick Is Greater When It Has Leaves

"Please don't harm us," the man said the traditional greeting to a Snake person of particular charm and serpentine powers. At first Ernesta thought he must be talking to her Aunt Three who stood in the doorway behind her watching as she sat beside the barely blooming nearly naked Belladonna in the months after her dramatic transplanting. While her grandmother is away on a journey feeling ribbons and other objects with the tips of her fingers she herself is gloomy and waiting for the empty places in her life to make sense to her.

Seeing that the man is addressing his formal greeting to her as though she is a full grown woman of the Snake clan with charms and bearing, Ernesta explains that she is still considered a child, though nearly old enough for her initiation. However he is not interested in this, he is interested in whether she has a solution to a problem of his involving the bark or leaves of Belladonna and to Ernesta's satisfaction another solution comes into her mind until she is giving him the recipe and some of the bark scraped from inside the main fork of the scheming weed of her attention.

"Is it you that puts these ideas into my head," she whispers to Belladonna knowing it is true that her mother's gift to her is the bushy companion with the transformative powers of seeds, roots, leaves and bark and that the gift of the bitterly scheming weed to her is that her mother's companionship will never leave her but rather the voice of her medicine mind will enter Ernesta's mind whenever she needs it.

For her part the scheming weed who now contained the spirit of the dancing woman Donna as well as her own plantish one lost all her leaves and most of her root system in the great move from the meadow to the courtyard of the busy-fingered humans. Unexpectedly she had gotten her wish to move at last though she had never expected they would yank her from her bed of earth and carry her a long distance in the suffocating flightiness of pure air and no stability of earth with its more steady motion. Instead the lurching unsteady motion of the humans followed by the consistency of the new earth she was stuck into for her new existence had made her ill compounding her losses and lack of bearing.

Stuck as a stick in the dirt of a city yard she at first had felt the hopelessness of her position and of her ability to produce any more thoughts and ideas in the forms of flowers and seeds. However as she felt the truly passionate care especially from one of the younger of the humans, the watering and the addition of some alkali soil of her desiring and the passionate discussions late into the night she had begun to revive her naturally bitter optimism and to engage her roots with the new clay as her leaves began swelling into new ideas in the city air.

Perhaps she had been correct all along, the mobility of the humans would ultimately move her precious seeds out into the world of variegated dirt and lushness of plantly existence.

Under the direction of Aunt Three, Ernesta took some of the seeds her mother had given her for her necklace pouch and put them into soil in the Moon Temple, sprinkling them with water gathered the night before from the courtyard well as her mother Donna had taught her the difference between kinds of water. Soon the seeds had sprouted and been tucked in flat trays of Aunt Two's making, slender stalks of young scheming weeds. She took these sprouts to visit their mother Belladonna and was happy to feel rainbows of the plant's optimism waving out over their wavering baby stalks.

If Some Are Happy Enough
That Is Not So For The Oak Tree

Members of the human city may have been content enough after the flood panic left and they could see that many of their crops had in fact survived and none of the livestock were harmed. Members of the ant city were content enough because now that they had been forced to relocate into above ground dwellings they were irresistibly moved to indefinitely tunnel through the clay and straw walls built by the humans, exploring the changing landscape of natural cracks and then too, there was always the possibility of constructing many of their own. In such ways the discovery that the humans have enormous storerooms with ingenious methods for preserving the most amazing numbers of delectable goods has encouraged the ants to rapidly increase their own numbers with the enthusiasm of the possibilities of gathering.

For her part the oak tree having been extremely pleased during the rain to be washed clean again and to have her roots cooled and ripened deep underground as well as in the rapidly refilling well now faces a dusty uncertain future. In the days after her initial clean-leafed delight she has become dustier and dustier in the absence of the colony of ants who having lived at the base of her body seemingly forever cleaning and dusting her out to the very tips of her nether extremes now have departed for the walls of the human buildings.

Now when gall wasps came around there is no one to challenge their egg laying let alone carry away the thousands of eggs left by travelers from all corners of Mundane's world since everyone loves to leave a little something on the oak tree of their own deposit. These deposits can begin to be a burden after several weeks of them as the oak tree feels she lives in such a dirty house of her own making, becoming depressed over it as anyone would. In addition she has begun to have minor inflammations and infections from the continual infestations and fissures caused by so many feet, bellies and jaws continually prowling about on her body.

For their part the ants did not miss the oak tree at all having found Aunt Two's storehouse to be particularly lucrative as a gathering place with the walls of human construction being pleasantly warm in the day time and cool and dry at night. However the aunts did not reciprocate this feeling when they discovered the columns of gatherers marching through the store room from an increasing number of directions.

"Lids," Aunt One said, and in the next few weeks Aunt Two became an expert on the manufacture of lids.

"Sealer," Aunt Three added when lids failed to deter a single ant from a single chore of the carrying away of goods, and so the air over Aunt Two's workplace filled with the odors of melting pitches, saps and waxes.

Having adopted the drastic runaway child of Gedda they had welcomed Margedda into the Snake clan informally and were preparing to initiate her into the company of the Spider Society of predictors along with their niece Ernesta who had long been recognized for her possible medicinal ability and power of transformation based in her wandering eye and subsequent capacity to see on two levels at once.

Margedda having recuperated from a fever of high determination and change had lately become very concerned with her appearance. Not only did she aggravate Ernesta by cleaning up their mutual room several times a day, lately she had taken to doing almost nothing except fuss with her big head of red hair.

"Let's go gather wild herbs and watch the mother ducks with the ducklings at the river," Ernesta would suggest one of her favorite activities that Margedda would sometimes do with her except lately when she preferred to sit with a comb and items she had asked the Snake aunts to give her such as ribbons and pins.

After a few weeks Ernesta noticed that Margedda was drawing a great deal of attention in the city simply by walking around displaying the power of her hair.

Margedda's Hair Is A Beautiful Storm

Margedda's hair is the crest of a male bird at the height of the mating season, the season of show-off. Things do not go into her hair so much as they appear constantly to be popping out of it—long rods of metal, huge wooden or tortoise shell combs, intricate gold panoramas suspended on stilts walk about easily in Margedda's hair, which is also like the sea in a beautiful storm; Margedda's dangerous hair. It rises and foams and ebbs, forms caves, plains, peaks and tendrils that drip down her neck and the fronts of her ears like simple vines.

In its many forms it changes by the hour, extending herself so far in any direction that to imagine Margedda without her hair is like imagining someone else without a face. Margedda's hair is horns and antlers, mane, crest and peacock tail, elephant ears, and cities seen from a great distance. Nothing extraneous to her comes near it, out of respect; it is not meant for touching, it is for the eyes to see what they dare; the hands could learn nothing from it.

Margedda's hair speaks of what is possible, and what is not. She makes of it an organic sculpture, careful as if it were granite and could only be done once, temporary as a one day moth. Nothing can change Margedda's hair, change is its only name, incorporating wind and straw, dust and rain into its body, giving them meanings they would never think of themselves, without Margedda. . . Margedda can be very simple when it is a simple day, but looking into Margedda's hair especially if anyone is concentrating, is to see the many wonders of your own mind and the transformations of your life. Since this can be dangerous, everyone uses Margedda's hair with precision and thoughtfulness.

When Ernesta saw that Margedda was attracting a great deal of attention she thought that perhaps if she was to become a woman of thoughtfulness and bearing she too ought to attract attention through the offices of her elaborate hair. All one morning she sat with Margedda's borrowed combs and basket of hair decorations until she had shaped her own coiled mass into something resembling one of Aunt One's harvest baskets filled with lettuces and bean plants, as Aunt Two said to her at noon, "Most of them upside down with their roots going everywhere."

The elaborate effect not being at all what she had intended Ernesta jerked the tied ribbons and bone decorations out of her hair that will never turn into Margedda's hair and going instead down to the river by herself to watch the mother ducks and the small boats landing and unloading their wares for sale in the market of the city, glad to be free for a little while of the numerous chores her aunts had put her to lately.

She was sitting on the wooden landing post watching her Uncle Jon in his bartering with one of the ship captains in behalf of the Snake clan when she leaped into the air and yelled at something cold and gurgley almost getting into her ear. Whirling, she was even more startled to see a very odd-looking brown and pink animal with tiny eyes and flat, broad, fleshy nose staring directly at her after scaring her half to death by smell-

155

ing her ear.

"You rude beast," she accused it. "Don't you have any manners?"

For a moment she believed she had fallen into a day dream and the beast was not of the earthly world at all, but of some other plane beyond mere imagining. Then she was staring at an old woman with a walking stick who stood behind the odd animal looking at her seriously without saying a word, and as Ernesta saw the snake tooth necklace around her neck, the Snake clan sash at her waist and the two men who looked exactly like her cousins she began to cry just before she was swept into her grandmother's greeting arms.

"Mama Mundane is back!" the cry went out as Jon came running over from the dock to greet his mother, and word spread so quickly that by the time they had finished their initial greetings and turned with the long gone travelers to walk them home the three aunts could be seen in the distance hurrying along the river road toward them with the great smiles and outstretched arms of terrible longing.

A Basket Makes A Different Kind Of House

"I knew my daughter had died and I started back then," Mundane said fingering the leaves of Belladonna's body. "Though it wasn't time to get all the way here until now."

After the celebrative feast of return that all three aunts and their brother spread out for their returning mother calling in relatives from the outlands to dance all night singing old songs of childhood over steaming bowls of familiar grains and vegetables from the storehouses and fresh meats traded from the few remaining hunters on the plain, Mundane discovered that the living quarters of her family in the Snake clan had shrunk in size now that she herself had done so much free wandering.

"I don't want to live in a clay house anyhow," she said. "They are trying too hard to be a permanent form. I would rather live in a lively basket full of light than in a tacky house made of clay."

Ernesta, finding since her grandmother's return that everything was speeding up, went down to the river delta with Margedda to gather thin reeds while Aunt Lattice and Uncle Jon cut some thicker posts and Aunt Gladys went out to the fields of the Tortoise clan to select some special straw sheaves to be delivered to the Snake household.

156

Soon Mundane and her eldest daughter were out in the largest Snake clan courtyard in the corner opposite from the standing place of the oak tree making a basket shaped like a house. They needed help with this, so Margedda and Ernesta were continually being asked to keep the soaking bowls filled with water and to hand wickers to them as they wove and wove, and tied and tied over the frame that was set into place by the two sisters Gladys and Caddis, and Uncle Jon.

Mama Mundane had already moved into her straw house before her daughters had finished adding a little overhanging porch at the tiny entrance so her pink and brown companion could lie sleeping in the shade in front where everyone in town who came to visit could see that Mundane had been blessed with the singular company of a pig.

Inside the straw house was a new sleeping platform with the best family rugs and sheepskins piled on it and a big fire pot for cooking and heating that Aunt Two had made, with a tall pipe that went out the top of the roof to let the smoke from the hot coals out into the night air.

"I don't mind cooking in clay," Mundane said. "But I don't want to live in it. Clay slows life down too much." Mundane liked life to be fast, she said the pace of stone was centuries too long for her, her favorite building material was straw. "With straw for a house," she said, "you stay alert and avid in the dance with transformation, as the snakes do."

Aunt One nodded quickly whenever this was said, and Aunt Two frowned. Aunt Three brought up the subject of her outlandish friend Sonia who wanted to build everything of stone so it would hold still and catch the sunlight and starlight in patterns so the Bee clan people could tell exactly what time this place is, relative to other places. Mundane thought this was a very funny idea, and rolled laughing on the ground the first time Aunt Three said it.

Mundane sat in her straw house for days after she first returned, dreaming and burning and chewing herbs and traveling around in her mind. She sat with objects that had belonged to her daughter Donna. She sat with Belladonna's leaves crushed in her palms and let her own tears fall onto them.

Then she began to have visitors as people she had known all their lives came to see her and bring their presents. She also gave them her presents from the bundles and packages that had been carried by her one strong grandson. During this period she kept Ernesta on one side of her and Margedda on the other as they waited for the dreaming and the smoking and the visiting to be over so she would at last begin to talk to them and after a while she did.

Everyday after they had eaten their morning meal the two girls went to the large courtyard and spoke to the oak tree and spoke to the pig and then crawled through the tiny opening into Mundane's house where they sat next to her making things for her house and listening to her talk about her former travels and the current traveling ruminations from inside of her mind. Her house was very light inside as the weave was loose to allow air and light to stir through from every direction.

"A house that breathes is a house that can talk to a person," she said.

She had them making nets to hold her things in as nets were important to learn about, she said because in a net the spaces are as important throughout as the cord. "Space ties everything altogether," she said.

"Now you will sing better, knowing about cords and spaces," she said.

They liked to look at her clothing and the other materials she had around her. Every day lately she wore a black shawl woven entirely from human hair, straight and black and given to her by the same people who had given her Little.

"This is how everyone's hair looked when I was at the furthest point east on my journey," she said. "Afterwards my own hair went as straight as this. I stayed with those people for a long time because they wore pointed wooden hats and they gave me Little."

Little was the name of the pig who every day lay in the shade in front of Mundane's house and walked around the city with her when she went out shopping and touching.

Being back among the Snake clan of her own origin she no longer wore a necklace of Snake teeth to remind herself where she had come from. Around Mundane's neck now hung a set of long sharp ivory-colored fish teeth, double rows of snarly snippers that had turned yellow while still belonging to the fish, and since the cartilage jaws were hinged and intact she had tied them with strips of leather and used them as scissors for doing her weavings.

Sometimes some of the Spider Society women stopped by the straw house to use the snarly snippers if they were making something of timely ceremonial significance wanting to use ancient cutting tools so the cords and strings and threads would stay cut and not be tempted to unravel or reconnect in some fashion of their own.

Ernesta and Margedda had never seen Mundane take the scissors off, though the aunts whispered that she did not sleep with them around her neck for fear of snipping off a piece of herself during the night, keeping them instead on a soft cotton pad next to her bed.

Ernesta told Mundane the important parts of the story of her time without her grandmother, how the well had dried up, how Jessi-ma had gone off in a fury with her mother Sonia when everyone blamed her for the water problems and the botched up festival. Most importantly she told Mundane that she had witnessed something at the river on the day that Lillian died that she did not understand.

Mundane set fire to more herbs when she had finished her stories and clicked her scissors in the air and did not say anything.

A Weed Among Humans May Still Be Wild And Wily

If the pig loved to lie in the shade created by the humans, Belladonna who had schemed all her adult life to get out of the overheated meadow and into a shady place was greenly comfortable now that the shade of the buildings built by the humans and the other plants in Aunt Two's garden provided her with some head covering. For her part Ernesta by bringing special soils to put around her stem and by taking careful cuttings as well as seeds to the Moon Temple for sprouting under Aunt Two's guidance was increasing her happiness.

In one generation Belladonna had succeeded in having both the portability accomplished by the nettles of her youth and the protective care lavished on the millet stalks in the great standing human fields without having to give up either her independence of form or the inherent wild bitterness of her fat purple juices.

No one was allowed into Aunt Two's garden without her permission because of her many herbs so poisonous if overeaten and with Belladonna having overtly consumed her sister Donna this rule was even more stringently enforced. Ernesta had begun staying out in Aunt Two's garden most of the time when she wasn't in the straw hut with her grandmother, caring for Belladonna, talking to her spirit and in addition learning the natures of the other plants that Aunt Two cultivated.

Grinding the black seeds and trying to imitate Margedda in her desire to be looked at by strangers Ernesta discovered that a little ointment of Belladonna's berries rubbed around her eyes caused the pupils to dilate, which exaggerated her protruding eyes, making her look as though she were deep in a magnetic trance, and sometimes actually putting her there.

The effect of this was startling to other people who Ernesta noticed listened very closely to everything she said when she was in this state. She shared her secret with Margedda in return for roots and herbs that Margedda gathered on her own walks into the hills. Margedda's eyes being naturally small would suddenly appear large under the influence of the eye ointment changing her appearance considerably so that she, too, became someone people listened to in her entranced state with the result that she began to pay more attention to what she herself was saying.

Ernesta added blue-green coloring to her ointment and even her aunts noticed a difference in her appearance. The two girls now both took more care with how they looked as well as how they sounded

How Cooking Took A Long Time To Learn

Ernesta knew that cooking took a long time to learn because it took so much effort for Aunt Two to make the largest of her cooking pots. She began working on this one afternoon after talking a long time with her mother Mundane, coming out of the straw house with a long measuring line she and her sister Lattice held, drawing off the dimensions for a large pot in the courtyard on the opposite side from Mundane's house and at right angles to the oak tree.

First constructing a sapling frame which her sisters cut and put into place for her, Caddis next wheeled carts of clay and water from the river in to the courtyard location and set to work with clay up to her elbows and all over her face from wiping the sweat that came to pour down her face of intense working.

Ernesta noticed that she and Margedda were not allowed to help with the new pot although many others were, instead being told to stay in the straw house with Mundane and learn more chants.

One day as she was winding her way through one of the

longer and less interesting of the chants Ernesta began talking to her friend Jessi-ma, who was standing in front of her just on the other side of the pig outside the straw house.

"We had to walk such a long time just to get to the ship," Jessi-ma said, "I was afraid we wouldn't get back in time."

"What have you done to your hair," Ernesta said, and just then Margedda stopped saying her own less interesting chant and looked over at her.

"It's the same as it was yesterday," she said. "Why?"

"No, I didn't mean you," Ernesta answered, "I meant *her*," suddenly leaping out the door and looking around, but Jessi-ma wasn't there any more.

"I saw Jessi-ma," she said, feeling strangely bubbly inside her solar plexus, while Margedda stared at her with large eyes and Mundane's broom-shaped head with its white re-coiling though still somewhat fly-away hair bent casually to put more herb leaves on the little pile of coals in her cooking pot.

All month long Aunt Two supervised work on the great pot in the courtyard, a pot shaped like Ana lying on the ground, with a narrow waist and two swollen chambers like a queen bee mother. Ernesta also noticed women from the other clans helping Caddis, as well as gathering wood, huge piles of it stood under the oak tree waiting.

"What's going to get cooked in that huge pot?" Ernesta asked, and her grandmother laughed and tugged on her hair. "Maybe you are," she joked.

Ernesta laughed too though later she felt uneasy when Margedda said to her, "You've never heard of the Snake clan eating young women, have you?" and pretended she had only been joking when Ernesta scoffed, "No, of course not, don't be silly."

They both noticed extra cooking going on in the kitchens, even the bakery people seemed busy these days and they wondered if winter was expected early, was the city stocking up for hard times.

One morning on her way to Mundane's straw house for her morning of enchanting, she was stopped by Margedda, who often got up very early to go roaming by herself, and who had arrived first.

"Guess who's here?—Jessi-ma is back." Margedda was too excited by the news to play a good round of guess-again.

"Where is she?" Ernesta said, whooping with surprised pleasure.

"I saw them down at the dock unloading. They're going to be purified from their voluntary exile and allowed back into the city. The Spider Society is down there smoking and enchanting them now."

Ernesta knew that if the Spider Society waved smoke over the returning exiles their magnetic field would be changed so they could fit back into the city without bitterness on anyone's part. She felt bubbles in her solar plexus again, and when she saw Jessi-ma walking past the Snake clan house that evening she was not surprised to see that her hair was totally changed. Instead of a large fuzzy mass sticking out of her head like a lively beehive her hair now wound around her head in metrical coils and then hung in three dozen tight shining braids with elaborate beadings at the ends of each strand.

Jessi-ma was glad to see her and her hair was impressive in its new design but she looked tired and sad. "We had to walk so far to get to the ship we almost missed it," she said.

"I know," Ernesta said. "You came to me and told me."

"I didn't know if I would get back in time."

"In time for what?" Ernesta asked but Sonia and Jon Lilly came by just then and came to give her a hug of greeting.

Three Can Come Back
If They See Cooking As Dreaming

"Mama sent Jon after them weeks ago," Aunt Three explained. "She didn't tell any of us. He hooked a ride on a commercial fishing boat clear down to the metropolis of Celeste and just asked around for days until he found them. Sonia was doing fairly well, living with some relatives, though of course not as happy and active as she was here. Getting that temple built here has become her whole life's focus, the focus of her entire priesthood."

Aunt Two snorted as she lifted breakfast cakes from her flat cooking grill. "I can't understand what Mama is up to. She certainly doesn't want a stone temple built here. She thinks the Bee clan is entirely too single-minded in their measurement. She says they're only seeing lines and forgetting spaces. She says one creature's line is another's space."

"She told Jon to tell Sonia that if Jessi-ma would undergo the blood ceremony with Ernesta everything would fit into place for them to come back." Aunt Three chuckled. "Then she had to give the Tortoise clan practically everything she brought back from her trip to get them to listen to her plan. They agreed to

162

stop cursing Sonia, though, just as they agreed for us to take on Margedda and prepare her for the Spider Society."

Ernesta drew in her breath and her aunts looked at her where she stood in the doorway to the common kitchen still in her nightclothes. "I found blood in my bed," she said, and an endless hush followed by electric ripples of excitement fell into the room as though from a great distance.

Certain Events Of Cooking Take Time To Dress For

Ernesta threw the beads back into the bowl in disgust letting the desultory impatient braid uncoil once more in Jessi-ma's long fingers of friendship and oil and the sharing of style. "This doesn't feel right at all," she exploded, "I don't think it's going to work for my hair. Besides, it's taking all day long."

"Well of course it takes all day," Jessi-ma said with a new-found patience that irritated Ernesta.

The beads of Jessi-ma's hair have such mathematical significance of measurement and counting as to be breathtaking in their coordination. Blue, red and black beads of emotion for the heart, head and overall strength and certainty of feeling lay along the careful spiral coils of fascination on her head and down her neck. The journey she had made by ship was present in a set of parallel coils that led to a diamond shaped bed of beads on the crown of her head.

In addition, as she explained to Ernesta, the shapes and colors of the beads have significance. Triangle, round and rectangular beads gave indication of the shapes and figures she would use in her life as a Bee clan woman of architecture and a shaper of numbers of material matters. Blue beads indicate hundreds, red tens, and black means zero if it occurs in the bottom row, or one if it occurs between rows. In addition, she explained, each placement of each bead means a syllable in the language of the singing priesthood of the metropolis that is the place of origin for the Bee clan, before they made their sojourn to Mundane's world to mark a geodetic center for measuring the surface of the earth. "Certain spirits are honored by certain configurations," she explained.

"The beads just don't mean the same things in my hair as they do in yours," Ernesta told Jessi-ma. "They don't even want to stay there."

Since Margedda had also begun to bleed, just a few days after Ernesta's first showing of menstrual blood, the aunts had explained that the great pot in the oak tree courtyard was for the menstrual initiation that all girls undergo in the city of Mundane. Since two other girls, Dee and Fran-keen, had also begun to bleed and were scheduled for sponsorship by the pan-clan Spider Society rather than the more local women's societies within their own clans, everyone waited only for Jessi-ma's womb to release the full wash of its adulthood for the blood ritual to begin.

"You'll spend four days in the pot with the other girls," Mundane explained to Margedda and Ernesta, "dreaming together on a bed of hot rocks."

"So you do have a way of cooking us," Ernesta said.

"Yes," her grandmother laughed, "We have a way of cooking up girls into women."

Margedda was sure she could predict the very hour that Jessi-ma's periodic bleeding would start, hardly letting her out of sight so she could readjust her current predictions as needed. The three girls spent hours together each day now, preparing their clothing with the help of Ernesta's aunts. They took lots of time to hunt for special feathers and flowers to dry, for shells at the river's edge and other valuable decorative items. Margedda watched her owl companion like a hawk, catching each discarded bit of down for use in her dress, that had tufts of feathers woven over the front to attract the power of birds of prey. No longer living in a slatted box the owl preferred standing on furniture dropping tiny feathers in a welter of fast scratching.

Ernesta found two perfect buzzard tailfeathers lying in a bush on a shale beach near the river that had changed shape since the night of flooding. They were as though waiting for her and she put them on the end of the sash she had woven for herself on Aunt One's small belt loom, along with some acorn shells given by the oak tree.

"The oak tree offers her acorns to all and sundry," she said, "but for a buzzard to give me these feathers is a rare event, for they are stingy with their feathers."

For Ernesta the clothing was not at all difficult, she easily chose the heavy brocaided dress that her mother had worn for her own blood ceremony, and Aunt One altered it for her. For Ernesta the difficult part was deciding on a configuration for her hair that would suit the bearing and the balance of her being.

"How you wear your hair has to do with how you wear your own life," Aunt Three said, and everyone else agreed.

Margedda easily arranged the tendrils of her populated wilderness hair and sat for two days out on the roof carving a ceremonial comb to wear of fragrant sandalwood using Aunt Three's carving tools and Aunt Two's pottery polishing stones. She had no trouble arranging the power of her hair, however her dress was another matter, nothing she could think of made sense for her to wear.

Sonia had made her daughter Jessi-ma a yellow, blue and black dress with geometric designs for this occasion years ago and many commented her hair had never looked better than with the rearrangement of it that Sonia now did at great length, of twenty eight moon braids spiraling from the crown of her head with beads signifying names, facts and measurements of time according to the geodetic time keeping in the temples of the Bee clan of architecture and measurement. Jessi-ma spent her preparation time worrying about her residual childhood clumsiness and making up musical songs to accompany the Celestial star stories told in her beaded hair, as her first blood began to come down on the morning following a dream Margedda had had of seeing drops of blood on fingertips that resembled the silver surface of the moon.

Transformation From Place To Place May Involve A Headband

Walking along the long high wall in single file, then down carefully through the dark convoluted tunnel passage that requires so much fumbling and side stepping, always having to know where your companions are in relation to yourself, then bursting up one by one through the tiny opening onto the hill, then more cautiously down the slippery path made by the ones who always go first, and across the hard packed clay that has been beaten down by so many of the giant feet that use it everyday and who built it to begin with, or so the old ones indicate in their stories of explanation.

Finally as they reach the huge pot of destination and enticement it is not necessary to go single file anymore; the overwhelming almost smoking odors of the substances contained in the great clay pot would lead any of them to it unhesitatingly.

What remains now is primarily the repetition of cultural motions, done for the good of everyone, of filling the mouth without chewing, of doing the very careful balancing of selecting and then carrying and extracting, walking and following, and then repeating, without getting so tired and overburdened that you collapse and must be nourished back into vitality by your companions. By means of this careful collective repetition, they had found over the millenia that many of the contents of one city can be methodically transferred into another city altogether.

Busy in their efforts they are not interrupted by the unbelievably deep-toned drum of giant feet on the hard packed clay beyond the pot walls nor by the vocal vibrations throbbing in the air of consternation though they are disrupted when the entire pot swings up into the air and vanishes with some of their membership still on board.

"Look what they've done," Margedda exclaims. "They've taken all your eye ointment directly out of the jar."

"Oh no!" Ernesta says, taking the jar and staring down into the crumbs at the bottom. "I was going to wear it tomorrow."

"So was I," Margedda says. Ernesta had made up a special eye makeup for the blood ceremony and ritual, made of green malachite in a sesame oil base and with a strategic amount of the eye-opening hallucinatory effects of ground Belladonna seed.

Now she peered at the small line of ants dispersing rapidly out of the jar and up her arm. "What on earth are you going to do with my eye ointment?"

"Probably use it for their own dark moon rites," Margedda laughed, watching Ernesta blow insects off her forearm.

"At least I finally know what I'm going to wear." Ernesta had gone into a frenzy of hard wondering as she more and more realized that neither Jessi-ma's hair style nor Margedda's would stand for her own. Only days from the full moon that started tomorrow she had talked at length to Belladonna and had finally gotten a vision in her mind of what she wanted.

A headband, she thought, a really simple headband around my forehead with a certain small amount of beading, and then a loop in the back for a heavy clasp. Because, she thought, I am always taking baskets out anymore as I go wandering to gather herbs and seeds for my solutions, and I never have enough pouches to put them in. I really could use a basket carried on my back.

"And then," she described to Aunt Gladys, "we could put a lid on it so nothing falls out, maybe a removable lid in case there are a lot of branches sticking up over the top from the plants I gather." Already Aunt One was sorting through her stacks of gathered branches and reeds for the appropriate sort of materials to frame Ernesta's carrying basket. As they set to work on it, Ernesta continued, "I think it needs a plant decoration on the outside, but just one."

"Do I need to guess which one?" Aunt One asked, and they both knew it would be a picture of the body of the scheming weed that gathered in colored patterns onto the outside of Ernesta's basket to accompany her on all her gatherings.

"You mean a headband something like this," Aunt Three said, pulling out one that she had made for herself years ago. It too, had a clasp for attaching a basket down the back for carrying.

"Yes, like that, except mine, with a portrait of Belladonna colored brown and green with purple-black berries that go with me everywhere I go."

Rarely had the fingers of Aunt One woven so fast, or the dye gathering fingers of Aunt Three or the small-loom weaving fingers of Ernesta moved so fast as in the last hours before the gathering of the blood ceremony and ritual at the great pot of Ana that Aunt Two and some Spider Society helpers had made.

When all the carefully washed, dressed, combed and decorated girls were assembled on the morning of their first collective bleeding, at the time of the first full moon since Jessi-ma had spotted blood on her clothes, they found the courtyard filled with Spider Society women standing around a number of fires of their own building. Wide stacks of burnable material stood around the oak tree, who seemed especially present and interested in the human doings in the courtyard of her current lengthy existence.

The House Of Ana Is Painted Red And Black To Honor Women's Blood

Aunt Two's lying-down Ana pot was the size of two of Mundane's straw houses hooked together, one being the head and thorax of Ana, the second being her great abdomen. The two were joined as if by a waist, and everything was painted red except the doorway vulva that entered her abdomen and that was painted black. The Ana pot of blood ceremony was built anew for each fresh group of girls and took a different shape on each useful occasion. This time she was bee shaped in honor of helping to resolve the Bee clan's problems.

For days Spider Society women had gathered herbs in the wild fields and from their gardens, piling leafy stacks in baskets near the entrance of the Ana pot. They had carried flat rocks from the courtyard fence, rocks Ernesta had often noticed looking burnt and had never thought to wonder why.

Now she saw that the Ana pot was lined with rocks taken from the fires. On top of the hot rocks were layered large soft leaves of pungently fresh herbs, steamy and already going to her head. Her heart was pounding so she knew she wasn't going to miss the eye-expanding effects of Belladonna. There would be plenty to dream from here.

Margedda kept trying to hide behind Ernesta and Jessi-ma since her dress was not suitable to her and she had settled for a borrowed one that was not of her liking. She was at first uneasy and then excited to see her mother Gedda at the gathering with her arms filled with platters of small raisin cakes she had made, and a special wild mushroom dish of her childhood remembering. Gedda looked for a long time into her daughter's uneasy face and then turned to a tall old woman standing near, a woman with smooth hair bluegrey as sea mist and even more tattoos than she herself had.

"This is your grandmother," she said to Margedda, "who has come all the way to the city with Mundane to find you and be here for this occasion." Margedda screamed with amazement as she fell onto the old woman's chest and outreaching arms. Edda, which was the name of the old woman of the north, carried a beautiful and simple leather dress with bone and fur decoration, and taking off Margedda's borrowed clothes she wrapped her in it. Ernesta and Jessi-ma were amazed to see how handsome and completely at home Margedda looked in the leather clothing with the bone decorations.

Then Edda put a necklace of long curved teeth on her granddaughter's neck. "A bear tooth necklace. For fertility of attraction and for fierceness," she announced to everyone, and they laughed and ohed in appreciation of the long yellow teeth, and the ability of fertile provision the teeth could bring to the wearer.

Ernesta thought this meant that Margedda would be a woman of true bearing, and she touched her own headband to make certain it was still in place for her own acquisition of bearing wondering if her heart would ever be quiet again in her chest.

The next gift Gedda and Edda had brought was also from the north, a ladle and bucket of special gathered stream water to go inside the Ana pot. "In our land this rite of the first bleeding is done with water ladled onto the hot rocks to make the

168

steam of transformation between worlds. We would like Marged-da to be able to use it today even though we know this is not your usual custom."

Briefly the oldest members of the Spider Society discussed this and began to nod. "That's agreeable with our customs too," Mundane said.

The procession and admiring of clothing lasted only a little while, just long enough for all five girls to see how each other had imagined themselves for the occasion, for Fran-keen to show her knife in its new tooled leather sheath, and for the striking lines of a black tortoise that splayed over the entirety of Dee's spectacular yellow linen cloak to make them all gasp.

Leading women of the courtyard procession sprinkled water everywhere, on the firewood, on the oak tree, on the rocks and ground, specially gathered water that was the sacred blood of Ana herself.

Then the women gathered around the five girls, taking off their clothing until they were naked except for the slender belt of shells at the waist of each of them. Mundane, Edda and three of the other oldest women painted triangles and stripes in red, white and black paint on their bodies, for life, death and the transformations dancing between these two great gates.

They were to stay four days and nights in the Ana pot. Once a day and once a night the rocks would be exchanged for fresh hot ones and the herbs changed. The young women would be led out for bodily eliminations and given some water and a little salt. They would eat nothing else. They would lie together in the body of Ana, dreaming, and their dreams would blend together and have great significance not only for themselves, for everyone they knew in the world of Mundane.

Cooking In The Cooking Pot Of Blood, Sweat And Dreams

A large shapely Ana pot for cooking girls up into women was now rapidly becoming a hot bed of activity. Wisps of flavor from the steaming herbs that had been layered onto a bed of hot rocks wafted through the vulva door as Mundane sprinkled drops from Ana's own fresh waters of menstruation onto each of five rapidly changing girls before they entered the dream chamber womb leading to their own adulthood.

Fran-keen and Dee went in first, crawling through the womb abdominal chamber into the second, upper visceral chamber. Stooping to peer inside Margedda could barely see shadows of their feet as they lay curled into pockets of herbs in the dimness. She herself wanted to go in last because she had to drag the heavy bucket of water bequeathed to her at the last minute by her grandmother Edda. However Mundane had last minute instructions for her own granddaughter Ernesta and so Margedda went in after Jessi-ma, following the light reflecting from her swinging, shiny meaningful hair beads.

Now wearing only a string of small shell beads at the waist, they would rearrange the shells throughout their lives on every important occasion. Their former finery was folded in piles on woven mats in the courtyard near the food that the gathered older women would eat during the long rite of passage accomplished by dreaming together inside a menstrual pot.

Mundane pulled a deftly woven cloth over the vulva doorway that had been twilled last year for the occasion by Dee's mother and older sister. Although the young women inside the Ana pot are now wearing only paint and a string they are so immediately hot their breath is swept away and they feel suspended in an airless place of no resistance.

Densely smelling steam from the soft plants giving up their water fills their nostrils with a spirit of serious dreaming yet they are not ready for this yet, they are still thinking of resistance. Giggling, Dee has begun sitting up first complaining of feeling just like a baby sitting on diaper moss with bare buttocks and before long all of them are sitting up giggling and pinching each other secretly in the dark to hear the comfort of awake squeaking before the effort of lying down and dreaming.

In compliance with the customs of Edda and the northern people of her place of origin, Margedda ladles water onto the hot rocks near her while her two close companions in the vulva chamber groan with the excess heat and water slavering over their skin of bearing.

"My paint is running down my face," Jessi-ma says, "I never had a chance to get used to wearing it."

Thick steam everywhere condensed in blazing drops down the bodies of the maidens, who collapsed laughing until their ribs hurt when Dee said she felt as though she were being licked everywhere by a huge sow with a hot, wet tongue.

Then gradually they ran out of resistance and past their own laughing as they heard from outside the clay walls of the Ana womb a rising chant being sung by dozens of women who are outside the pot at any given time, taking turns keeping watch with them. Night and day during the four days of their collective dreaming the older women would take turns dancing and chanting, telling in song form the stories from their own dream journeys to keep watch with those within the Ana pot.

Ernesta listened to the singing for a moment, hearing Jessi-ma begin singing softly along with them. She was about to say a joking phrase to Jessi-ma about the nature of her singing when she realized that the dark light of not seeing had vanished. She can see perfectly and what she sees first are not the walls of the clay pot but rather her own body. She can see that she is presently standing, and that the pot is a different shape than she had thought. Mundane must have had pulled aside the cloth over the vulva opening to let sunlight come in to them, revealing that the secret of the pot lies in its ability to change shape. If you just stand up it will become tall enough to fit you, for instance.

She was looking down at her own feet with a feeling of revulsion, for they were grey and scaley with very long toenails. I must have been in here so long I need a bath already and some clipping, she thought and then was startled to see downy white clouds spreading up her thighs. Margedda's steam bucket had gotten out of hand, perhaps she had thrashed around tipping it over. Then the leg clouds flattened and solidified into a second layer, this one dark blue-grey and shaped into flat fingers.

Feathers, she recognized, I'm rapidly being feathered from the bottom up. Someone else was already here, some other being standing beside her, and inside her body.

"Who are you?" she asked sharply, for having someone else living inside your physical being is a frightening sensation.

"Yes, you may," she hears, as though in answer to a different question. "I'll just step outside for a while."

The feathering is spreading up her body and over her stomach and as she turns her head to the side she is gaping down at her own proceeding feathers with one eye. Her eye seems to have wandered off to one side of her head. Now she is seeing something different at the same time out of the other eye, which can see the dark and light outlines of the ceiling, and that it is no longer made of clay. Crystals imbedded in rock flicker reflections down at her upward turning eye.

"My wandering eye is fully developing," she thinks, opening her mouth to laugh out loud and astounded when the sound comes out Roark, rather than her regular laugh.

"I don't sound entirely human," she thinks. She straightens her head, pulling her neck down into the bed of large curved feathers she can currently see spreading up over her shoulders on both sides. Without moving her face she is able to see both of her shoulders and down her feathered arms.

"Do you mind if I borrow your body for a while?" She can hear her voice say this although it seems to be a memory, not a current event. She believes she had actually said it earlier, before she said, Roark.

Odors of the herbal leaves rose to her nostrils with a keen awareness of ravenous hunger and that her stomach had gotten agitated and tight. I'm suddenly so hungry that the steaming leaves smell so wonderful I'm ready to eat them, she thought.

More light fell on her from the entry of the pot. Mama Mundane has opened the door for me, perhaps we're all finished inside here, she thought. She moved her large foot to step outside.

Her foot did not move forward but sideways, swinging her around and her heart nearly stopped dead when she saw two moving feathered creatures behind her. They were small and naked to the neck where newly sprouted feathers showed how young and tender they were.

These are my children, she thought.

The children were moving on a bed of sticks lined with downy feathers and seeing one portion of the stick nest dislodged Ernesta reached out to push it back into shape so the two tender creatures wouldn't fall on their faces onto the hard floor. Only when she finished the rearranging did she realize she had done all the moving with her mouth.

I wonder where my hands are? she thought, but before she had time to look for them someone else arrived, another bird just like herself, and as she gazed into the face of this one she recognized that this one was the mother of her children. She felt an intense connection and sense of obligation.

All my life I will live with her, she thought, and we will make more than one nest like this and work hard to feed and socialize these hungry young ones.

Her Ernesta-self knew then that she had taken the loan of the body of a large male vulture. She recognized that the keen, delicious, delicate, pungent smell that she thought was herbal leaves was actually remnants of meat scattered in the nest under the children's feet. Rotten meat, not herbs, was smelling delicious to her now.

"Did you get anything?" she asks, using the beam of her eye to talk with, and her mate replies in kind, "No, nothing is ready to be gathered yet. Why don't you try."

Behind her the children are moving agitatedly with growing hunger, so that she feels propelled to the doorway, and without wondering whether she will fly well or not, she lunges out.

Pure air lay beneath her as she left the cave of the carrion birds shooting out and down a long cliffside until her terrified brain began screaming, "Hands! Hands!" and the wings came out at last, broad and strong and catching at the air like elongated tents. She pushed against the solidity of the wind, feeling it as a changeable though thoroughly sturdy wall with its own will. In great relief she slung her body up on it, and began to sail.

Singing Is More Than Sounding In A Cliff Of Cells

Jessi-ma could hear Mundane's voice beside her, guiding her with directions, and whether this was currently happening with newly spoken words or was a memory of instruction given yesterday in the straw house with the pig sleeping out front was cause for a good argument beginning with the meaning of the idea, "yesterday," for if yesterday meant "the day before this one" how could anyone know if this one were really "this one" or "some other one," and if she was hearing the words how could they not be happening now, and not "before" anything?

"You are entering all-time now," the old woman's voice said, "soon you'll be in the layer of it we call 'eventual time.' You will be able to do this without losing the ability to come back into the part-time you are used to, and the relative measured time so treasured by your Bee clan."

Jessi-ma's immediate impulse was to sing the sentence as she lay curled on her side, head tilted up so the sweat steam gathering from Margedda's duck-shaped ladle would run down her tight braided cords of hair and not into her eyes. Holding her hands together against her heart she interlaced her fingers and moved them back and forth to keep the rhythm of her new song. Because of the sweat and the herbal leaves underneath her body she kept slipping sideways and losing the rhythm. Clutching her interlocked fingers more tightly to her heart she tried to maintain the song even though she had slipped so far she could actually see the river shining silver along her peripheral vision.

I have slid completely out of town on my own sweat, she thought.

Slipping more rapidly sideways and spreading now in several directions Jessi-ma lost complete track of her hands, her heart and her essential rhythm in a myriad of sparkling interlocking cells and sounds that hummed out over a broad surface of beach facing out to the sun and the moon. She found that her cell sounds and surfaces were spreading and interlocking with the face of a tall brown cliff, a shimmering shale cliff presenting not at all a solid surface, rather many chambers for sounds and cells reaching eagerly and easily to interlock with hers.

The beating of her heart reappeared, resounded and became her song, and she could hear it now as a humming, a giant pulsing humming that the cliff was putting out into the atmosphere, then much farther out into the diversity of sky and stars.

Somewhere in the sounding cells freely floated a conglomerate that was still the person Jessi-ma with a memory of part-time and she felt at once an overwhelming interconnected well-being pervading the matrix of shale that now was her flesh. Even slabs of herself that had fallen from her tall broad face onto the beach below hummed the same tone that was her current song.

She was immediately aware of her enormous resonant memory, a song she could sing herself that seemed nearly endless as it stretched backwards and forwards in time. Her resonant song hummed back and back until it tripped into an exhilarating memory of all-consuming mother-fire and strong feelings of early family. When the song hummed forward in time tiny explosions of fire occurred in conjunction with activities of humans who were gouging at her innards with portable shovels, and later still were aiming long fiery refined mineral projectiles at each other, as they stood along her long shale-skin body.

Her rock flesh did not feel firmer to herself than her human flesh had, however everyone that stepped or landed on her felt softer and very lightweight. She was most interested in the content of their inner minerals, finding she instantly and very personally connected with them.

What interested her most about the humans was the enormous proportion of moisture in their bodies, immediately evident as their feet bounced plushly over her surface with the same consistency her once-human self had perceived in jellyfish or the squishy boneless bodies of caterpillars. Human motions were plush, though rapid and their song fluttery, brief and high-pitched.

They're kind of cute little waterbags, she thought, of the groups of women gatherers who rolled light-footed over her body on their way to more lucrative tree groves, and of the men humans who sat wetly on her surface discussing the hunting of doves in high chirping voices.

174

However, the humans and other overly active creatures were of not more than sporadic interest to her, compared to her intense memory life that consisted primarily of a complex and busy network of talkative relationships between herself and some of the more active and creative mind/bodies in the universe.

Between her surface and that of every other major body of significance such as the moon, lay nets of energy/sound, grids of communication beams that constitute a living screen between the two containing a continuous flow of event-thoughts.

As she beamed her own song out onto the energy grid she recognized that rock formations everywhere on the earth's surface are in "touch" with each other through the projections of their songs onto grids a mile or so out from the earth surface. Information from surfaces on the anterior side passes along the net simultaneously. She herself, she perceived at once, was only a small portion of the net of grids sent out by rock surfaces all over the earth, and she could hear that her particular hum differed somewhat from her neighbor rocks, yet the whole makes up a giant harmonic song that mingles and transfers with songs of other mineral beings across the sky that now seemed to her no larger than a courtyard.

Across the courtyard sky, facing her on her revolving axis, beaming a life-song in her direction, was the moon, as close now to her ken of comprehension as her mother had ever been, and more so than a donkey or an oak tree, when she was Jessi-ma the human being in part-time. The moon spoke to the earth as a daughter to a mother, she realized, and knew that some of the song pouring through her was the intense love, need and connection between them.

In addition other nets extended through the centers of rock bodies for internal communications. The restless fiery center mind of the earth sent continual beams upward to the cooler outer bodies such as herself and she in turn beamed the thought-song out onto the energy beam grid for interaction with other stellar bodies. I am certainly in Ana's mind now, she thought, and her thinking was a song that hummed strongly out of her being.

The earth's surface, as she easily perceived by entering the energy net and looking back at herself, was heavily populated by parasitic life forms with no independent song-nets of their own. They grew in a variety of cellular forms from rooted green dependent growths to smaller flying and crawling beings who even more dependently ate the green beings and roamed in a limited band of perceptive existence between the outermost rock and water surfaces and the cloud-mist band defined by the wind.

Children of the earth, she sang, and yet they do not grow up to be other earths. They are dependent thought-cells of the earth, she sang. They modulate the skin of the earth even as they are part of the skin of the earth.

Some of these life forms recognized the energy grid and sang into it, connecting to the earth-star memory conversation while others, including a few of the humans, who as a group were the most dependent of creatures, were forgetting about the energy grid, and becoming disengaged. These, she could hear from the simplicity and occasional discordancy of their song, were lacking in imagination and interconnection, and to her shock her Jessi-ma self recognized that some of the most severe local disconnection was among members of the Bee clan.

Beating Arms Are Needed
If The Song Of the Wind Is Illusion

Draped over the wind Ernesta glided toward her own greater understandings. She found that the air easily divided into channels that she could see. These paths swept in curves graceful and natural according to the contours of the cliff face and the forces of movement coming off the flat land and the water. By riding the paths she found she rarely had to flap her big wings though by changing their angle she could switch onto different paths and thus formulate her own direction. The paths had shapes, some being concave tunnels sucking her along their courses, others being convex tubes she slung herself over to ride like waves of water.

Draped over such a convex tube she began having a conversation with it as she was very curious about its nature. And as her questions continued she felt more and more familiar with some thing about it until finally it revealed that in addition to its own essential windy nature it was currently also occupied by the spirit of a human she knew very well, one Fran-keen.

"Fran-keen, you have entered the wind?"

"Yes," a voice replied inside Ernesta's head. "I came in here looking for a song. I thought to find a song the way Jessi-ma has found hers, and so the wind seemed an obvious choice for my part in our dream visioning."

176

"And so you are finding your song in there?" How exciting this is, Ernesta thought, to communicate this way, and forgot to tip her wings for balance, momentarily falling off of Fran-keen into windless air, beating her arms in a frenzy.

"Go easy with the sharp turns," Fran-keen said, coming up underneath her in another path course and lifting her again. "No, it's very disappointing. The wind has no song of its own at all. The wind is only mind."

"But everyone has heard the wind's song," Ernesta said when her buzzard self had caught its breath from her fall. "The wind sighs, and howls, sobs and laughs everywhere it goes."

"No, not really," Fran-keen said. "The wind carries the songs of others, that's all. The sounds are from the rocks or trees, from the intensity and passion of their substance and shape; the wind just amplifies their own songs and carries them. The wind itself consists of mathematical progressions, too many to enumerate to you, and coordinations of the synthesizing of every miniscule emission of heat and cold, fire and ice, yes and no, up and down, here and away. And all with no particular passion."

"But that's what makes all the other songs possible, isn't it?" Ernesta continued and Fran-keen grudgingly agreed, "Yes, the air-borne ones at least, and I'm closely coordinated with the rock-borne wind of heat and cold as well. I just didn't expect to suddenly be part of one centralized wind mind with so many patterns, and all so mathematically formulated whereas I thought it would be more expressive, and emotional. The wind is not at all emotional. It's computational. There's Jessi-ma now," she said as they sailed across the river toward a beaming cliff face.

The energy grid of thoughts streaming from the cliff were instantly recognizable to Ernesta, and her buzzard self remembered engaging with the inter-stellar dialogue many times a day to ease the tedium of long coasting while searching and gazing and waiting between meals.

As she sailed over the rock containing Jessi-ma she envied her the endless dialogue of ideas she must be having with the greatest stellar beings visible to anyone. While Ernesta herself was chained to this temporary mobile form of carrion bird, flying over a limited area of physical territory. Then as she saw the city of humans come into view in its entirety it occured to her that in her human form Jessi-ma had no capacity to understand the intricate workings of the city of Mundane as Ernesta did. She had no way to get the perspective Ernesta was now getting, and furthermore she had no real interest, her mind always being preoccupied with measurement and distances between great mineral forms.

As Ernesta coasted over the city on its broad plain she understood the memory of its history, that ancestors far older than Mundane had settled here first gathering and hunting from the countryside and then slowly over the generations staying closer to home base and depending on the gardens and the fields.

She could see the splitting of the clans when those who wanted only to farm separated themselves from those who like her grandmother wanted to stay connected to the older ways of gathering and hunting. She saw how the splintered clans had agreed to live together in a city and in mutual respect for each others' functions. She saw the ages-old connections her people had to the snakes of the territory, and how the underground activities of the snakes were of primary interest to so many living creatures that not only the humans but others told stories about them.

Floating over her own household she could see that the scheming weed was busy even in her absence making connections between herself and those who in the future would come to her for advice and medicines. She saw that the children of Belladonna would be with her children and enhance their powers as Snake people, though never easily because of the occasional sudden greed of the plant to take all the human energy for itself in one surge of overdose.

She saw how carefully her aunts had tried to prepare her for this day, and how thoroughly her grandmother guided her into it. She was amazed to see that the courtyard of the oak tree was empty, with no large painted menstrual pot filled with five sweating and sleeping young women herself included and surrounded by chanting older women keeping the rhythm of the dream.

This is a different day, then, she thought.

As always, the oak tree stood quietly in her own centrality as a city of her own especially to the multitudes of insects who lived so much of their family lives in her boundaries. While they ran, crawled and were born all over her she stood dreaming in her own oakish reveries, including her lifelong connection to Ernesta's Aunt Three.

Oh I understand what happened, she thought, as her big-bodied bird self circled the courtyard, Aunt Three dreamed her children from the spirit of the oak tree, and that's how they are related.

By looking into the oak tree's reveries she saw that the current house of the snake clan had once been moved from a different part of the city so it would stand closer to the oak tree of Aunt Three's dreaming, and that Mundane had advised them to do this to strengthen the connections of the Snake medicine clan to the living plant world.

"How rude of us if we make connection with them only when we gather substances from them several times a year," Mundane said. She slapped her hands together for emphasis.

"Dialogue, dialogue, dialogue. Talk to them all the time, every day, maintain the friendship, don't take it for granted. Once they lose interest in speaking to us, they will no longer tell us their healing secrets," she said, "and we will fall down a pit of stupidity and loneliness, we will lose our powers, and our intelligence, and rightly so. We will become blind mechanical counters and educated guessers. All our powers of knowing come from conversations with the earth, and for us especially from the snakes and the plants."

Now passing over the Moon Temple where the snakes lived much of the year Ernesta remembered that she herself would now be expected to enter the temple and hold continual conversations with the snakes. She would learn where they lived in the wild, and go with baskets to invite them to the gatherings of her people in which they had participated with the humans for as long as the snake clan had lived in the area. Generations of the snakes had dialogued with generations of her people, she saw, and she would continue this conversation.

She nearly stood stock still in mid air looking down to see her mother Donna walking gracefully up the steps of the Moon Temple. This is a particular day then, she thought, during a time before my mother entered the scheming weed.

Turning in a wide arc at the east end of the city and climbing high to get onto a westward bound channel of Fran-keen's wind mind, her buzzard self registered keen disappointment that no body was laid out on the charnel platforms. An image of two newly feathered hungry children stirred in a nest of her mind.

She passed slowly over the city again, and saw in a distance a woman walking along the road that led to the river. This figure was not someone she knew well and yet her features were familiar, and her person completely riveting. She was carrying a cage containing two black doves who struggled to maintain their perches during the journey.

"That's Lillian," she exclaimed so loudly that another "Roark" sound came out of her buzzard throat. She felt completely exhilarated, and followed the walking woman who had been Jessi-ma's aunt from high overhead.

Perspective Is Watching Yourself
From Grids In the Sky

From the grid of beams she is projecting into the sky overhead Jessi-ma can perceive clearly over a large geometric portion of the landscape, can see Ernesta floating over the earth, and her own aunt Lillian walking toward the river on the dusty river road. Jessi-ma can also see that her aunt is doing all her living in one straight line. All her energy beams out in one single axis, not a grid, certainly not a four or five dimensional cube that bends in time as it merges with other rhythms it meets in the worlds outside its own human body.

Aunt Lillian cannot keep any time with any being except her own, Jessi-ma thinks. And she now seems frantic to make an artificial connection to others' times by mechanically measuring angles of the stars and moon by means of this newly planned temple. She can see from the way Lillian constricts her beam that she does not trust interconnection, that she can only follow her own single stream of energy without reference to the multitudes of beams around her, and that this singleness of focus also terrifies her because of its incompleteness so that she acts out of fear rather than connection.

More importantly Jessi-ma from her grid in the sky can see the temple site at the left of the main river landing, and that the site is in the wrong location. Sonia and Lillian had marked out the temple base with measuring ropes based in mathematical computations they and others of the Bee clan had made over a series of months. A temple-shaped pit has been dug in the earth and heavy stone foundations blocks have been laid.

But now Jessi-ma can see that the location is situated directly in the center of a complex lateral power grid necessary to a number of the animals and birds who live in and pass through the territory of Mundane's world, and who use it to orient themselves to the turning of the seasons as well as spatially to other locations on the surface of the earth that they might use for migratory or other purposes.

Totally unneccesarily the new stone temple will block some of the information of orientation used by local creatures as well as the flocks and herds of passers-by in their migrations.

Simultaneously she can see that in the south bend of the

river lies another crossroad of horizontal energy grids that interconnect and carry beam songs directly from deep in the center of the earth. A temple situated on that spot would magnify fundamental earthly information directly out to other major stellar bodies of the cosmos.

The two sisters of the Bee clan were placing the temple inappropriately, she thinks, becoming very excited as she realizes the possibilities fulfilled simply by relocating the temple site, and the more her mind explores this situation the more necessary the relocation becomes. All she needs to do now is communicate her understandings to the human architects who are in charge of the project. What fine conversations they can have now, based in these rock-formed observations. Moreover, as soon as Lillian understands the situation she can reverse her perilous course, and her death will not need to happen. Then the overdone raindance, the flood and subsequent cursing of her sister Sonia, none of these events will need to happen.

Eagerly Jessi-ma hums her growing excitement of understanding toward her aunt, trying to magnetize her attention and draw her off the road and across the path to Jessi-ma's stone body. Once here, the older woman can sit quietly absorbed in the stone's sound aura gaining information that easily appears in her mind already translated into human language.

But Lillian's singular mind beams do not change direction, do not become magnetized to turn toward Jessi-ma. No small matrix of human thought reaches toward Jessi-ma's greater stone matrix of song and interlocks with it. Lillian's use of all-time appears to be completely dysfunctional, as the beam of singularity and disconnection continue fearfully and stubbornly along its unresponding track.

As she increases the intensity of her singing appeal Jessi-ma in frustration thinks, something is wrong with my aunt, for she has no capacity to sit dreaming with another being, she is trapped in a singularity of partial time.

Predators Use Great Passion Of Their Being

Margedda lay dreaming in the Ana pot, far from the river and its growing excitement of gathering persons. The extra steam that rose around her, filling her nostrils and then dropping onto her skin in sheets from her grandmother's water bucket pressed her off into a different dream state than that experienced by her four companions.

She did not know where she was for a long time in the welter of strong sensations, rough cloth against her cheek, a bobbing motion, heavy breathing, the sparkle of moving bright lights in the distance. Only gradually she remembered the last sight of her grandmother Edda years ago, and her mother's crazed flight from their old life as wild gatherers in wooded, hilly country-side. Thick smell of loam, mushrooms, ferns came to her and a vision of what deer look like, big eyed and sudden-bodied, graceful in spite of their monstrous ears. People dressed in green, carrying small bows. Berries popped with broad fingers into her plump mouth. Then the terror of her mother's journey, their tiredness, her own angry fevers of protest and desire to stop moving, if only for a day.

When she came back to the Ana pot after her childhood memories the other dreamers had gone. She followed the trail of their beings to the river, already knowing they had borrowed the bodies of others, wondering what creature would share its physical space with her own mentality. Yet almost before she could complete the wonderment she was eyeball to eyeball with a large owl, easily recognizable by its curved, sharp beak.

For one terrified instant Margedda thought she had turned herself into a mouse and was about to be devoured, but then she heard herself asking permission to enter the owl's body, and heard the affirmative answer, and was suddenly peering out at a world of dazzling, obnoxious white light. She blinked, trying to see more than vague outlines in the stark whiteness. A smaller, fuzzier replica of herself pressed against her breast feathers and she saw she was standing on the rim of a nest with one fledgling, who was currently opening a giant yaw, and she knew she would go hunting even in this piercing uncomfortable light.

She found flying no problem at all, circled the tree once to remember the location of the nest, and then circled higher. Immediately she spotted a human of interest on the river road below her. Her Margedda self also immediately recognized Ernesta in the form of a buzzard high over her head, apparently following the woman.

However of particular interest to Margedda's new owl self were two plump little doves in a cage on the woman's shoulder. They looked marvelously vulnerable and breathtakingly beautiful. She felt such a passion for them as she had never in her life felt for anything. The passion rocked her body in waves from the crown of her feathered head down through her great beating body and down further through the hinged and gleaming talons of her curved, heart-piercing feet. She knew that for the fulfillment of this overriding passionate feeling she was willing to do absolutely anything.

Is the human going to let them out of the cage? she wondered, and set out on a zigzag following course that kept her landing in the shelter of various groves of trees along the way. The shade was easier on her eyes, and the woman obviously did not sense her, although Ernesta, she felt, certainly did, and so did the doves, for they began an uneasy flapping in their cage of human talons.

High above the owl version of Margedda, Ernesta was also following Lillian, who continued walking until she reached the site of the new temple. She rechecked the ropes of its layout and did some remeasuring with a rope instrument she had brought with her. The cage of doves stood on the ground in the shade, while Margedda crept above from limb to limb, waiting for the release of the plump seed eating birds.

Apparently Lillian brought the doves with her because she didn't trust the rest of the Bee clan to watch them for twenty four more hours, Ernesta thought from her high vantage point.

Margedda's machinations amused her. So much effort exerted to create edible flesh when all she had to do was wait until they died of their own courses, and then there was plenty. She was surprised and pleased with how much insight she had from this high vantage point. Motives, secret thoughts, all manner of energy patterns float up, she thought. She could also hear Jessima's cliff song to the moon clearly, and understood it.

Suddenly over the temple site she lurched, lost her balance completely, and fell spinning down toward the surface of the water. As before, Fran-keen had to swoop into a much lower path to get under her and lift her. Yet again, Ernesta flew over the temple and a second time plunged out of the sky in a dizzy spin.

"If you were a real buzzard you would realize at once that no one in the great blue sky would attempt to fly over this spot twice in a row," Fran-keen said, coming supportively up under her. "Without my interference you would be a bunch of wet feathers clotting up the river."

"There's some interference there in my balance," Ernesta said. "Otherwise, I was doing just fine."

"You don't have to get huffy," Fran-keen said. "I've been instructed to stay near you in all your explorations, and I'm simply advising you."

Ernesta realized that her ability to fly was not based solely on the office of the wind. She also was orienting to some kind of very regularly spaced magnetic sound grid with north south, east west alignments. The temple base appeared to interrupt these signals at a junction crucial for her sense of land-water orientation.

"That interference place knocked me out of the sky twice," she said angrily to Fran-keen. "A person could get killed by that stupidly located human contraption."

Then she remembered that the building of the temple had been a main focus of the festival. "What a good thing that was postponed," she said. "Just wait till I tell everyone what I just learned about it. The location needs to be replanned."

"Dee and I are concluding that ourselves," Fran-keen ruminated into her mind. "There is a human-designed magnetic disturbance in that area that effects much of the population."

"Dee? Where is she now?" Ernesta asked, circling the temple base and cocking one eye down toward the earth.

"She's in the river, having a great time being water."

"I wonder what time water is in?" Ernesta said. Then her attention was taken by Lillian's screaming. Something had flashed out of a clump of trees and was running straight at her.

"Is that Margedda?" Fran-keen asked.

"No, it's too big for an owl. I believe it's a lion. I saw one coming down river toward the delta when I passed this way earlier," Ernesta said. She could see a disturbance in the air from the force of the lion's roar. She saw Lillian run for her dove cage, then drop it on its side as the lion charged again. Screaming in complete terror, Lillian ran with her arms waving over her head further south on a path that led directly to Jessi-ma's flat surface overlooking the river beach of shale fragments.

Her feet clenching the limb so tight they were cramping, Margedda watched through intense glistening lenses of her eyes as the first dove wiggled its soft body free from the broken slats in the fallen cage. As it made its first arc into the air flying almost directly toward her she unclenched her feet and like a sky-borne cat flung her whole tensile self at it, shocked by the force of her own will.

Locking her claws precisely into the dove's soft breast, she found that her powerful wings easily stalled her forward motion for a moment in the hollow air and held both their bodies up as she turned and mounted the wind higher to return to her treetop nest. By the time Lillian reached the shale cliff, Margedda was already stuffing fresh chunks of the measuring dove into her single baby's eagerly swallowing gullet.

At first Jessi-ma thought that Lillian had at last connected to the humming magnetic field that lay between them, and was coming to greet her understanding, but the woman was running too fast to be making any kind of connections. Her face was twisted with panic such that instead of facing the lion and making any attempt to enter its time and decipher its motives, she was admitting the extent of her disconnection by running heedlessly away without once looking back.

Jessi-ma began a last loud song of instruction, humming directly at the woman whose feet plopped rapidly across her shale surface. "The lion is no longer following you," she sang. "Your own fear is what is out of control. Oh simply turn and look, turn around and look."

The running woman hearing nothing except the song of her own breathing and wailing did not attempt to change course until her feet skittered from under her and she skidded on her side directly over the side and down the cliff face of Jessi-ma's tall humming body. Lillian's grasping fingers did not hold her for a second as she fell heavily onto a projection of rock less than halfway down. There she lay deeply unconscious bleeding from the head. Her eyes were half open and her face was contorted. One sandal trembled on Jessi-ma's shoulder, caught in a small bush. Jessi-ma's human self wept helplessly.

Infinite Splitting Leads To Splitting Infinity

Margedda waited for what seemed decades of time for the second dove to emerge from the broken cage where it crouched stubbornly, having seen murder. Unused to her owl body Margedda had chosen to sit in a tree with small branches causing her long toes to continually cramp so she that shifted back and forth from foot to foot, feeling foolish and very visible.

Then it occurred to her that perhaps she could split herself once again, entering the dove without leaving the owl entirely, and giving the dove some courage to continue their encounter. She asked the dove if she could enter.

Immediately she found herself peering out fearfully from the slats of the cage. Her beak was delicate, slender and long, and her heart thumped painfully against her breast. Using all her Margedda will against her inclination to stay still, she forced her trembling body to crawl out of the cage.

"Now," she thought, "all I have to do is get back into the owl."

But she had forgotten Mundane's warning injunction: "Just remember that they won't let you in if you don't ask first." She had made no arrangements with the original owl mother about trading places with a dove in the middle of the exercise, and when she looked back at the tree, the owl, eyes glaring greenly as a cat's, was already in mid-plunge.

Margedda had time for one shriek before the claws gripped into her throat and chest and began lifting her dying body off the ground. Then, as the great wings spread and dipped to turn them both toward the nest something hard hit the owl, so that she grunted and dropped straight to the ground, carrying Margedda with her. There they locked and flopped together in the dust, drops of blood flying in all directions.

As her eyes began to glaze over in weakness Margedda saw human feet standing hugely beside her and she heard a human voice saying, "Oh look what we've done, we've shot an owl!" There was more voice, from too far away for her to hear.

High above Ernesta saw Margedda enter the dove. She saw too the owl's dive and she also saw two boys from the city of Mundane, out hunting with bows and flint arrows in the old hand-fashioned way of the men's Arrow Society that met at the round-house. She could see that they thought they were shooting the dove, owls being sacred to the death side of Ana, and untouchable to hunters.

Circling, she watched them as they piled stones around the owl to mark their mistake and pacify the owl spirit. Then they made an old-fashioned fire, using flint to strike sparks rather than coals brought from the city as any one not in the Arrow Society would have done, and they began roasting Margedda's dove body to eat uneasily.

Ernesta was shocked that Margedda had split into two parts and both were now dead. "She made a mistake, don't you think?" she asked Fran-keen, but the wind was now silent. Her companion had gone elsewhere, and she was alone in the sky. She felt pulled to coast down the beach, past the ever-singing Jessi-ma, then out over the river.

Some dark bobbing dots on the water turned on close examination into human girls who very foolishly were floating out too far into the current. They had borrowed a pigskin raft, and now it was sinking.

Dissolving Can Be Completely Absorbing
And Then Reforming

Dee dissolved when she entered the water, spreading apparently indefinitely, shaped by being continually swept by everyone else's waves. She became accepting of everything, dissolving everything into her own substance, helplessly like a huge unattached stomach.

She was moved by everything. When the earth's gravity said, "down," she rolled and dripped and wiggled down, when the moon's gravity said "up," up she went with the saltier tidal waters that backed up from the sea. When the sun pulled on her, out she went into the air in a mist aimed toward the sun. When the creatures lapped and sucked, in she went to the cells of their flesh. When the humans channeled and irrigated, off she went skin-thin into their fields.

At first these amounts of total and apparently willess acceptance of utterly everything asked of her were disturbing to her, then gradually she began to appreciate the extent of her popularity and ability to alter whatever came her way. Everyone loved her unequivocally and wanted to carry her everywhere with them. The humans even carried her around outside their own bodies. She enjoyed so much traveling, especially the exhilaration of evaporating into cloud forms, and then later regathering herself from the dews, mists and light rains that returned her substance to the main river bed.

Then she found that she not only dissolved other substances into her own body, they often reformed themselves in her presence, and this was of some interest to her. Her life was completely absorbing, and her popularity was universal and complete. Every act was one of appreciation for her substance and her habits and her being, every exchange benefitted and enhanced the lives of those around her. She began to feel alone in her all encompassment and an endless tedium with her total popularity.

After listening to the magnetic waves coming from the cliff sides around her she recognized Jessi-ma's voice, and then Frankeen's in the undulating wind. She absorbed their information, discovering that she was full of information gathered from everyone else, and because of her ability to travel she was in continual dialogue with the other forces, including the distant celestial ones who spoke through the grid net in a kind of continual mumble.

When the humans took the pigskin float out across her surface she recognized them as an event from her human past at once. She knew that the girl Jessi-ma was going to drown if she didn't take some action, and as a matter of old habit she began talking to the wind about this business, as she and Fran-keen had been in dialogue all their lives about one thing or another.

"I'm so bored with being loved by everyone at every moment that it's very tempting to drown them," she said. "Just so I can have a different feeling directed at me."

"Put them back on the shore, Dee," Fran-keen said, "or I know you'll regret it."

"Don't worry, I'm only joking," Dee said, feeling Fran-keen rippling her surface against the force of her own undercurrent. Under the influence of the sucking channels of air, the humans were carried back to shore on the strength of the lapping waves and their own swimming efforts, and dumped up on the shale beach.

From her place in the cliff Jessi-ma watched her former girl self dragged up onto the beach with sorrow. "If she doesn't get connected to the rest of herself and to the grid net of celestial communication she won't be any more successful as a Bee clan architect than her poor aunt was."

She sang out to her human self on the beach but the girl was too proud of herself for not drowning to listen to a cliff trying to tell her to look up and see a woman dying on the ledge above, although the children did look around uneasily as the song rippled in the air around them.

In a last attempt to make contact, Jessi-ma's cliff self shrugged in waves through her shale shoulder, succeeding in dislodging the sandal Lillian had lost in her fall, and when it fell the humans did come over to it, and Jessi-ma picked it up, and examined it. She also noticed a bloody dove wing that Ernesta dropped from the sky as a clue to them.

"Well", Jessi-ma's cliff self thought, "at least it's a start toward communication with ourselves."

High in the air Ernesta watched, realizing it was the appropriate time to leave the buzzard's body completely, and reenter her former child self on the ground below. Otherwise the children wouldn't have sense enough to get out of their dilemma by swimming around the rocky point to the sandy beach that she could see lay just to the north of them.

She wanted to take something with her to remember her time in the buzzard, and turning her head, yanked two long grey feathers from her lush tail before saying "Goodby and thank you, and I hope you didn't mind," to the real buzzard who waited to reclaim his body.

"Not at all," he said. "I will grow new ones. That takes good balance," he said, "pulling them from your tail in mid-air like that." He turned himself toward his cave home across the river. The feathers floated to the ground beside her Ernesta self and she quickly shoved them into a bush before engaging with the other children.

"Let's swim around the point," she said, taking the lead among them as was proper, since she was the oldest. Soon they were safe on another beach and gathering reeds, with all of them back in their human bodies.

"I guess we're ready to go back to the city now," Ernesta said as they walked single file up the path that led to the river road.

Suddenly she was nose to nose with a mother lion. Her scalp prickled all over with fear and her mouth went dry as she thought about the location of Fran-keen's knife. Then she remembered everything she had been taught by her mother about animals and began to examine the lion with all her possible senses.

She's not going to hurt us, she thought. Her wandering gaze caught the lion's eyes as she felt a jerk of recognition. She gasped.

Is that you? she thought and the lion sent a thought back to her, I always look out for you and for all the grandchildren of my city.

Ernesta tapped her hand against Jessi-ma's thigh, standing behind her, to signal the rest of them to back up into the river. She heard Jessi-ma stifle a groan that she had to get wet for the third time on the same day.

The groan continued as a long sound with no end in sight and seemed to consist of several voices. She herself was soaking wet with hot water and had been for days. Someone was shaking her shoulder.

"Come back from your dream, come back to those of us who live in the world," someone said repeatedly in a sing-song. Irritated, she brushed at the hand, opened her eyes and stared into Mundane's amber lighted eyes. She jumped, trying to remember when she had ever seen such eyes. She saw the opening of the pot, and sunlight harsh as bad news.

After she stumbled outside while other women shook her

still dreaming companions, Mundane put something around her neck, a necklace with one snake fang.

"This is the first day of the first year of your life as a woman," she said. "You have shed your girlhood skin, and every month you will shed something of your old self and grow something new."

Ernesta would have babies now, two babies, and male companions as well as female. Perhaps a lifelong companion. The periodic bleeding of her life would repeatedly remind her of her connection to the moon and to other enormous beings. She would dress differently and be welcomed into the Spider Society. She would be in charge of many events and decisions in Mundane, and would take her place as a Snake clan medicine woman. Her gathering basket with Belladonna's portrait awaited her. If she lived long enough, she would replace Mundane herself as the central mother of the Snake clan.

And like Mundane, she too would watch over others. She turned toward her companions as they stumbled from the Ana pot into the company of the women who had borne them. Gedda was holding the familiar owl that was Margedda's obligation of connection to her disparate selves. Margedda would be shamanic with her ability to let herself die and return. Sonia held conventional measuring tools for Jessi-ma, who looked intently into her mother's eyes, having now the difficult life long task of persuading the Bee clan to sing with the new voice of comprehension she had gained from a dream in which they did not participate. And Ernesta saw Dee with a new seriousness and Fran-keen laughing at the joke she had played on herself, as they were welcomed into the company of their mothers and aunts.

Everyone knew the five of them together would now be lifelong peers, ruling together, exchanging and squabbling as Sonia and Lillian and her aunts and mother and Gedda had, trying to find answers to the riddles of human living on the earth, and in the pull of the moon, and in the midst of other creatures. But they would be much closer than that generation had been, for they had dreamed together in the blood ceremony, they would know each other better than they knew anyone else. They knew each other's fragilities and strengths, perspectives and fallings. They were woven together in the images and events of each others' dream minds.

Cold water pours deliciously down the skin of Ernesta's new body as they are all five washed by the other women in the last bathing they will get from someone else until the births of their babies or unless they fall mortally ill. Ernesta is ready now for

190

however her woman's life unfolds around her. Even when she falls off course she now knows she has both bearing and balance, for the great bird of death has told her so.